REALLY THE BLUES

JOSEPH KOENIG

PEGASUS CRIME
NEW YORK LONDON

REALLY THE BLUES

Pegasus Books LLC
80 Broad Street, 5th Floor
New York, NY 10004

Copyright © 2014 Joseph Koenig

First Pegasus Books cloth edition August 2014

Interior design by Maria Fernandez

Library of Congress Cataloging-in-Publication Data is available.

ISBN: 978-1-60598-581-7

10 9 8 7 6 5 4 3 2 1

Printed in the United States of America
Distributed by W. W. Norton & Company

This book is dedicated to the memory of

Ferdinand Joseph Lamothe

CHAPTER ONE

Call it the law of diminishing returns. The yield from a pre-dawn roundup in the Marais was several Gypsy pickpockets, two real Frenchmen released with full apologies, eight Dutch and Polish Jews. Brought to a police station off the Place des Vosges, they were lodged in the crowded holding pen. One of the Jews, a neurasthenic Amsterdamer with blood clotted under an ear, hung back at the bars to distance himself, if only a little, from the mob. By the weekend the lockup, packed to bursting, would be emptied, the inmates gotten rid of with others like themselves from all over the city.

Time, passing slowly, nevertheless moved too fast. Friday night an open car, an elegant Mercedes 770K cabriolet, arrived at the station, and officers in leather trenchcoats giving off the scent of mink oil brushed past flics demanding to see papers. Downstairs, they surveyed the prisoners in their cage.

"These pigs make my eyes water," said a lieutenant, fanning the air. "How are we supposed to pick the right one out of this stink?"

His superior, a Wehrmacht major, shouted "Goudsmit!" A man on the other side of the bars barely lifted his eyes before lowering them quickly. "Here he is, right under your nose," the major said. "The biggest stinker."

"We'll take this man," the lieutenant said. "We will issue a receipt."

"Take any you want," said the jailer. "Take them all, I wish you would. I don't know what to do with these I have, let alone the new ones we catch every night."

Flics unlocked the pen, and Goudsmit dove back into the mob as they rushed in. They caught him by the wrists, pulled him out with his arms twisted behind his back.

"Idiots," the lieutenant said while Goudsmit struggled. "If he can't use his hands, I'll see that you will never use yours again. His kidneys—persuade him there."

A knee to the small of his back dropped the prisoner on all fours. The police hoisted him under the shoulders and loaded him onto the back seat of the Mercedes. Propped between the major and lieutenant, he stared despondently beyond the headlights.

"Where are you taking me?" he asked in lightly accented German after they had gone a few blocks.

There was less curiosity than resignation in his tone. No destination, in the company of these two, was a good place to be. He clasped his hands in his lap conspicuously, a reminder that they were not to be damaged en route.

"For a night on the town," the major said. "We are going to have a high time. The entertainment will be supplied by you."

Goudsmit kneaded the sore spot in his back. Every bump in the road produced groans. The lieutenant stuffed a Gitane between the prisoner's lips, kept him lit up till the big car stopped on Place Pigalle.

The plaza was enclosed on all sides by bistros, nightclubs, *boîtes à chanson*. Since the occupation reached Paris, the area had lost its luster. Tourism was dead. Few Parisians could afford to take in a show or cared to linger at nightspots that had been their second home. But the red windmill on the roof of the Moulin Rouge still was bathed in floodlights, and the streets were clogged with German cars. A new crowd was not shy about rubbing shoulders with the viceroys of French industry from Berlin. Goudsmit understood why he had been brought here. He spit out the cigarette. If it was entertainment the German bastards wanted, let them play Russian roulette.

The Mercedes rolled past the Theater of the Grand Guignol toward La Caverne Negre. Over the entrance, a neon savage draped in a leopardskin loincloth, a banjo-eyed, knuckle-dragging man-ape, wielded a knotted club. His other hand twirled a lion by the tail around his head. The sign wasn't an accoutrement of the Nazis. It had been there a decade before, when La Caverne was The Jungle Room.

The major, whose name was Weiler, produced a flask from his trenchcoat and instructed Goudsmit in using brandy to dissolve the blood around his ear. "You still smell," he said, "but more agreeably. We can't have you turning important stomachs, can we?"

Goudsmit accepted a pocket comb and used it to re-craft his pompadour. With every hair accounted for, he offered the comb back to Weiler, who ordered him to toss it out of the car with the brandy-soaked handkerchief.

The Germans escorted him to the entrance of La Caverne, where he balked. An involuntary twitch, wondered the lieutenant, or was he about to make a break? In the sinister alleys of the red light district there was a fair chance that he might make a successful getaway. Goudsmit planted his feet an instant before the sound of a jazz band reached the street. He seemed to have second thoughts, making an adjustment to his tie before walking inside.

Twenty tables cloaked in checked tablecloths and lit by candle stubs in Chianti bottles were clustered around a low bandstand. Papier-mâché stalactites tapering from the ceiling evoked a vaguely subterranean atmosphere. But it was the damp chill that made Goudsmit feel he'd been brought underground. Paris had lacked warmth since the Germans arrived. He was shivering even before the occupation army seized much of the stocks of coal and heating oil. His hands began to stiffen as Weiler shoved him to the front.

A seven-man combo—"Eddie et Ses Anges" was stenciled across a celestial sunset on the bass drum—was mired in a desultory arrangement of "Chasing Shadows." The musicians were ragged and uninspired, not trying to hide it. The leader, the trumpeter, was the exception, linking the lackadaisical ensembles with inventive solos. Goudsmit frowned at his improvisations. It would be obscene to admit to enjoying himself even for a moment, even to himself.

An extended guitar riff petered out, and the piano picked up the melody with the ham-handed drummer. Goudsmit was prodded onto the bandstand by Major Weiler, who laid a hand on the piano player's shoulder, patted it, and jerked him from his stool. The music ground to a halt, the sound like a needle dragged over the grooves of a spinning record.

Goudsmit took his place at the keyboard. The Bentside spinet had been a beautiful instrument in its day, but that day had come and gone. The ivories were scorched by cigarettes. Spilled drinks had washed away the finish. A wobble in one leg was partially corrected by a cheesebox splint. Fingering the keys, Goudsmit discovered two of them close to dead. The evicted pianist was led away as the crowd hooted. Just another night under the new order at La Caverne Negre.

The trumpeter announced the next song to Goudsmit, who turned to Weiler shaking his head. "I don't understand a word he says."

"Why not?" Weiler said. "He's speaking French. You speak French. What is the problem?"

"His accent. It's incomprehensible."

"Don't jabber. Play."

The guitarist strung together chords that Goudsmit shredded with his right hand and reassembled as the intro to "Manoir De Mes Reves." He was no Django Reinhardt, but his playing lost its sloppiness behind the new pianist. The drummer, switching from sticks to brushes, demonstrated a confident touch. The tenor saxophone assumed the lead, and the trombone and clarinet added embellishments. Goudsmit lingered over the melody, laying down a walking bass line with his left hand. The trumpet player brought his instrument to his lips, depressed the valves soundlessly, and then, squeezing his eyes shut, he began to blow.

Goudsmit struck a wrong note. No European jazzman played with the trumpeter's sly brilliance aside from Django, and Django, a Gypsy, was laying low. Goudsmit had been in Paris for close to a year since the Germans chased him out of Holland. But he had never gigged with anyone as accomplished as the front man for Eddie and His Angels.

The other musicians held back while the trumpeter matched Goudsmit hot lick for hot lick. Every idea that Goudsmit introduced, the horn man explored on fresh ground. His night out with Nazis was turning out be a memorable occasion in ways he hadn't anticipated. At the close of the number, the trumpeter pronounced the next title, keeping Goudsmit guessing till the first notes of "Avalon" poured from his horn. Goudsmit joined in, driving the melody, taking it into areas he'd never considered until, abruptly, his concentration vanished.

New customers decked out in black with death's heads on their uniform lapels had entered La Caverne. SS. None of the German occupiers were to be trifled with. Not for a Dutchman, a jazz musician, a Jew. But these were the deadliest, charged with implementing the Nazis' racial policies. They marched (yes, Goudsmit thought, that was how they always moved—in lockstep) to the front and took the table closest to the band. Goudsmit hit a dead key, wondered how many more he might be permitted before it was his turn to be yanked off the stool. Steadying himself, he played for all he was worth—played for his life.

Under the Thousand-Year Reich, jazz was disparaged as the mindless noise of animalistic Negroes. For unknown reasons, the SS were defiant partisans of the forbidden music and went unpunished for deviating from the party line. Goudsmit survived in Paris because the murderers whose job it was to destroy him needed him to hear the music as it was meant to be played, a delicious irony, but tortured logic that eluded him as he concentrated on fitting his fingers on the right keys.

If this was to be his last night on earth, he would spend it doing what he was born to do. His fears were for nothing, though. He hadn't been put in the spotlight to be killed. The Germans hated him but loved his jazz, and didn't it mean that he had them over a barrel? The drummer looked intently into the audience, and Goudsmit glanced back as the SS settled their bill and marched out. Now he could relax, even get to know the trumpeter and find out where he had learned to play. Paris had been a haven for American jazzmen before the war. None were left, but the hornman with the idiosyncratic French seemed to have picked up their style, and become nearly . . . no, every bit as good as the best of them. Possibly—Goudsmit smiled as he pictured it—an interpreter could be found to translate.

Because he hadn't rehearsed with the band, every number came apart as a jam session with the piano and trumpet leading the charge. "Someday Sweetheart" closed on a bluesy coda by the sax, and the trumpeter called out "Wrap Your Troubles In Dreams," his English also colored by a peculiar accent. The trombone was stating the theme when Weiler carried a bottle of Champagne onto the bandstand. Rather than award it to the musicians, he poured a glass for himself and moved among them, listening, then placed it on the piano and slammed the lid down over the keyboard. Goudsmit screamed as his fingers shattered. He was grabbed from behind and lifted from the stool as the original piano player reclaimed his place.

A police van was double-parked beside the Mercedes at the curb. Goudsmit was dumped in back and driven away. Inside La Caverne Negre, the trumpeter asked his pianist where he had been.

"Next door, having a drink with our German masters. They said they had brought Goudsmit for a command performance for the SS, and I would have my old job back."

"Goudsmit? That's his name?"

"Was he very good, Eddie? Someone I could learn from?"

"Not bad. A shame what they will do with him."

"A bigger shame what they would have done to me if he was not disposable. There are things I could have taught him."

"I'm not sure."

"About staying alive," the pianist said. "Let's not think of it."

"If you say so. It's the easiest thing, once you put your mind to it. I do it all the time."

"What will we play?"

"Do you know 'Didn't He Ramble'?"

The piano player shook his head.

"Fake it—it's a funeral march from New Orleans," Eddie said. "Play it like a dirge. Play it for Mr. Goudsmit.

"Un, deux, trois," he whispered, and waited for the drummer to beat out the time. Tapping his foot, he blew a mournful phrase, built two somber verses around it before tucking his horn under his arm and singing the chorus in his odd English.

"Didn't he ramble . . . he rambled

"Rambled all around . . . in and out of town

"Didn't he ramble . . . didn't he ramble

"He rambled till the butcher cut him down."

Eddie Piron was back at La Caverne Negre at four the next day for breakfast. Most of his musicians wouldn't show up until they were due on the bandstand at 9:00. One or two might not be there even then. Eddie liked to get to the club well ahead of time to hang around, talk to Pete Roquentin, the manager, and take advantage of the free meals for employees.

He sat where the SS had been the night before. The Parisian dailies hung on sticks on the wall, and he took down *Paris-Soir* and, turning past the war reporting, studied a weather forecast of afternoons in the mid-40s and clear, dry nights fifteen degrees cooler. The news pages in the collaborationist press scarcely merited a look. It almost certainly was true that the Wehrmacht was advancing across Europe without encountering significant opposition. But about more than the weather, he didn't really care. As long as he had a steady gig, the world could keep going straight to hell. Eddie Piron, at thirty-two, had achieved everything he dared to dream of when he arrived in France nine years ago, aside from a recording contract, a movie-star wife, and bushels of money, and these he was resigned to forgo until the fall of the Thousand-Year Reich.

"This is a jazz club, not an auberge," Roquentin said to him. "When I hired you, I didn't anticipate your moving in."

"It's only because I'm underpaid that I piss away my life in this dump. If you gave me what I'm worth, I could afford to live in keeping with an artist of my genius."

"You don't fool anyone," Roquentin said. "You're here all of the time because you have nothing other than to wait to play your songs, play them, and then to wait to play them again. Which reminds me . . ." He went to the office in back, returning with a large accordion envelope which he put down beside Eddie's eggs and ham.

"What's this?"

"From the piano player the SS brought in last night."

"He left it for me?" Eddie said. "Why? We never spoke."

"It came from the police," Roquentin said. "He had been lodged in jail in the Marais. After the Germans took him away, this was found in the cell. He can't use it where he is now. Someone thought that you might."

Eddie untied the cord, shook out pages of sheet music which he laid flat over the newspaper and made a show of examining carefully. It was no one's business, least of all Roquentin's, that he barely could read the notes.

"These are no good," he said.

"What are they?"

"Written parts for an orchestra with full brass and reed sections."

"What's wrong with them?"

"You won't pay for more than seven men."

"For six. Janssen is quitting."

"Well, I can't use the arrangements in any case."

"You wouldn't use the trumpet part if it was written by Satchmo himself," Roquentin said. "You won't play a note that isn't your own."

"So why did you bring them?"

"I'm only the messenger. Don't kill me." He watched Eddie sprinkle confectioner's sugar over a beignet. "Goudsmit was a huge improvement over Philippe. Too bad we'll never hear him again."

"Maybe the SS will provide another like him," Eddie said. "They know where the best musicians . . . where they can be dug up."

He leafed absentmindedly through the obituaries, the soccer scores, the results of the races at Longchamps. Behind the sports were the want ads. In these hard times, people were parting with prize possessions, even priceless antiques, for a song. He told himself that he would rather have a good song. In English it was almost funny.

One of his musicians came into the club, accepted a small check from Roquentin, and stepped onto the bandstand. He walloped the bass drum with the pedal and began disassembling the kit.

"You're leaving?" Eddie said.

"That's right," said Janssen.

"You might have mentioned it last night."

"Last night I wasn't sure—before that business with the Jew."

"Where are you going?"

"Back to Copenhagen."

"Family?"

"No, I have no one. A girl in the eighth arrondissement, who's staying."

"You've got a job lined up?"

"The jazz scene is dead there. Very dead."

"What do you have?"

"Peace of mind," Janssen said.

"How much food does that put on the table?"

"A better question is why you don't require it yourself."

Eddie read the advertisements.

"You didn't answer the question," Janssen said.

"You haven't answered mine."

"The Germans are lethal critics of the music. I didn't come to Paris to be made a nervous wreck."

"Once you loved it here," Eddie said.

"Once there were no Germans. How much will you give for my kit?"

"Roquentin says you are irreplaceable, or, I should say, that he won't replace you. I can't use drums without a drummer." Eddie tapped the paper with the back of his hand. "Run an ad."

"Musical instruments are going for next to nothing. These are practically new, you know, hardly broken in. I thought you might come up with a few francs."

"Leave them," Eddie said. "You might change your mind."

Janssen shook his head.

"Well, it's up to you."

"You're not a Frenchman, Piron. What keeps you here?"

"There are worse places to be."

"That's hardly a recommendation."

"Good enough for me."

"Living under the Nazis? What's good about it?"

"Nazis don't have a monopoly on nastiness. You haven't been around."

"What hellhole are you from? You never say."

"Take your drums and get out."

"Eddie's American," Roquentin said.

Janssen disconnected the pedal from the bass drum, watching the trumpeter. "You're telling me Roosevelt's another Hitler?"

Eddie topped off his cup, added cream.

"An America Firster, huh?" Janssen said. "That's your gripe with Roosevelt?"

"I've had my fill of the States, that's all. I'm not political."

"I get it. A Heinie-lover. You talk like one."

"Been to America, Janssen?"

"For my eighth birthday I sailed to New York with my favorite uncle. We took the train to Chicago, and then out west to see the Grand Canyon. America's the most beautiful country on earth.

The people are the friendliest, the common folk are, always with a smile and a friendly word."

"Since you like it so much, maybe you should move there."

"If I had a U.S. passport, I wouldn't return next door to Germany."

"You're wrong about the States. You don't know about a place till you've lived there as an adult."

"I was wrong about you," Janssen said. "You've got some Nazi in you, yourself."

"You were a stupid judge of people when you were eight. You haven't gotten any smarter." Eddie picked up the paper, buried his nose in it.

Janssen leaped from the bandstand, tossed a punch that Eddie caught against the newspaper. Eddie kicked the table over, and as he lunged at the drummer Roquentin saw blood on the trumpeter's chin. He threw himself between the brawlers and muscled them apart.

"I'm not saying that crack didn't call for it," he said to Janssen, "but you can't pick fights with my meal ticket. If anything happens to his lip—" He looked to Eddie to back him up, shouted "Oh my God," ran to the kitchen, and came back with ice wrapped in a cloth napkin that he pressed to the trumpeter's mouth. "Look at what you did to him."

"I should have done more."

"You musicians are thick in the head, fragile where it counts. Eddie's no Nazi. Nazis don't bleed. He's just trying to get your goat. It's something Americans do that you must not have noticed when you were there." He winced as the trumpeter probed his lip. "How does it feel?"

Eddie stepped in front of the back bar, inspected his lip in the mirror as the slight swelling of a moment ago blew up. "It's numb."

"You look like you've been stung by a bee. By the whole hive." Roquentin jumped onto the bandstand and stopped Janssen, who was back to taking apart his drums.

"What are you doing?" Janssen said.

"Eddie can't perform like he is. And I can't give the customers a band with just five men. Philippe will take the spotlight, but I need you to fill out the rhythm. Will you stay on for the next few days? The mess you put me in, it's your fault."

"I'll be glad to." Banishing him from the bandstand was his triumph over Eddie. But when he looked for him, the trumpeter was gone, hurrying past the window with the ice pack against his face.

Eddie went out into the neon dusk surrounded by the waiters and bartenders, prostitutes and thieves of Montmartre on their way to work. Twice he started back to La Caverne to finish what Janssen had started, but decided that what he owed the drummer was a favor. For at least a year his lip had been killing him. His embouchure was bad, the mouthpiece of his horn seated in such a way that it felt like he was touching a hot iron to his lip every time he blew. He needed a trumpet lesson. A beginner's lesson that would be his first. A smile stretched the swollen lip, and pain traveled around his mouth. He was a professional musician who had never studied music, or his instrument. A pity that he couldn't decipher Goudsmit's arrangements. If they were any good, perhaps he could find players to do them justice. It would be something to have his own orchestra like Benny Goodman's or Duke Ellington's. Big band music—swing—wasn't his style, but a chance at the success he craved could persuade him otherwise.

Paris had changed, not for the better. In his heart remained the city between the wars where everything was possible. But Janssen was right. It would be a crime against the conscience to love the Paris of today. The German Paris. Hitler's. Definitely not Eddie Piron's.

A Citroën 7A rolled by, filled front and rear with men wearing black berets and khaki shirts. French fascists, they did the Germans' dirty work pro bono, rounding up Jews, communists, other antisocial elements, and anyone with whom they had a grudge. People turned away in disgust, but not all did. What he had in his heart for those Frenchmen and their supporters was more unpleasant than what Janssen would prescribe. How he felt about France or the French, however, was nobody's business but his own. Other than how he played his music, Eddie Piron was nobody's business.

At an apartment house on the Boulevard Victor Massé, the doorman was asking whom he was here to see when suddenly he was ushered in with an embarrassed "Good evening, Monsieur Piron." Eddie touched his fingers to his lip, which had begun to throb. That the doorman hadn't recognized him was due only in part to his injury. It was a time of day when he never showed up here. When he should be at La Caverne getting ready to take the stage.

He rode the lift to the fourth floor and rang a doorbell. The peephole opened, and he felt compelled to say "It's Eddie," not certain that it was convincing, because footsteps moved deep inside the apartment. Soon they returned, and the door was inched back by a woman wrapped in a bath towel. Another was twisted into a turban around her head. "What happened to your face?" she said.

"You don't like it anymore?" He said it with a smile, the smile unlikeable to judge by the frown it prompted.

He dropped his hat on a chair and walked into the bathroom. Water was still standing in the tub, and the woman watched him scrub fog from the medicine cabinet mirror and examine his lip. "Aren't you working tonight?" Carla said.

"I can't play with my mouth like it is. Thank God the lip isn't split, or I'd be out for months."

"How did it happen?"

"A difference of opinion," he said.

"About the political situation? The war? What?"

"About the divine wisdom of the head angel of Eddie et Ses Anges."

She snuggled against him and tried to kiss him. Directing her lips to his cheek, he peeled back a corner of the towel.

"You need to see a doctor," she said. "Not my breasts."

He unwrapped her all the way. "I know what I need."

The other towel went over the shower curtain rod, and she stepped back into the tub while he got out of his clothes. When he was undressed he looked at her again and said, "Wait in the bedroom, I won't be long," and sat down in her bathwater, soaked in it, then emptied the tub and refilled it with water so hot that he barely could endure it. Lately he was taking two, sometimes as many as four baths a day. If a doctor was what he needed, it should be a psychiatrist, he thought, although it wouldn't take a Dr. Freud to tell him why he might be starting to lose his grip.

In bed she was tender and solicitous, suppressing the abandon which he normally provoked with words and specific motions of his body, which she would demand more of until she was driven to wild paroxysms that gave him greater enjoyment than anything besides his music. By nature Carla was selfish only in love-making, Eddie encouraging her greed and taking advantage of its excesses. If he wanted tame affection, she would step aside for other girls. Today, mistaking his best medicine, she let down both of them, achieving only a call for a premature halt.

She said, "How soon do you think it will be before you can play again?"

"Play well?"

"Yes, of course."

"I don't know that I have ever played well."

"I've heard that before."

"I was thinking I would like to break down my technique and start over. To learn the trumpet from serious musicians."

"From the Paris Opera? The symphony? I've heard that before as well."

"I have the time now."

"And if they are not selecting new pupils from the graduates of La Caverne Negre?" she said. "What will you do?"

"I haven't gotten that far in my thinking."

"Go there."

"In that case, I would like to travel in the country."

"You've been here ten years. Certainly you've been around."

"I want to see all of France. Before it changes permanently."

"You mean because of the Germans?"

He reached across her for her cigarettes, shook one out of the pack, and was striking a match when the pain registered, and he put it back without lighting up.

"They're only men," she said, "not gods. Despite what they believe about themselves. The mountains and lakes won't be different because they're here."

"Everything else is," he said. "Including me."

"What prompted this reappraisal?"

"The SS brought a piano player to sit in with us last night. We jammed for ninety minutes, he was a lot better than Philippe. When they were tired of listening, he was taken away. He's Dutch. A Jew."

"It doesn't mean they'll kill him," she said. "He may be spared, or escape. They might want to hear him play again."

"They already killed him," Eddie said. "I watched it happen."

"In the club? In front of everybody? That's bestial even for them."

"They smashed his hands," Eddie said. "It's the same thing."

"They wouldn't harm you. They wouldn't dare."

He rubbed his lip.

"Would they?"

"It makes me think," he said.

"You're not a Dutchman, or a Jew," she said. "You're France's greatest jazzman."

"Second greatest," he said.

"Have it your way." she said. "Isn't it protection enough?"

"The greatest, a musician I can't hold a candle to, is running for his life. If they can do that to him, they can do it to—"

"To anybody?"

"To me."

At the usual time the next day, Eddie was at his usual place at La Caverne. Roquentin told him, "It's as I say, you can't keep away. I should charge rent. Better yet, I should charge you to play."

"How was last night's show?"

"Magnificent. Fantastic. The best ever. I never knew that Philippe, Janssen, and the others were such virtuosos till I heard them without you hogging the limelight. Stay away as long as you like. Please . . ."

"Is that so?" Eddie said.

Roquentin shook his head. "I can't tell you they actually drove away many customers, because I didn't have a single reservation after word got out that you can't perform. A handful of tourists, Spanish priests, walked in off the street. What they know about jazz you can fit on the head of a pin next to the angels they are trying to count there. I thank my own angels for Janssen. He is atrocious, and so he keeps the rest on their toes covering up for him."

"They're my angels," Eddie said. "Where is he?"

"He'll be in by eight to run through the song list and assign solos. Unlike you, he leaves nothing to chance."

At 7:30 Eddie went out for a walk and to pick up lip balm at a *pharmacien*. When he returned an hour later, Roquentin ran out of the office, cursing.

"Oh, it's you," he said to Eddie. "I thought you were Janssen. He told me, he swore I can depend on him. It's time to go on, and no one's seen him. You musicians, not one of you is a humanitarian. You'll drive me to an early grave."

Three minutes before nine, the band trooped in, all but Janssen. The club was a quarter full, a better crowd than Roquentin had anticipated. He told Philippe that tonight would be his big break. Again. Philippe said he would happy to play extended solos, to sing, and to crack jokes, even to tap dance if the audience wanted it, but the music would sound tinny with only five players. Roquentin told him to forget about dancing, and asked Eddie to sit in on the drums until Janssen showed up.

"I've never held a drumstick except on Thanksgiving," Eddie said.

"I don't understand."

"What do I know about playing drums?"

"You've watched drummers play them. Flail your arms, work up a heroic sweat."

"I'll give it a try."

"Hit them with the sticks occasionally," Roquentin said. "It's a nice touch."

The applause when the lights went up was cut short when Eddie kept to the background. The band opened with "Alligator Crawl," Philippe's specialty number. If it was the one tune you heard him play, thought Eddie, you'd think he was the second coming of Fats Waller, but it was the only piece where he shone. Eddie punished the snare drum, hoped no one was offended by the spastic beat. What was keeping Janssen? Roquentin was having fits.

So would Carla if he didn't get back to her apartment before dawn. When she demanded where he'd been, he'd summon the requisite contrition, keep it to himself that he could have begged off to Roquentin, but agreed to sit in knowing she was waiting up for him. In particular he would keep silent about how much he was beginning to enjoy himself. Roquentin was right. He would pay to play. Even the drums.

The applause withered, the crowd thinned. After the set ended at 11:00, Roquentin dimmed the lights and came onto the bandstand.

"Let's call it a night, boys, okay?" he said. "We're not doing anybody a favor with the music. You'll be paid in full."

Everyone but Eddie seconded the idea. He suggested they stay for one more set.

CHAPTER TWO

The Olympic games awarded to London for the summer of 1944 had been cancelled because of the war in Europe. Undeterred, the oarsmen of Le Société Nautique de Paris put their boats into the Seine every day to prepare for the next Olympiad seven years away. On a cold, drizzly morning they worked the stiffness from their back ahead of a misting tailwind; single sculls, two-man boats, fours, and an eight, which, generating the most speed, overtook and passed the lighter craft. It was the coxswain reading the river from the back of the eight who noticed the corpse washed up against a stone pier of the Pont Neuf and barked commands through his megaphone to detour for a look.

Suicides had become an everyday phenomenon in Paris, so common that the police were called routinely to investigate lost wet wash, bundles of old clothes, and the occasional mannequin discarded in the water. The body under the Pont Neuf wasn't the first encountered by a crew from Le Société Nautique. None of the rowers grew used to them. Practice was stopped and a single-sculler who hadn't actually viewed the corpse, the least shaken, was sent to bring the flics.

A car from the Sûreté stopped shortly alongside the bridge to allow a first look at the scene before officers parked at mid-span. There they hung over the rail, pressing their broad-billed kepis to their heads.

"A jumper," said one.

"Not a flyer, that's for sure," said his partner. "He dropped straight down, deadweight, and dashed his brains out, if he had any to begin with, on the stones."

The current animated the corpse. A wobbling arm seemed to signal to remove it from the river fast, but the flics were in no rush. At any second the body might dislodge from the pier and become the problem of officers downstream. At great length they debated methods of retrieving it without getting themselves wet. The corpse refused to budge. They were running out of time when carp fishermen sailed by in a small motorboat and were enlisted in throwing a rope around the remains and hauling them to shore.

Short hair and a V-shaped torso had made it apparent that the victim was a man, a fact reiterated when the corpse was raised from the river nude above the waist. Sergeant P. Bourassa turned the pants pockets inside out to find keys, a few coins, and a handkerchief, and then arranged a guard to keep the dead man company during the wait for a wagon from the morgue. Returning to the Pont Neuf, he sighted upstream for the next suicide. If it was on the way, he might save a return trip. There was nothing on the water but cardboard flotsam, and it was with feelings of a job well done that he drove back to the station.

Attendants at the morgue, meat inspectors reassigned to assist with the heavy workload, shared the on-scene assessment of suicide. They noted little damage to the skull, but no doubt a broken neck would be discovered, or a concussion that rendered the victim unconscious when he hit the water. The dead man appeared to be in his mid to late twenties. A handsome, well-groomed man, he hadn't been in the river long. Because rigor mortis was present, the coroner, Dr. Laurent, assigned an approximate time of death of twelve hours before the body reached him at 7:45 A.M. A man with blond hair, a thin moustache, light stubble on the chin that could have been the beginnings of a goatee, and blue eyes clouded now, 183 centimeters in height, 71½ kilograms. The attendants undressed him. The pants, made of an inferior wool blend, were not custom-tailored, and might have been part of a medium-priced suit. The label was foreign, the name of the designer, or possibly the store where it was sold, unfamiliar, as was the language in which it was stitched. The same for the plaid boxer shorts.

The recent suicides often were foreign Jews, refugees running out of money, luck, hope, and the will to live in the City of Light. This man wasn't one of them. Not a Jew of any kind unless there was an uncircumcised population that hadn't previously turned up on a slab. The remains were well-nourished, also uncharacteristic of Jewish suicides. Despite wounds to the head, Dr. Laurent concluded that death was unlikely to have resulted from an intentional leap from the Pont Neuf. If he were to choose a Seine bridge from which to end his life, he would reject the Pont Neuf for not being sufficiently high above the river. The coroner, brought out of retirement in his seventies to deal with the rash of violent deaths, speculated that the corpse had gone into the water somewhere else and become lodged against the bridge after traveling with the current.

As the attendants turned the body over, Dr. Laurent saw a slit under the left shoulder blade made by a narrow instrument, a screwdriver or the blade of a stiletto-like knife. Two more like it were between the uppermost vertebrae, inflicted when the victim was crouched or kneeling. While still a medical student, he had given up using a pen to fill out autopsy reports. Erasing apparent suicide as the cause of death, he penciled in probable homicide.

A baby dead with six adults in a gas leak at a Boulevard St. Michel tenement was squeezed against the back wall of a refrigerated unit to make room for the blond man placed at her feet. Space at the morgue was at a premium. Days went by before the murder investigation began with an examination of the victim's clothing. The mysterious label read "Dry Clean Only" when translated by a professor of Swedish from the Sorbonne. The label was photographed, as was the victim from the neck up, and the pictures distributed to the daily papers.

Roquentin slipped *Paris-Soir* off the sticks and kept it close at hand. When Eddie came in, he ambushed him, shouting, "I've got something to show you. He was murdered."

"Janssen?" Eddie said.

"How did you know without a look? Did you kill him?"

"Are you serious?"

"You didn't get along. Tell me how you knew it was him. I'll tell you how serious I am."

"I read the paper at Carla's. Is that a good answer?"

"For me. I wouldn't mention to detectives that you fought."

"I have no intention of mentioning it to anyone ever," Eddie said.

"Someone must identify the body."

"Why us?"

"You, you mean. If you don't, his girlfriend will. When she tells them you were enemies, it will mean the third degree for you, the rubber hose, the rack, the guillotine. Tell the detectives she wasn't happy about his going back to Denmark. Point the finger of suspicion at her before it is turned on you."

"He was stabbed in the neck and his body thrown in the river. Do you think she did that?"

"What I think is that you know more than you let on. I'm giving sound advice."

"You just don't want to get involved with the police yourself."

"You have all the answers, don't you?"

"Not even one," Eddie said.

"How did you come to hire Janssen?"

"You were there. You don't remember? He walked in one morning after we lost Yves and were short a percussionist and said he was our man. I gave him a tryout, you know, and he played the Krupa solo over the Goodman recording of 'Sing, Sing, Sing,' not badly. He got the job."

"What did you know about him?"

"He could play like Krupa, if he had to."

"That's all?"

"I confess to overlooking the target on his back. He wasn't the only stranger in this city wearing one."

"Did you know who his friends were? Where he'd performed before? What he was doing in Paris? Did you ever meet the girlfriend? For all you know, she doesn't exist."

"He could play."

"Tell that to the detectives."

"If they were interested in the music—but we have nothing to talk about."

"You're afraid of them," Roquentin said.

"You're being ridiculous."

"Why are you afraid?"

"Now you're making me mad."

"Will you force me to kneel before you and stick a knife in my back?"

"Get off my back," Eddie said.

He'd brought his horn. He removed it from the case, tried it against his lip, and ran through the scales. The pain was excruciating. When the band came in, he took his new place at the drums. Janssen's place. His discomfort under the lights in the murdered man's seat was excruciating, too. The crowd was the largest in weeks. How much did it have to do with the drummer's murder? All publicity was good publicity. Murder might be the best. He settled down, reminding himself that the public didn't know yet that the Pont Neuf corpse was Janssen from Eddie et Ses Anges.

Roquentin counted the house, grinning at him. By this time tomorrow the murder victim on the front pages would be identified as the drummer at La Caverne Negre. Roquentin would have to find extra tables to handle the mobs.

While the beans soaked, Eddie sautéed the onions, celery, and garlic and diced the vegetables, plump bell peppers more precious than gold since the occupation. Dumping them in a pot with thyme, cayenne pepper, and pork bones that the butcher had let him have for free with a promise that his dog would love them, he set a low flame and prepared rice, ham, and andouille. He considered himself in most ways to be a normal Frenchman. Yet often he cooked up a mess of red beans and rice like the poorest Creoles in New Orleans, following a recipe handed down over the generations by his mother's people—the family jewels.

Behind iron shutters, the tenement flat was still but for the pot simmering on the stove. Eddie touched his lip. The pain hadn't gone far, a jolt sufficient to discourage him from going back to bed. Not that he could. Someone was pounding on the door.

"Police! Let us in."

"A moment," Eddie said. "I just got up."

Someone snickered. He heard "Now!" in a different voice.

He dressed, opened the window, and cranked the shutter. The afternoon sun was harsh on his eyes, and he readjusted the angle of the louvers. Enough light remained to pile up between four gray walls in need of paint, the gray ceiling, a bare floor tilted away from the door. The cold-water tenement at 43 Rue des Terres had gone up not long after the Revolution, one of thousands that lent Paris timeless charm and minimal comforts.

The two men who stormed inside when he drew back the bolt were bigger than Eddie and quicker on their feet, slamming him back against the wall. He had the same rights as any real Frenchman, so he'd crowded them to slow the stampede. Except that he had no rights here. The French never had as many as they boasted, and let a lot of them slip away. Now they had none.

"Edouard Piron?"

Eddie shook his head.

"Don't lie to us. We know who you are."

"Then you know I'm not Edouard."

"You deny you're him?"

"I'm Eddie. It's the name on my birth certificate."

One of them put his hand out for it.

"You'll have to take my word."

They weren't here for his word. Their flashlights played against every surface, and corner. He saw blood on his pillow. It was his own, but he didn't want to explain how it got there.

They'd announced that they were police, and because he was expecting the police he'd let them in. Watching them tear apart his place as if they owned it, owned him, he realized his mistake. Flics were obsequious civil servants, their badge an outstretched palm, giving off the sweaty aroma of functionaries suspicious of everyone above their station in life and below it, the politicians who were their bosses, and the public who paid their salary, fearful of the criminals who provided them with work. Many entered the municipal ranks in other departments, gravitating to the Sûreté because that was where opportunities for easy advancement and graft were greatest. These two were different, efficient and enthusiastic.

"Let me see identification," he said.

They looked at him as though he had declared for a padded cell in Charenton asylum. One of them—the one who'd snickered in the hall—said, "You know why we're here."

"I have no idea," he said. Blurted it, giving himself away.

By now so had they. Their French came with a German inflection, but they weren't the military. Gotten together as they were in well-tailored mufti and bad haircuts, they had to be Gestapo. In occupied France it was impossible to disguise what you were after opening your mouth and visiting a barber.

The snickerer said, "How did you know Borge Janssen?"

They'd come for information, and told him more with one question than he could give them. So Janssen's first name was Borge.

"He was my drummer."

The other said, "You haven't answered," while the snickerer looked through Eddie's stuff.

"He walked into the club one night and told me I needed to hire him. He played for me, and I did."

"When was this?"

"Six weeks ago? Two months?"

"In that time you became friends?"

"I never saw him away from work."

"That isn't what we asked."

"No, we weren't friends."

Socks, underwear, dirty shirts, his clean one and only tie, never worn, were strewn on the floor while they ransacked his chest of drawers. Under a sweater they found treasure, a heavy envelope.

"They're musical arrangements I've been thinking of using," he said. "That's all they are."

They flipped through Goudsmit's book and tossed it onto the pile.

"But you know his friends?"

"None."

"His girl?"

Eddie shook his head.

"The people he worked for?"

"He worked for me."

"But you knew his friends?"

His answers wouldn't be different the second time around, the third. The Dane was a capable drummer when the mood struck him. It wasn't Eddie's business that he'd been killed.

"The girlfriend's name is Anne Cartier."

"Means nothing," Eddie said.

"She lived on the Rue du Faubourg Saint-Honoré, in the eighth."

Eddie shrugged.

The snickerer opened the bottom drawer and goosed blue wool bathing trunks. "You haven't asked why we're here."

"Janssen was killed," Eddie said. "You want to know who did it."

"Very good. You're American. Where in the United States do you live?"

"Chicago, Illinois."

"I have first cousins in the suburb of Oak Park that I visit every other Christmas," the snickerer said. "You don't sound like anyone I've heard there."

"I was brought up in New Orleans."

"Why are you in France?"

"It's my home now."

"Why?"

"I don't understand."

He understood that responding transparently would cast suspicion on himself. Braced by a cop in the States, it had been safest to craft his answers to sound truthful. Here—now—that was dangerous. He was expected to lie. Didn't everyone have something to conceal from the occupation?

"Why would an American prefer to live in occupied France than in his own country?"

"There's no law against it," Eddie said.

"You are a musician? A jazz musician?"

"Yes."

". . . who left America for Paris to find work? We find this hard to believe."

"The jazz scene isn't what it used to be there. Swing isn't for me." Damn it, they had him telling the truth again. "I like Paris," he said. "Don't you? Isn't that why the Germans grabbed it for themselves?"

"How long do you intend to stay?" they asked at the same time.

"Until the music runs out."

"When do you anticipate that will be?"

"Never."

They concentrated on his belongings, toed the pile of clothes making tsk, tsk, tsk sounds with their tongue against their teeth. They didn't approve of his reading, French translations of American detective novels, but there was nothing officially subversive in it. They went through his pantry, ice box, kitchen cabinets, and the milk boxes in the closets where he stored hundreds of phonograph records, and which they shoved back so hard that he would need to take inventory of how many they cracked. The snickerer got down on his hands and knees to look under the bed, said "Ah-hah," pulling out a hinged case covered in faux alligator hide. When he popped it open, Eddie's trumpet fell out, and he snagged it by the bell.

"This is your instrument?"

"Yes. What else?"

"Janssen was a member of your band. Were you also a member of his?"

"He didn't have a band. He performed exclusively with me."

"Did I say anything about music?"

The other one stopped poking around to listen to Eddie's answer.

"I haven't any idea what you're getting at."

What did he know about the drummer's life aside from the sorry way it ended? When the next question was slow in coming, he said, "What do you think he was doing when he wasn't playing for me?"

"We are not here for your edification. Answer the question yourself."

"Eating and sleeping," Eddie said. "Practicing. Making love to his girlfriend in the afternoon. Musicians are lucky to have time for that."

"I wouldn't want his luck, or hers. Not yours either. If you don't give us something substantial, we will make things miserable for you."

"You're already doing a good job."

They laughed. Eddie wished that he could get his players to come in on the downbeat as crisply as these two.

"We haven't begun," the snickerer said. "Tell us why he is dead."

"When he leaped off the bridge, he took his reasons with him."

"What do you suppose they were?"

"No one was as surprised as I. I'd seen no sign that he was depressed."

"He killed himself because he was happy?"

"All suicides appear happy right before the end, don't they, knowing their troubles are over?"

Eddie never felt suicidal. Possibly, he thought, he was too unhappy. He would sort out his feelings later, after he was rid of these men.

After another tour of the apartment, they started toward the door.

"You had better not be holding too much back," the snickerer said.

"You're holding back something of mine."

The snickerer studied his reflection in the trumpet before tossing it on the bed. Eddie caught it on the bounce as they went out and took it to the window. Across the street they made a call from a café. He was still watching when they drove away. Without cleaning up the mess, except to extricate the sweater from the tangle on the floor, he hurried to La Caverne Negre. He was boiling over, and the dim, mid-day quiet of the club was the right atmosphere in which to cool down. It wasn't called La Caverne for nothing.

Roquentin was studying the paper but didn't say anything. Eddie went to the kitchen to tell the cook how he wanted his eggs, and then went to the bandstand and pounded Janssen's drums.

"Practicing?" Roquentin said.

"Getting rid of my frustrations."

"With a girl like Carla you've got frustrations?"

"Fewer than without her. But still—"

Roquentin didn't laugh. Eddie didn't smile. Ironic conversation substituted for candid talk about their situation. Parisians had stopped speaking from the heart while they waited for the Germans to leave. Eddie was waiting as fast as he could.

His eggs came. Roquentin put *Paris-Soir* beside his plate folded back to Page 3, which was headlined with the account of another suicide, the twenty-fourth that the authorities knew of that month.

"Read it," Roquentin said.

"These stories give me indigestion."

"I'll digest it for you." Roquentin took back the paper. "It says a woman in the eighth put her head in the oven and killed herself out of despair. She was just twenty-two, quite beautiful if witnesses are to be believed. It's unthinkable that she should decide that life is hopeless at her tender age."

"Everyone feels like that to a certain degree these days," Eddie said.

"Not everyone turns on the gas in a sealed room. A neighbor came to find out about the smell and switched on the light. The spark triggered an explosion that brought down the building. Two more died, eight were injured, and forty are left homeless because of her thoughtless act."

"Tragic," Eddie said.

"The reporter says she became despondent after her boyfriend was pulled from the Seine. He likened them to a modern Romeo and Juliet, although the boyfriend wasn't a suicide as originally thought, but was murdered."

Eddie pushed his plate away, went back to the bandstand.

"Borge Janssen, it says here, was the drummer for Eddie et Ses Anges at La Caverne Negre. The authorities are looking for any scrap of information and demand the cooperation of every citizen."

"I've already been questioned," Eddie said. "I came clean, which is to say I gave nothing."

"They'll be back for more, you know," Roquentin said. "A foreign national killed to look like suicide. It's not something they'll give up on until they're at the bottom of it."

"What's really going on?" Eddie hammered the tom-toms, punished them. "Who gives a damn about a dead jazzman in Paris?"

"Other than us two?" Roquentin turned up his palms. "Well, I don't suppose the publicity will kill us."

CHAPTER THREE

The tri-motor Ju 52 broke out of thickening skies above the north approach to the runway. The wheels were down, flaps raised, when a smaller plane escaped low clouds three hundred meters below. The tri-motor was descending at a steep angle when the pilot noticed the other aircraft, a mail plane from the provinces, and pulled up abruptly. After circling the city, the Ju 52 made its second approach over Orly. Cars assembled on both sides of the fogbound strip, headlamps blazing, to light the way.

Before the tri-motor stopped rolling, a Mercedes cabriolet pulled out of the formation and followed it to the end of the runway. The ground crew wheeled stairs to the left side of the fuselage and arranged them under the door. A delay of several minutes ended when the hatch was flung open and flight attendants emerged, chill blondes with swastika clasps holding brown ties against shirtfronts. They were followed by the captain, co-pilot, several businessmen from Berlin, four honeymooners, and a stout, sweaty man whose blue button eyes were distorted by Coke-bottle lenses. Stepping down onto the macadam, the man surveyed the skyline. From Orly it was possible to make out the Eiffel Tower disappearing into the clouds. He was looking there when the Mercedes pulled up.

It was Major Weiler who called "Herr Colonel." The man on the runway, intent on the horizon, didn't acknowledge him. It seemed he would never have his fill of the view.

"This is all ours now," Weiler said. "Its acquisition is Germany's greatest achievement to date."

The man turned his head, evidently displeased with something he saw. "What do you propose we do with it now that we have it?"

Weiler held himself stiffly, and saluted. Then he took the colonel's bag and walked alongside him to the open car.

"Other than your close call on landing, Colonel, how was the flight?"

"How does it matter? What have you found out about the corpse in the river, Janssen?"

Colonel Heinz Maier was notorious for answering questions with questions of his own, a Jewish trait. Behind his back it was whispered that the colonel was Jewish himself, at least in part, a part sufficiently large to put him in Dachau, or one of the camps less conducive to a good outcome for a Jew. There was to be considered the chance that he was not a Jew, but had Jewish friends while growing up near the old ghetto in Frankfurt am Main, and had acquired his bad tics there, and that if suspicions about his origins reached him, it would not be Colonel Maier who landed in a place not conducive to good outcomes. So, the whispers were never voiced.

"From his fingerprints we determined that he is a Danish national, one Borge Janssen, forty-one, from Copenhagen, a Heidelberg graduate in political science."

Maier was distracted as the road passed one of the sixteenth-century palaces that littered the city. Perhaps an extreme fascination with French architecture and historic locales was also a Jewish trait.

"The identification was confirmed through Borge Janssen's dental records. The dead man is him."

"You didn't know that his fingerprints also are on file in Heidelberg, where he was arrested in 1934 while a graduate instructor, and again three years later for the bombing of the National Socialist party headquarters?"

Weiler was hot. The atoms in his cells went into motion; he felt them crashing into one another.

"A year ago he was sentenced to beheading for a similar outrage in Hamburg. Sentence delayed when he escaped from Santa Fu Prison."

"This is the first I've heard. But why is the investigation ours, and not the Gestapo's?"

"Janssen's record of political intrigue and of direct assaults on the organs of Reich power is as long as your face is now. You believed that the killing of a drummer in a jazz band would bring me to Paris?"

"Until yesterday all we had were the facts of his death, and those were disguised to look like something else."

"To look like what?" Maier said.

"Suicide, sir. His body was thrown off the Pont Neuf into the Seine after he was stabbed."

"Suspects?"

"None."

"Promising witnesses, or clues?"

"The other musicians and the owner of the club where he worked on Place Pigalle deny knowing his true identity. They are assumed to be lying until proven otherwise."

"They were his primary acquaintances here?"

"A girlfriend. But she—"

"But she is believed to have been killed in a gas explosion at the building where she resided with Janssen."

"Yes, Colonel, that is correct."

Weiler doubted that he could present a single fact about Janssen that the colonel didn't already have. Maier had come from Germany with more information about Borge Janssen than anyone on the scene had been able to obtain, and enjoyed making him feel like an idiot.

"Do you wish to refresh yourself at your hotel?"

Weiler was curious as to how Maier would turn a simple courtesy into an interrogatory.

"I am perfectly comfortable," Maier said. "There is nothing as refreshing as beginning a complex investigation, wouldn't you agree, Major?"

Weiler nodded. So that was how it was done.

Swastika pennants fluttering from the cowlings of the Mercedes cleared sparse traffic to the former Musee du Jeu de Paume at the northwest corner of the Tuileries Gardens. Across the classical façade an enormous banner flapped like wet wash in the breeze. DEUTSCHLAND SIEGT AUF ALLEN FRONTEN GERMANY VICTORIOUS ON ALL FRONTS. The Eiffel Tower was cloaked in a banner like it. Weiler began to believe that it was the city's celebration of German war aims more than its landmarks that caught Maier's eye.

"Why are we here?" Maier said.

"Military Intelligence for the Paris district is headquartered in this old museum, along with much of the army administration.

Your office is on the second floor, with a splendid view of La Place de la Concorde. Across the river you will see the Palais Bourbon, the former home of the chamber of deputies, the French lower house, which voted the Third Republic out of existence after we took the city. I will be pleased to show you to your office and introduce you to the staff."

"Did I ask to be brought here?"

No, Maier wasn't a Jew, but something worse, the member of a race, species, or genus deserving to top the Jews on Germany's list of despised elements. Weiler had been acquainted with him for half an hour, and already the colonel merited consideration for that rating on his own list.

"I assumed—"

"I will make the assumptions, Major Weiler. I did not travel all this way for you to do my thinking."

"Very well, Colonel, where would you like to go?"

"To see the place where Janssen lived."

"It was destroyed in the gas explosion after his death. Nothing remains."

"Then the inspection shouldn't take much of our time," Maier said.

Our time? Does he think I'm to be his Paris coat-holder? Weiler kept his thoughts to himself as they started in the direction of the eighth.

"Initially, it appeared that Janssen wrongly thought the Sûreté was closing in on him for illegal residency, and chose to end his life rather than submit to arrest and interrogation," Weiler said. "The post-mortem examination revealed he had been murdered. Berlin believed the Gestapo had killed him in the course of an investigation about which it knew nothing other than that his name appeared on a list. It would be keeping in character for those sadists to have their pleasure from him and make it seem like suicide, rather than arrange an intelligent inquiry into what he was doing in Paris. They never troubled to find out if we might be interested in speaking to him."

Maier nodded. "That is how the case became ours," he said. Amazing, thought Weiler, the colonel not only agreed with him, but didn't respond with an interrogatory. "The Gestapo chief here promised an investigation into the machinations of his bureau, and an investigation into his investigation is under way to determine if it is a cover-up. He will be the first to say that it is not advisable for anyone to point our work in a particular direction in an effort to make himself look good."

"No, Colonel," said Weiler, deciding it was also not advisable to investigate who was secretly a Jew.

On the Rue du Faubourg Saint-Honoré, Maier ordered the driver to stop beside a crater ringed by heaps of broken brick. Scummy water had pooled in the bottom, well below the level of the sidewalk. The building that had stood here, to judge from what remained, wasn't old, but had gone up not long after the Great War, an example of the modern residential blocks that had revived a decaying neighborhood.

"The girlfriend lived in this corner?" Maier asked.

"On the second floor."

"How do we know?"

"The structure is collapsed here," Weiler said. "Her apartment was the *nullpunkt*, the ground zero of the explosion."

"If so, why is the apartment house damaged from the ground floor up?"

"It was a very powerful explosion."

"It was," Maier said, "but without defying physical laws, which direct the force of a blast upward. For her apartment to have been the site of an explosion that brought down the building, she would have to have lived on the lower floor, and you say she lived—?"

"On the second floor," Weiler said, "on and off with Janssen. This has been established beyond doubt."

"You've identified her remains?"

"Victims and body parts are still being sorted out. None have been conclusively proven to be Mlle Cartier—Janssen's girl."

"So the evidence that she was a suicide—?"

"Comes from what is left of the neighbor who apparently entered her apartment after smelling the gas and turned on the light, triggering the explosion."

"No better theory?"

"What better one can there be?"

"That the building was destroyed intentionally in the detonation of a bomb built by Janssen and his woman, or by enemies of theirs, or was the result of the ignition of explosive materials stored in the ground floor or basement," Maier said. "I count three, no?"

"Everyone smelled the gas," Weiler said. "The police, firemen, and rescue workers reported noticing it as soon as they arrived."

"As well they would have," Maier said. "The blast completely tore apart the apartment, gas lines included. It's a good thing the walls came down, or someone lighting a cigarette would have triggered a real gas explosion, and—" He made a blowing sound between puckered lips. "Poof, no police or firemen."

Weiler stepped out of the Mercedes and held the door open for Colonel Maier, who sat tight.

"Two distinct suicides that were not suicides. What would be learned about them by setting foot on the rubble?" Maier pushed his sleeve over his watch. "It's time for lunch."

"May I recommend a restaurant?" said Weiler. "The food in Paris is uniformly excellent. But we—the officers of the general staff—have found a bistro not far from headquarters that is beyond anything else in the city."

"I will take my lunch at the hospital."

"Hospital, sir?"

". . . where the victims of the explosion were taken for treatment."

At L'Hôpital des Soeurs de Saint Hubert the radiators made angry spitting sounds, and the windows were sealed against the hint of fresh air. Major Weiler untied the sash around his coat, and was unbuttoning it when Maier grabbed his arm.

"Leave it on."

"I'm already drenched in sweat," Weiler said.

"It projects the personage of a formidable investigator. No one will mistake you for a bleeding heart when they see you in shiny leather."

Maier took him past signs pointing to the cafeteria to a nurses' station, where they were intercepted by a nun in a gray habit and starched wimple who looked aghast when Maier told her what they were here for, repeatedly shaking her head as if she were refusing a lewd suggestion while the colonel walked ahead onto the ward and to a bed farthest from the windows.

Madame Ruth Sarle, grievously burned in the explosion and resulting fire on the Rue du Faubourg Saint-Honore, was swathed in bandages oozing the yellow unguent that eased the pain of injuries that otherwise would be unbearable. Major Weiler was immediately reminded of a mummy, not from an Egyptian sarcophagus, but by way of Hollywood, trailing the loose wrappings of its shroud as it pursued the living. Patches of charred hair were rooted among running sores on the top of her head. Stubs ending at the knuckles remained of the fingers on her right hand. She gave no indication of being aware that she had visitors as Maier pulled up a chair.

"Madame?"

The woman didn't answer, although her eyelids fluttered.

"Madame Sarle?"

The fluttering became agitated.

Maier reached around to the foot of the bed and cranked her into a sitting position. "I am Colonel Maier," he said. "This is Major Weiler. We have a few brief questions about the incident at your apartment house."

The colonel's French was flawless, colored by a slight accent from the Alsace region. It surprised Weiler, who felt intuitively that bigger surprises were in store.

Maier turned the crank again. When they were face to face, he said to the patient, "I would like you to tell me about the lamentable girl who lived in the apartment where you were injured."

The woman shook her head as insistently as had the nurse on the ward. It seemed strange to Major Weiler that a man who seemed to generate this reaction from everyone would choose detective work for a career.

"There, there, there," Maier said. "You have nothing to fear from us. We want only to get to the cause of the accident to prevent others from occurring."

The woman raised her hand. Weiler glanced over his shoulder to see the nurse step near. He kept her away as Maier captured the hand and pressed it against Madame Sarle's side.

"Whatever you need from the sister will be waiting for you after we have your answers." Maier turned his head sharply, and took a deep breath of air. Weiler was puzzled until he began gulping air himself. Madame Sarle had defecated in bed.

Maier squeezed her hand tight. "Your neighbor—"

"Anne Cartier," Weiler said.

"Mademoiselle Cartier, she lived alone in the apartment?"

Weiler was about to correct Maier, a highly intelligent man with a short memory. Moments ago he'd mentioned that the Cartier woman lived with Janssen, and already the colonel had forgotten.

The nurse had pointed out that the patient had inhaled flames, losing her voice, and scarcely could make herself understood. Weiler heard her whisper, "With her boyfriend. He was there most nights."

Colonel Maier seemed delighted. "Isn't it easy? A few questions more, and we will be gone. The boyfriend's name was Janssen?"

"I need the nurse."

"A loving couple, no doubt. What did the young man do for a living?"

". . . musician."

"Did Mademoiselle Cartier work?"

The woman started to shrug, but was brought up short by the pain.

"Don't worry if you don't have answers for every question," Maier said. "We want honest answers, those are what we want. Did you see Mademoiselle Cartier in the company of other men besides Monsieur Janssen?"

"Never."

"Ever see Monsieur Janssen with friends?"

"No."

"Take a few seconds to think about it."

"Please let go of my hand," the woman said clearly. "My burns— You are hurting me."

Maier stroked her arm, petted it, squeezed her hand.

Madame Sarle shook her head.

". . . In the company of other women?"

Maier squeezed her hand again, must have squeezed it hard, Weiler thought, because Madame Sarle's mouth twitched. Maier put his ear next to her lips, and Weiler watched them move as if they were lovers; she was nibbling at him affectionately while he smiled and nodded, encouraging her with soft words, never releasing her hand. After nearly five minutes, her head fell back. Maier looked at her. Where her shoulder curved into the left side of her throat was a place the flames had missed. Maier leaned close again, kissed the healthy skin, and then turned away with Weiler at his heels.

"I'm famished."

"I've lost my appetite," Weiler said. "What did she tell you?"

"Lies."

"You seem pleased."

"A lie is something to work with. Before, I had nothing. A lie is usually founded in truth to give it the ring of believability. What we must do now is strip away the untruthful aspects of her story and concentrate on the useful information."

"Where do we begin?"

"She began by telling me that Janssen and the Cartier woman fought like cats and dogs, she heard them shouting through the walls. Another young couple, newlyweds, had lived in their apartment previously. With them it was the sounds of love-making that kept her up all night."

"Did she say what the harsh words were about?"

"Anne Cartier accused Janssen of seeing women behind her back. If his infidelities didn't cease, he was going to end up with his throat cut. At the time his body was pulled from the Seine, she told Madame Sarle that Janssen was a cad who must have treated his other lovers with the same disdain he had for her, and that it was another lover, or perhaps another lover's other boyfriend, or husband, or brother, or even a murderer for hire, who killed Janssen. She had begun to hate him till she learned of his death, when she forgave everything and grieved for him. That is why Mrs. Sarle believed she killed herself."

"Did she tell you what prompted her to enter the apartment?"

"She smelled gas," Maier said.

"You said the explosion wasn't caused by gas. She changed your mind?"

"I suggested she was mistaken and had become confused after being injured. She conceded I was probably right and changed hers."

"Probably?"

"Allow the woman her dignity, Major Weiler. She had been caught in a fib."

"After you challenged her, did she give a different account of why she went in?"

"She confessed to worrying constantly about Mademoiselle Cartier. It was her way of admitting she is an old busybody. When I asked why she was worried, she told me again that she thought the girl had become despondent over the loss of her boyfriend."

"But she heard them fighting. It hardly seems either woman would have been displeased if he walked out."

"She stuck to her story and demanded the nurse. Her pain was returning, and she needed her pills."

"I wasn't aware."

"I was," Maier said. "It was unpleasant to see her suffer so. I asked once more about these loud arguments, and she admitted that possibly—there is that word again—she was mistaken, and not all were between Janssen and Mademoiselle Cartier, but involved outsiders siding against one or the other or both of them."

"Who are they?"

"Would I know?" Maier said. "I just stepped off a plane."

Weiler's stomach growled. They had wasted time tormenting a dying woman when they could have been enjoying lunch, and at a better place than a hospital cafeteria. "Do we have a single piece of conclusive information about the girl?"

Maier shook his head. "Inconclusively, I would say that Mademoiselle Cartier is alive, and in hiding, and ready to resume the activities interrupted on the Rue du Faubourg Saint-Honore."

"It's thin," Weiler said.

"Do you care to bet against it?"

Minutes before the start of the first set, six SS came into La Caverne with a new trumpeter for the Angels. Gert Weskers had acquired a following in Paris as a competent, if unspectacular, jazzman in the years before the war, and as an occasional collaborationist ever since. No one had an enthusiastic opinion of him aside from the Germans, and theirs had little to do with his playing. Eddie didn't want him sullying the bandstand, but there was no politic way to keep him off, and Roquentin didn't object to the Nazis who had come to celebrate their protégé with magnums of his most expensive Champagne.

Weskers didn't embarrass himself, and the set closed to modest applause. More German officers showed up during the intermission, so many that Roquentin had to dispatch a waiter to other clubs for fresh stocks of bubbly.

In the second set, Weskers's chops let him down midway through a run of high F's during the coda for "Swing That Music." The SS didn't mind, calling for more Champagne and endless encores till Eddie thought his arms would fall off pummeling the high hat. It was close to five when Weskers announced that he couldn't blow another note, and the SS left. Busboys were stacking chairs on the tables when a sweaty man in a linen suit and white vest, and with a straw boater under his arm climbed onto the bandstand, grabbed Eddie's hand, and began pumping it.

"Want to compliment you on the swell combo you put together," he said. He was raspy-voiced, his English assuming a familiarity that Eddie denied to his musicians. "I'm sorry I didn't get to hear you on the trumpet, but you're an okay drummer, damn right you are, and that new fellow wasn't too shabby. What's his name?"

"Gert Weskers," Eddie said.

"Gonna file it away in the memory bank, and make a note to catch him next time he plays with you. I'm Thad Simone, your newest biggest fan." He laughed. "Guess there ain't that many left in Paris that don't speak Kraut, and what do they know about music?"

There weren't, but Eddie kept it to himself rather than second an idea that could get him in hot water if it reached the wrong ears. A half smile was all he had for Simone, who could consider himself lucky to get it.

"Me and the missus just hopped off the *Normandie*. I know, I know, most Americans are headed back the other way. There's talk it's only a matter of time before Roosevelt takes a flyer on this European war, but I'm not convinced. I mean I don't see why. We got no gripe with Hitler I can put my finger on. It was up to me, we'd knock these Europeans' heads together, and settle the thing here and now. But that's just one fellow's opinion."

There weren't so many customers for his music left in Paris that Eddie wanted to antagonize a single one. But he didn't care for Simone, or to be around him. He said, "I'm bushed. I've got to be back on the bandstand in fifteen hours, which translates into, before I know it. So if you'll excuse me—"

"Sure, sure, know the feelin' myself," said Simone, pressing close. "Now I've discovered this Caverne Nigger, I'm gonna be a regular. I like the atmosphere, and I like the crowd. I like the music. My only complaint is I don't get to hear you toot your horn. Did you give it up for good?"

"I injured my lip," Eddie said. "It's getting better."

"Glad to hear that, I'm making it a point to be here when you pick it up again." Simone started away, got a step or two before he stopped and stared at Eddie. "We met someplace before," he said.

Eddie shrugged. Simone continued to stare.

"Ain't no doubt. I've got a great memory for faces, ask the missus. Seen yours up close. It just don't register where. Any ideas?"

"I've gigged, must be a million different places," Eddie said. "You say you love jazz. It could have been any of them."

"Yeah, I guess—Well, I don't want to keep you up past your bed-time." Simone stayed put. "Say, ever play the Dog Pound by Decatur Street in New Orleans?"

"That's a Negro club," Eddie said.

Simone grinned at him. "What was I thinkin'? What would you be doin' there?"

"You tell me."

"Say, don't take it wrong. The Dog Pound is integrated now—or what was I doing there? There's plenty of shines—Creoles passing for white in New Orleans that are as lightskinned, hell, lighter'n me and you. Listenin' to your outfit I naturally was reminded of New Orleans. And then I remembered the Pound. You boys play the good old good ones I ain't heard since I was last there."

"It must be that," Eddie said.

"My mistake, no offense intended. Say, been back recently? I'm from Galveston myself, only a few hours away from New Orleans across the state—"

"It's late. I'm going home."

"Sure, sure," Simone said. "A musician got to keep current with his shut-eye. Next time, you'll let me buy you a drink, that a deal?"

Eddie slipped his sticks in his back pocket and walked out. Simone was watching him go when he noticed Roquentin carrying a crate of empty bottles to the curb. "Let me help, mon ami," he said.

"Much obliged," Roquentin said as Simone got his hands under the load.

"Say, that house band of yours really knows its stuff, makes the hottest jazz in Paris. I was talkin' to Eddie, and I asked him did he ever play a particular joint in New Orleans, but I didn't get a thoughtful answer. His eyes were already at half-staff. Did he, huh, I'm talkin' about the Dog Pound."

Roquentin backed onto the sidewalk. Looking over his shoulder, he made his way toward the curb.

"I asked—"

"Did Eddie play a New Orleans club called the Dog Pound? He's from New Orleans. He didn't leave home till he was twenty. Unless he didn't pick up a horn before he left, he must have played somewhere. Any good reason why he wouldn't play there?"

"I don't know," Simone said. "I'll ask him again."

"You can. But it won't get you anywhere."

"Why do you suppose that is?"

Roquentin put down the case. "Thank you, sir. Good night."

"I asked why it won't get me nowhere."

"Eddie doesn't talk about much besides his music. Not even to me, and I'm his friend."

"'Scuse me for repeatin' myself, but why do you suppose that is?"

Roquentin was starting back to the club when he stopped and turned around. Bending his wrist, he rested his chin on the back of his hand in the pose of Rodin's *Thinker*. "I would say it's nobody's damn business."

Simone had an answer, but Roquentin cut him off. "You would say, why do I suppose that is?"

"I probably would."

"What business is it of anyone's what he did before he came here?"

"Not mine," Simone said. "However, you might have the idea I'm on a busman's holiday."

"I am not familiar with this expression."

"Must be because the buses don't get you where you want to go here. It means I'm a cop, a detective with the Galveston, Texas, police, whose business it is to look into things that might not be what they appear to be, and get to the bottom of 'em. I'm here on an extended vacation, but that don't mean I leave my instincts at the pier. Couldn't if I wanted to. I thought I might've heard Eddie back home, but he stepped out so fast I didn't even get a chance to ask if he made any phonograph records. Me and Mrs. Simone, we enjoy fox-trotting around the living room when we're stuck indoors on a rainy day. He acted like I was prying into some dark secret he had."

"If he does, they don't concern us. Eddie's a brilliant musician, that's all we need to know about him."

Simone nodded. "I wouldn't want him thinkin' nothin' else."

CHAPTER FOUR

When Eddie stepped out of the cab at the apartment house on Boulevard Victor Massé, the door was wide open for him, the doorman saluting with his free hand. "Good evening, Monsieur Piron, it's good to see you again."

Eddie's fingers were at his lip before he jammed them in his pocket. It had been only a couple of days since he'd been here. What the doorman meant was that he was looking like himself again. Soon he would be able to play the trumpet and really would be the old Eddie.

Carla was always herself, in a mild fever even before he was out of his clothes. It wasn't as if he kept her love-starved, but tonight she couldn't have enough of him. When he lay back on drenched sheets, she snatched her cigarettes away from him and said, "I'm not done with you."

"I should hope not."

"I mean now," she said, and forced him on top again.

During a truce in their skirmish under the covers, he said, "What's gotten into you? Are you trying to kill us?"

"You don't know?" The hint of a laugh came with nothing in her face that wasn't serious. "*You* got into me." Not an especially clever joke, and still without a smile. "I should never trust you."

"You can always count on me," he said.

"Count on you. Never trust you. They amount to the same thing," she said.

"Stop being mysterious. I don't know what you're getting at."

She put her hand behind his neck and pushed his face close to hers. Taking it as his cue, he was burrowing between her legs again when she said, "I'm pregnant," and he dropped off her like a sack of potatoes.

"What? Not in the mood?" she said. "I know what you're thinking. The baby is yours. I've been completely faithful."

Something had been going on with her. He'd suspected she was seeing someone behind his back but hadn't mentioned it because he hadn't been entirely monogamous himself and didn't have the moral high ground. Her assertion of loyalty, normally a protestation of love, was a troubling fact today. He would do the right thing by her, though, because . . . because doing the right thing was the right thing to do.

"You find it funny?" she said.

Baby, the word sounding over and over in his head. He couldn't have been taken aback more if Carla had unleashed a stream of obscenity at him instead. He didn't know if he wished she had.

"Yes. No—of course not," he said. "What do you intend to do?"

"About the baby? I'll have it. Isn't that what mothers do?"

"What mothers do. Not every pregnant woman."

"Beasts," she said. "Don't you want to be its father?"

"Not knowing you were pregnant, I hadn't given the subject any thought."

"It's a strange thing," she said.

"What is?"

"That men don't."

"I didn't expect—"

"You never heard of the birds and the bees? Playing the innocent doesn't become you. Consider my surprise when the doctor told me."

"I'm feeling a little of it myself," he said.

"A little? The baby is as much yours as mine. Everything I feel is yours in equal measure, except the pain."

"The pain of childbirth?"

"Leave that to me," she said. "You'll marry me?"

"Have you told your parents?" he asked, to the point when the situation called for poetry.

"They're understanding when it comes to their only daughter, which may explain why I push the limits, but they'll be scandalized. Should I confess that my baby's father is an impecunious jazz musician on the next boat back to the States, the scandal won't be small. Papa hates jazz music, though he has never actually listened to it. He is an admirer of Dr. Goebbels, with whom he met last month in Berlin, and—Do you know what Dr. Goebbels has to say about jazz?"

"No, and I don't care."

"Now you must," Carla said. "He says it is Americano nigger kike jungle music. As you are neither a kike or a nigger, or from the jungle, a proposal of marriage will repair some of the damage you've caused. There is no getting around that you are American, and that the baby will be one as well as an early bird. But when I am Madame Piron, you—we will avoid all but minor recrimination."

"When is it best for me to be introduced to them?"

"Is that a real yes?" she said. "You're not going to make them disapprove of you?"

"I doubt I'll have to go out of my way. I should start preparing."

"Not before you agree to a wedding. How will it be if they become fond of you, and there isn't one? We won't only be talking of scandal then, but of a disgrace I can never live down."

"My parents aren't like that," he said. "Any girl I bring home, they would love because I did."

"They are poor," she said.

"I'd forgotten."

"The de Villiers are an old, proud family. Before the Revolution they were among the largest landholders in the Île-de-France, giving their sons to the nation as archbishops, cardinals, and chevaliers. They are staunch Catholics, politically conservative, pro-German, anti-Semitic." She stopped talking. "You're frowning. Are you going to tell me you are secretly a Jew?"

"I'm not Jewish."

"It's one of the first things I noticed about you," she said, "getting to know you. I just wanted to hear you say it. What's wrong, then?"

"It's hard to envision myself as a blueblood."

"It won't take much. All you will have to change are your opinions. I don't care for Germans myself, or Jews. I'm as conservative as my parents, but am going through a stage, as they put it, sowing my wild oats as you've evidently sown one of yours in me. At heart, I'm like them, but will be more demanding of our child, though never of you." She leaned back, and kissed him. "How could I be?"

He had met her six months ago at the bookstalls on the Seine embankment. Thumbing through a biography of Toussaint L'Ouverture, who led Haiti in revolt against Napoleon, he caught a slim but chesty girl eyeing him from the philosophy shelves. He took it for an idle glance but double-checked a moment later, and saw himself getting the once-over. She came by as he was rehearsing pickup lines and demanded to know who he was, remarking immediately about his accent and reacting with disdain for all things American. Fifty minutes later they were in her bed, where he was persuaded that in a hundred years he'd never find another like her.

She insisted on his phone number. Informed that he couldn't afford a telephone, she made him write the address of the club where he performed. She wasn't interested in jazz. Negro music was artless; she chided him for his love of it. Her tastes ran to the bittersweet ditties of the music halls, and light opera. The next night, she was at La Caverne to satisfy herself that the story he'd told wasn't just a story, paying greater attention to the crowd of German officers than to the playing.

Only during his solos did she concentrate on the bandstand. Her contempt for his music irritated him. Later, he understood that it clinched his feelings for her. Carla de Villiers wasn't a fan, not of him. Till he'd gotten to know her, he doubted that anyone in Paris would ever view him apart from his music. With Carla there was no mention of jazz, except when she dismissed it as piffle.

She hated speaking about herself. A week ago she'd suddenly confessed that she had been engaged to a captain of infantry in the First Army group who was killed in the German invasion, one of the few French units that remained steadfast.

"He was a brave fool," she told Eddie. "When everyone ran, he fought for French honor, and his, and what did it get him? What did it get me? Prove to me you are not like him, Eddie. Be a coward, and I will follow you to the gates of hell."

Without her (and sometimes between assignations even now) he would be back to one-night stands with new fans in his dingy flat. So he promised that he would never do a brave thing, nothing more courageous than to perform a song of his own composition at La Caverne.

Stroking the inside of his thigh with her fingernails, she said, "What are you thinking of?"

"Of us. What else?"

"Of the three of us," she said, and kissed him again.

The kiss didn't feel the same. How many kisses would there be if the baby resembled its American side rather than the French? If it carried the genetic legacy not of its mother's line, or of Eddie's mother's— Pirons, Frenchmen from Limousin who came to New Orleans in the early 1700s, making several fortunes in sugar cane and slaves before losing them in Confederate bonds—but of Eddie's father, tribespeople from modern Dahomey, fierce west African warriors and hunters, the slowest afoot run down by Arab traders and bartered to French sea captains who took them to Louisiana via the middle passage and turned them over at a handy profit to planters like the Pirons at the Tuesday and Saturday slave auctions in New Orleans? This part of his history he'd learned from his father's uncle, Cephus Sutpen, born on Aurore plantation in May of 1859 or 1860, not long before the war that advanced the Pirons' ruin, family lore which the old man related on the porch of his estate, a plank shack in the canebrakes. Eddie never tired of hearing how his forebears spent their free Sundays making music with other slaves at Congo Square north of the French Quarter, where his great-grandfather, a redhaired octoroon, had become proficient on banjo and fiddle. He would plead ignorance of all this, accuse Carla if the baby arrived looking like Cephus. If it resembled his blue-eyed mother, the story would have to be told, but not before the child was waiting to become a parent itself.

Where he excelled in his predicaments was in stalling while hoping for the best. Carla might choose to end the pregnancy herself. The blame, the crime, the sin would be hers, and he could be appalled. And there was a better than even chance that the baby would be born the right color. Carla was pure white, and he was fair. He needed to consult a geneticist, talk to the Gypsies.

But there was a larger problem. If Carla was pro-German and anti-Semitic, her attitude toward Negroes was obvious. It was one thing to distance himself from other blacks, to make disparaging remarks about them to people who mistook him for white, occasionally to mouth the same disparagements to himself, but unforgivable in his wife. How could he live with her without becoming like her, become like her while learning to love the child? He would always be fearful that his secret would come out, and Carla would hate him, hate the child too, want them murdered.

She said, "Now what are you thinking of?"

"Of marriage."

"Is it such a difficult decision?"

"Look at us," he said. "Do you call this the proper setting for a proposal?"

She smiled opaquely. "There have been worse."

"Me, I'm a romantic," he said, and shut his eyes.

But he didn't drop off. When she woke up before dawn to go to the toilet, she was alone.

The sun was shaking loose of the horizon when Weiler's car arrived at the Tuileries. Dismissing his driver, he walked along an alley of London plane trees toward the old *musee* at the northwest corner. At his side was a soldier whose face and neck were a welter of scars, a quiet man who paused under the banner above the entrance. The hearts of men were stirred by different things. For this simple soldier, Weiler observed, it was a patriotic slogan. For himself, nothing could be as moving as seeing the City of Light under the control of the Reich. What captured Maier's heart remained a mystery, assuming the colonel had one.

On the bench outside Maier's office on the second floor, the soldier, a Corporal Schneuring, stared at the wall while Weiler fidgeted. Weiler was counting on the corporal for information that would cause Colonel Maier to quit regarding him as a lackey. Maier was due at 8:00. Weiler had shown up well ahead of time to impress the colonel with his devotion to duty.

At 7:40, as Weiler checked his watch for the hundredth time, Maier's door opened. The colonel seemed less surprised to see him there than Weiler did to notice a pallet on the floor. A suite of rooms had been reserved for Maier at the Claridge, Paris's swankiest hotel, but evidently he was an ascetic who preferred not to take his rest between clean sheets on a comfortable mattress. Was he a hater of Paris and its fleshpots, one of those career military men whose fondness for barracks living had instilled a distaste for luxury? Weiler debated it as Maier rolled up his blankets, heaved them into a closet, and opened the windows wide.

Aside from a large desk and several chairs, the office was unfurnished. The desk was a gorgeous French antique that had belonged to one of the Louises, taken from the museum galleries for Maier. There was nothing on it but a green blotter, some papers, a lamp. Not a coffee pot anywhere in the enormous room. Weiler hadn't been expecting an elaborate breakfast, but not to be offered even a cup of coffee and a croissant seemed inhospitable even from a man who preferred to sleep on the floor.

"Allow me to introduce Engineer Corporal Schneuring. He is a sapper who examined the scene on the Rue du Faubourg Saint-Honoré," Weiler said. "You will want to hear directly from him what was found."

The colonel sized up Schneuring with the same reverence for his scars that the corporal had for the patriotic banner over the façade. "Yes, please, Corporal Schneuring," he said warmly. "Tell me."

"I determined conclusively that the apartment house was destroyed in a dynamite blast. Chemical analysis of material retrieved from the rubble indicates that the explosive was fabricated from amatol, a mixture of TNT and aluminum nitrate."

"Yes, Corporal," Maier said. "And what do these facts tell us?"

"That the dynamite probably was obtained from our stores or from those of the French military, sir."

To Weiler, Maier appeared somewhat bored. "Have you—either of you—determined who detonated it?"

Weiler was ready with an answer. Schneuring had it faster.

"No one, sir. The blast originated in a storage locker in the cellar. The explosives were kept there, and probably were set off by accident."

"Yes, but by whom?"

The question was for Weiler, but Schneuring again was first to reply. "It is beyond my competence to answer."

"Wait outside while I continue the discussion with Major Weiler," Maier said.

Schneuring performed a crisp about-face. When the door had closed behind him, Maier said to Weiler, "Is it beyond your competence as well?"

"I am not an expert on bombs, or bomb-makers."

"Expertise is not a requirement for a sound opinion," Maier said. "A healthy intuition is."

"Begging your pardon, sir, but I don't—"

"You know that whoever placed it there meant it for use against us. We don't distribute dynamite as a matter of course to our enemies. You know that much."

"Which residents of the city can be identified as enemies?"

"First and foremost above everyone else, you mean? Those resisting the occupation, I should say."

"There is no organized resistance. Parisians are like most Frenchmen, only more so, docile and cowardly, concerned with nothing beyond their personal comfort. Ethnic psychologists tell us they are among the last peoples in Europe from whom we can expect organized resistance."

"Not all Parisians can be depended upon to accept German rule. The Jews, for instance, and the communists don't take kindly to having us here," Maier said. "Rumors of attempts to organize against us are common currency in Berlin."

"I've been stationed in Paris since the first days of the occupation, and have heard nothing. What do they know in—?"

Weiler's throat caught. A good thing, perhaps.

"Until now the threat has not been specific," Maier said. "I wouldn't like to consider what it might do to our position here if it becomes more pointed. We cannot allow an opposition to take root. An increase in the roundup of Jews and politically unreliable elements is a good first step, while you find whoever placed explosives in the apartment house and we continue to look for the killers of Borge Janssen."

"It seems counter-productive to interfere," Weiler said, "when they do our work for us so well."

"Janssen was not a friend of Germany when he died. It would be a mistake, however, to assume that his killers were out to do us a favor, or even that it is a good thing. I rather prefer that it had been the Gestapo that knocked him off. We could question the lot of the Paris bureau, determine the guilty parties, and return to Germany as bullets were being put in their brains. Unfortunately he wasn't killed by our side, but by the would-be dynamiters, killers more treacherous than he. And more dangerous."

"Why do you make that negative assessment, if I may ask?"

"In war, to prepare for anything less than the most calamitous possibilities is to court disaster. Bad enough that Janssen turned up in Paris, but his unexplained death made to look like suicide is more troubling than if it hadn't happened."

Weiler saw it differently. That was his opinion. He wanted to explain, but Maier's glance toward the door was a signal that he should leave. As he shut it, he looked back at the colonel studying papers at his desk. Breakfast could wait. Could wait forever if it was up to the Colonel Maiers of the world.

CHAPTER FIVE

Simone pulled on his pants, watching Mavis wriggle into her girdle through the half-open door. He wouldn't call Mavis shy, but there was never a time she got herself together that she didn't make sure there was a door between them. It was when she was out of her clothes that the lights went on and she did a star turn. He'd been with women with odder quirks, but none with Mavis's manners. She rarely used curse words in public.

Catching him peeking, she kicked the door shut. "Let me have my stockings," she said, and her hand came out for them. He was curious why she played the games she played, but didn't bring it up. It might cause her to reflect about herself, something he didn't want her to do.

She came out straightening her seams, and then she stepped into her heels, which matched the red of her hair. A shade darker than a fire engine, it got her noticed without being tossed from the best places. Her lipstick was a similar color, but violet eyes were her best feature, even with crow's-feet starting to show. Mavis was getting up in age, close to thirty. In a year or two Simone would have to cut her loose. But in the soft light she wasn't bad. He'd advise her to keep to the shadows, where he usually could be found himself.

"You're giving me claustrophobia," she said.

"What?"

"Quit standing over me," she said. "You've been on my feet since New York. You told me we'd be traveling in style, but that stateroom didn't have a porthole where I could catch a breath of fresh air. I couldn't even turn around without bumping into you. I'm black and blue up to my ankles."

"It was your first time on a liner."

"So?"

"That's how they are, a little cramped. You think it was different up on A deck for his royal former highness and the Simpson broad? I bet she had as many black and blue marks as you without raising a stink."

"I bet she did," Mavis said, "and some bite marks to go with them. But I bet she wasn't sick the whole way over like I was."

Simone backed away from her and was rewarded with a frown.

"This room," Mavis said, "it isn't any bigger than what we had on the *Normandie*."

"You ain't seasick now? Let me know if you are."

"I could be coming down with it again," she said. "It feels like the walls are closing in."

"Would you be seein' Paris if you weren't travelin' on my dollar? It's an expensive city to get around in. We got to cut back on some luxuries."

"All I've seen of it are various ceilings. I could have stayed home and done that without being nauseous."

What other woman complained about a free trip to the most romantic city in Europe? Mavis was an ingrate. A little green around the gills, he'd admit, but an ingrate nevertheless. "You look beautiful tonight," he said.

"Tell me something I don't know."

If she didn't show some appreciation fast, she could swim back to the States, or work off her passage studying ceilings over the shoulder of some of the Germans they'd run into. "I mean it," he said. "Beautiful."

"From someone else, I would take it as a compliment," she said. "Coming from you, it sounds dirty."

"It don't mean you're not," he said. "Learn to accept a remark the way it's intended."

She held out her arms, said "Come here," and undid his tie. He thought she was going to get lovey dovey, waste precious time. Instead she retied the knot and jammed it under his chin. "You look better now," she said. "I wouldn't say beautiful. Better. Are you ready to go?"

He dug a finger behind the knot for breathing room, didn't mention that he'd been ready for half an hour.

The language of the lobby of the Hotel LaBottiere was German. A young couple with tourist stickers from the Tyrol on their luggage was checking in. Simone appraised them as newlyweds from her shy smile and lipstick on the man's collar. There was plenty of traffic to and from the Carillon Room, the restaurant with sidewalk seating, most of it uniformed. Simone made himself comfortable in a sofa by the desk, while Mavis settled in an easy chair near the bar. She really did look beautiful tonight. Why didn't she take his word for it? Would he be here with a woman who wasn't?

A Frenchman using a walking stick and a straw boater to cultivate a lackadaisical resemblance to Maurice Chevalier offered to buy her a drink. Mavis shook her head, but the Frenchman kept on feeding her a line. Simone was about to wise him up that he wasn't wanted, when he figured it out for himself and walked off.

Next to try his luck was a man who pulled out a lighter as Mavis was putting a cigarette to her lips. Simone couldn't see his face, but the lighter wasn't a Zippo. A good thing. If Mavis would let him, he'd hang a NO AMERICANS sign around her neck. The man was definitely not American, probably not French either, judging by the stiff way he held himself. Mavis grasped his hand as she touched the cigarette to the flame, in no hurry to let go. He was taking her upstairs when Simone left. Mavis was set for the night. Her new friend seemed to be a gentleman who would buy her supper. Simone had time now to grab a few drinks and catch a show, maybe at La Caverne Negre.

The lobby was deserted when he returned to the LaBottiere at two. From the landing he saw a knife's edge of light under his door. Inside, Mavis was sitting up in bed, scribbling on hotel stationery. "Have a nice time?" he said.

"I've had worse."

"That's good."

"And better."

"Who was he?"

"A junior assistant something or other from the—" She flipped through the papers in her lap. "The M-E-S-S-E-R-S-C-H-M-I-T-T Company."

"What's he doing in Paris?"

"Looking for a location to put up a factory to build airplanes." She pronounced it aeroplanes. "Fighters, and bombers, and also some whaddaya call them, dirg—dirigig—hell, you know, blimps."

"Got it all in your head?"

"Not there." She gave him the papers. "I'm tight. I wrote it down."

"What good would you be if you weren't?" He leered at her. Before she could ask what he was getting at, he said, "You did all right. We'll take tomorrow off and visit the Louvre."

"What's that?"

"An art museum. They got *Mona Lisa* there."

Mavis pulled a face.

"Somethin' the matter?"

"I thought we could go up the Eiffel Tower and admire the view."

"Someone'll be happy to pay for this information. I'll take you when we're flush. It'll be more fun."

"Do you have a someone in mind?"

Simone nodded. "The other side."

"The other side? That's our side. The Germans, they already know about the factory."

"You and me, that's one side," he said. "The whole world, that's another."

"I don't care that we do business with Nazis," she said. "But if it's all the same, I don't want to fuck any more of them."

"Think of it like this," Simone said. "You're doin' it for America."

"Why can't we see the sights tomorrow? I spent the entire night looking at the—"

"The ceiling," Simone said.

"The floor. You don't know about Germans?"

"Thought I did."

"Don't take my word."

Mavis had met him on the fourth floor of the Michigan House on State Street in Chicago running naked and bleeding past his door. She was there for a singing engagement in the Stockyards Lounge, which had ended badly. Laryngitis had robbed her of her voice, and she'd been booed loudly and canned on the spot. Her manager/ boyfriend—Mr. Fifty Percent, she called him—gave her a beating that cost her a tooth and a deviated septum. She told Simone that she was an actress, a contract player at Monogram Pictures who had appeared in six Poverty Row oaters, had lines in four of them, and twice was kissed by Tex Ritter at the fadeout. Her career had stalled when the studio ran short of cash, and she had jumped at Mr. Fifty Percent's offer to reinvent her as a nightclub thrush. Left high and dry, battered and hoarse in a city where she didn't know a soul, she'd gratefully accepted Simone's invitation to show her the European capitals. He was tightfisted, but not a bad sort, keeping the tight fists to himself. She'd been excited about seeing Paris, and having seen what she had for six days was in a hurry to return home.

The walls were closer when she woke at eleven, alone. Simone had threatened to cut her loose, but why would he do that after reeling in their first big fish? Trying to make sense of it, she remembered something he'd said before they went to sleep, while she was in the tub washing the German out of her. He had to go down to the telephone exchange and ring up a fellow back home who would know what to do with information about a German aircraft plant on the outskirts of Paris. Eleven A.M. here meant it was late afternoon in the States, so that was what he probably was doing. And if he wasn't, and she never saw him again? Sleeping with a Nazi wasn't something she recommended, but that didn't mean she wouldn't do it again, do it as often as she had to to work off a return ticket from the most romantic city in Europe.

"I want you to know what this call is costin'," Simone said. "Seventy-five dollars the first three minutes, and twenty-five for every one after that. 'Less you care to reverse the charges, I can do without small talk. Am I makin' myself understood?"

"That little speech just set you back ten bucks," said the man on the other end of the line, whose name was Lem Perkins. "Whyn't you get around to what you want?"

"Don't expect too much till we have a deal. But I have learned," Simone said, "that Messerschmitt Aircraft, Inc. is lookin' to put up an assembly line outside Paris. As we speak, I'm workin' on gettin' my hooks on blueprints and other goodies from the junior executive scoutin' out a site."

"Hot stuff," said Perkins. "Someone will pay handsomely to have it. One thing you're forgetting, though."

"What's that?"

"We're not at war with Germany."

"Gonna let it get in the way of you becomin' a hero? Everybody knows the war's comin'. Congress'll declare it, the army'll be in the trenches before you pull your thumb outta your ass."

"You're a spy now?" Perkins said. "It's a ways from what you were doing last time I heard from you."

"Forget what I am. War is right around the corner. Can't hurt to jump the gun and guarantee a proper outcome."

"How'll the information get to me?" Perkins said. "You can't drop it in the mail. The Germans inspect everything going to the U.S."

"I can send it to Switzerland, Havana, Mexico City, anyplace you want. Bring it myself. It's up to you."

"Nothing is. Not even here in New Orleans. Washington decides on everything."

"You'll tell Mr. Hoover?"

Perkins's chuckle went on too long to suit Simone. At twenty-five dollars a minute, it was costing almost fifty cents a second to be mocked.

"Field agent like myself doesn't get to meet the Director except for a handshake when I collect my watch for twenty years' service. He especially doesn't want to know about a cashiered cop playing Mata Hari. I'll put word in the pipeline. Someone will notice it and bring it to the attention of someone with connections who knows someone a few doors down from Hoover. That's how things get done."

"Paris ain't cheap," Simone said. "I could starve waitin' to hear back. Makes me wonder what the Brits'll pay to learn about a Messerschmitt plant in range of their bombers."

"I can let you have some earnest money while I try to push this along the pipeline. How's that sound?"

"A thousand would sound about right."

"What?" Perkins said. "I didn't hear. Must be the connection."

"Wire what you can to the Hotel LaBottiere," Simone said. "Havin' any weather?"

"I thought the call was breaking the bank. You want to talk about the weather?"

"I intend to get my money's worth out of every second I'm payin' for."

"It's sticky hot, and we're expecting a big blow as we generally do this time of year. That use up the time?"

"I still got half a minute," Simone said.

"What's left to talk about?"

"Eddie Piron."

"Who's that?"

"Character I met the other night tootin' a trumpet on Place Pigalle. Know the name?"

"There's no shortage of Pirons in New Orleans," Perkins said, "a good many of 'em musicians. Most every Piron I'm familiar with is Creole. What's a colored boy doing in Paris now the Germans are there?"

"He don't look particularly colored," Simone said, "'less you have an eye for it. The Germans, they don't. They're too busy lookin' at noses to be concerned about nappy hair and such. I'm tryin' to find out what he's doin' here. It's why I ask."

"Asking me?"

"I suspect he's hidin' from the law. American law. Louisiana law. He's got delicate manners, so I would venture it's not for spittin' on the public sidewalk. Have his name run through the NOPD files. We still got friends on the force, don't we?"

"I wouldn't call 'em friends of yours. I don't believe I've ever come across anybody who knows you and calls himself that, with the possible exception of myself."

"Do it anyway. It'll give me somethin' to keep out of trouble when I'm not engagin' in international intrigue for Uncle Sam."

Lukas Schickle, thirty-two, from Cologne, with a master's degree in the philosophy of the European enlightenment from Humboldt College in Berlin, had been in the French capital for close to three weeks, time enough to start thinking of himself as an old Paris hand. Each day after work, he took a long walk in which he discovered the most interesting bookshops and art galleries, authentic bistros and out-of-the-way restaurants. His fiancée would join him shortly, and the city would be presented to Hilda as an intimate gift.

Turning the corner onto the Champs Élysées, he was struck by the splendid enormity of the Arc de Triomphe. Not long ago, the victorious Wehrmacht had paraded under the monument in a poignant scene that to his eternal regret he hadn't been here to see. Hilda would never have tired of his eyewitness account of the historic moment when Germany erased the shame of defeat in the Great War and Paris became an outpost of the Reich.

As he stepped off the curb on the Rue du Colisée, a black Citroën splashing through a puddle soaked him to the knees. His head whipped around with a furious stare for the idiot behind the wheel. The Citroën was the only car on the block. Prior to the occupation, the streets would have been clogged with traffic, but now, at 8:30, there was only the occasional vehicle, few pedestrians on the sidewalks. "Nique ta mere," he shouted, and was whisking oily water off his pants when the car skidded to a halt and two men stepped out.

Shickle started across the street with the pair from the Citroën on his heels. All he'd intended was to express his displeasure with thoughtless Frenchmen in a generic way. They seemed to have taken it entirely wrong, as though he'd seriously suggested fucking their mother. Big Frenchmen, he noticed—quickly glancing back—bull-necked and broad across the chest, nothing like the sniveling frogs he dealt with on the job. An apology probably would defuse the misunderstanding, but the idea rankled him. Besides, these two didn't look like they would be bought off with less than abject groveling, and that he was not prepared to do. They came up on both sides, grabbing his arms, and muscled him to the car. My God, thought Shickle, I'm being kidnapped for cursing at frogs. Forcing his head down, they threw him onto the rear seat. One got in back with him, and the Citroën careered around the corner, turned again and again until they were bumping along cobbled lanes, the authentic medieval lanes of Paris that he wished he'd never seen.

His captors said nothing, not even to each other. Using a collegial tone, he asked, "Où allons-nous?" They might have been deaf. There was nothing to do but to sit back and enjoy the ride. His hand was already inside his jacket, fishing for Gauloises and his lighter.

The butt was scorching his fingers when they rode around the Tuileries and stopped at a columned building that looked like one of the great mausoleums of classical times. A famous edifice with a long and colorful history, but without the Paris guidebook sitting in his hotel room Schickle couldn't identify it. Anticipating luxuriant carpets inside, he was instead marched along bare floors, his footsteps echoing against empty walls off-white in color, somewhat lighter in rectangular spaces where until recently paintings had hung.

Schickle breathed a deep sigh. Soon the misunderstanding would be cleared up. He owed his kidnappers an apology for thinking they were French. No longer afraid, he surrendered to outrage. No one had the right to loot precious artworks, and to snatch decent people off the streets. Occupiers had responsibilities, too.

In a high-ceilinged room lit by torch lamps, lightning flared at the edge of heavy draperies. The men who had forced him into their car now pushed him down on a chair within arm's length of a desk where a man in a tailored uniform was studying him. Schickle was the quicker study. Foppish officers and party hacks had counted for nothing much in Germany a few years ago. Now they had all the influence and didn't let you forget it. Schickle knew how to handle him. Senior Nazis had assumed a controlling interest in his firm, and he had done quite nicely, thank you, by being as imperious as they, and more obtuse, never caving in to their appetite for obsequies. This one, too, he would put in his proper place.

"Schickle, I am Major Weiler."

Schickle rose to his full height, leaned across the desk looking down at the major, and extended his hand. Weiler didn't take it. Bent over, grasping at nothing, he felt absurd. So much for his usual stratagem, but he had others. Mid-level soldiers did not have advanced degrees. He would probe Weiler's background and demonstrate the disparity in their education and cultural levels.

"Sit down," the major said. "Let us dispense with the preliminaries. We know what you are, and what you have been doing. Tell us what we don't know, and we—you will be spared the discomforts of the learning process."

Not a student of rhetoric, thought Schickle, or else plain stupid; the major didn't recognize a contradiction when he uttered it. If Weiler knew about him, there would be no reason for interrogation. Schickle searched for words to set Weiler straight, to rid himself of absurdity, and to attach it where it was the best fit.

"I don't know why I've been brought here. I've done nothing wrong."

Weiler made a note in a legal pad. "Is that how you view it?"

Schickle watched him fill the page and start another. Who knew that he was a gold mine of information? He'd merely expressed his puzzlement, and Weiler stupidly had turned the words around.

"Nothing wrong in conducting several meetings with an American agent?"

"Me, sir? What would I tell him?"

"Not a he," Weiler said, "as you damn well know. As your fiancée will be informed."

Schickle felt cold and clammy. At the same time, he was boiling over. Here were clues to what the major was getting at, the various pieces mashed together into something unrecognizable like the cubist works he had seen at the Degenerate Art exhibit in Munich four years ago, familiar colors and forms arranged monstrously.

"We know about your relationship with her," Weiler said, "as part of your workings to sell out the Fatherland."

"What?"

"Feigning ignorance is a dead-end street, Schickle. Don't go down it. I warn you, don't take the first step."

"I'd never . . . I wouldn't . . . betraying Germany is beyond anything I am capable of doing morally, emotionally, or in practical terms, even if I wanted to. Which I do not."

Weiler laughed out loud. Schickle immediately felt jealous. He didn't think that he'd ever be able to laugh wholeheartedly again. The picture was coming together now as a nightmare scene worthy of Hieronymus Bosch. In a moment of weakness brought on by loneliness for Hilda, he'd told foolish lies to a foreign woman, a tale of such preposterous invention that he'd had a hard time keeping a straight face. Somehow it had reached the ears of military intelligence, who were as gullible as she had been. Paris was infested with spies. He was one visitor who was nothing other than he claimed to be. No, that wasn't exactly right. Who was what he claimed to be now. Had he known that he was such a convincing fabulist, he wouldn't have set his sights as low as he had, but tried his hand with the beauties of the Folies.

"You gave away Messerschmitt's plans in France. You don't consider it betrayal?"

To be suspected of treason was his personal hell. But at last the mystery was cleared up. An admission to his indiscretion with the American was in order. He would add his sincere regret for his unbecoming actions with promises that they would not occur again, and then his ordeal would be over.

"I did nothing like that, sir," he said. "I should say, I mean, I mean I told a woman, yes, I confess I did, that I was a project engineer for Messerschmitt, but that was only to encourage her to, to get her to come back to my room. I know nothing about factories, or aircraft. I . . . I've never been in a plane in my life."

"Naturally, all foreign women are looking for a man professing knowledge of the German aircraft industry."

"More than are looking for a man with my real job. Trust me," Schickle said. "I'm a salesman in ladies foundation garments visiting Paris to oversee the introduction of our new line at the Galeries Lafayette department store chain."

"We know," Weiler said. "They've never heard of you at Messerschmitt."

Schickle sat back beaming as he had as an elementary school pupil when a teacher awarded him a gold star for right answers.

"We looked into your story before we had you arrested," Weiler went on. "Give us the rest."

"But that's all I am, a brassiere and girdle man. Why do you think otherwise?"

"What we want to know first and foremost is how a corset salesman came into possession of the plans of Messerschmitt Aircraft."

Schickle's hand rushed to his mouth. The picture had been rearranged into an image as lifelike as a portrait by a renaissance master, yet more horrific than anything by Bosch.

"I am unaware of any of them. I know how it appears, but I don't. Not one thing. I met a woman. I was feeling rather sorry for myself, bored and without friends in a foreign city, and I did not think, I mean I thought a heroic story about what I do was required to win her admiration. She was quite beautiful. Therefore I . . . I enhanced my background, you might say, and told her I was a big shot at the aircraft company."

"Do you expect me to believe that?"

She did, Schickle wanted to shout in his face. Fell for it completely, in ways he never would tire of although they left him exhausted. Just this morning he had sent a note to Hilda instructing her to delay her departure because he had his hands full here with the underwear.

"My parents, my friends, my comrades from loyal service in the Kriegsmarine, everyone who knows me, they will tell you I am a patriotic German."

"They cannot explain how you know anything other than about girdles. It leaves only one question unanswered."

"Yes, sir?" Schickle let out a deep breath. "What is it?"

"How did you know?"

Tears came to Schickle's eyes. It wasn't a strategy he had employed at his firm. He was a tragic victim of coincidence. Who would believe that a lie coming innocently to mind was a military secret? One more thing he understood about these vain men who had all the power today. When you gave them opportunity to crush you, that's what they did. He hid his face in his hands and wept. It would give Weiler the wrong idea, but he couldn't help it. Weiler would crush him to nothingness. Wait and see.

Three new restaurants were the talk of the Gestapo, a Greek taverna in the Latin Quarter, another that featured fine French rustic cooking, and La Vielle Amie off the Place de la Concorde, which already had earned three coveted stars in the Michelin red guide. Any of them would make an excellent place to meet with Colonel Maier, but Weiler didn't bring it up. He and the colonel were the occupying powers here, yet Maier spurned the little luxuries that went toward alleviating their heavy responsibilities. Suggest fine food to Maier, and he would denounce it, and you, as decadent. They could confer just as easily in the office. Over the phone.

"I've learned something about the fellows in the band Janssen was playing with when he died."

"This is about music?" Maier asked.

"Indirectly."

"Let me tell you directly that I have no interest in music."

"You should hear it anyway," Weiler said. "I mean what I've learned. It began when a traveler from Dresden representing himself as someone in the know about Messerschmitt Industries linked up with an American woman in the market for the secrets he seemed to be selling."

"How did you get on to them?"

"The woman had traveled to Paris in the company of another American, a former policeman in the city of New Orleans. The man, Simone, evidently is running her to fish for information."

"Information for whom?"

"For himself, I should say, to be packaged to the highest bidder. He made several calls to the United States from the international telephone exchange where just last week we completed installation of listening devices."

"This wasn't done immediately upon taking over the city?"

"We did it now, and found out that Simone requested a background check on the leader of the band. His name is Eddie Piron."

"You are telling me that Piron and Janssen are linked to the sale of Messerschmitt plans to an American?"

"Nothing came of that," Weiler said. "The man we believed worked for Messerschmitt was a liar." Weiler paused to allow Maier to berate him for leading him on about nothing, and for being late with the phone bug. Amazingly, the colonel had no comment, not even his maddening questions. "That was by way of preamble. I must say that it is in character for a man like Borge Janssen to be involved with someone like Piron."

"What character is that?"

"We checked on Piron, too, through Interpol headquarters in Vienna. They report that he is sought by the police in the United States, a man who is not what he seems to be. Not even *who* he seems to be."

"You are trying out a narrative for a movie trailer? A melodrama?" Maier said. "Or do you intend to tell me what the allegations against him are?"

"It is only by way of—"

"Preamble," Maier said. "Stop clearing your throat, and get on with it. Why does Simone care about him? Why should I?"

It was just as well that they hadn't gotten together at a restaurant where Maier would interrupt his remarks with a barrage of questions. He held the upper hand now. He held the phone.

"I will begin at the beginning. Piron is from a small town in the province of Mississippi near New Orleans in the American South, born there in the autumn of 1908. . . ."

CHAPTER SIX

Sunday was payday for the band. Monday was their day off, and by Tuesday when the players wandered back to the club a good many were broke, hitting up Eddie or Roquentin for a few francs to tide them over. This Sunday, after the last set, when Eddie handed out paychecks, Gert Weskers had a yellow envelope for him.

"What's this?" Eddie said.

"Open it and see."

Two pasteboards slipped out as Eddie tore the flap. He caught them as they fluttered to the floor, complimentary tickets to *Bonjour Paris*, a new revue starring Maurice Chevalier which opened for previews the following night at the Casino de Paris.

"You are lucky to be holding those," Weskers said.

"I wouldn't cross the street to see Chevalier."

"Chevalier is old hat. Youngsters mock his cornball antics. A friend of mine is his piano player and is papering the house. Otherwise they will be playing to the previous generation."

"This explains my luck?"

"Do you have a girl?" Weskers asked. "It's hard to accept, but women adore him."

"Not hard," Eddie said. "Impossible. You're right, though, they do." He slipped the tickets in his shirt. "Will you be there tomorrow night?"

"Me? I've got no girlfriend," Weskers said. "See you Tuesday."

Delighted with Eddie's invitation to a show in which he wasn't the attraction, Carla spent the afternoon shopping for him at the Printemps department store. When he arrived at her apartment, she presented him with a hand-painted silk tie, which he held up against his chest to show off how nice it looked but refused to wear. Carla wasn't insulted. She knew that he would never put on a tie. Tomorrow she would return it and buy a maternity gown for herself. Tonight, though, he was quite the romantic, even paying for the taxi that took them to the Casino on the Rue de Clichy.

The house was packed when they claimed their seats ten minutes before the curtain was due to rise. Chevalier had regained his status as a drawing card, or else Weskers's friend had done an excellent job distributing tickets. Eddie stretched his legs into the aisle bordering the pit where the orchestra was warming up. The pianist, a stranger, picked him out of the crowd and smiled like they were old pals.

The orchestra struck up a number, and the curtain rose. The show was a plotless trifle, an excuse for the performers to trot into the footlights to do their star turns. Chevalier came out in spats, a straw skimmer, and twirling a bamboo cane, hammed it up before breaking into "Ca Sent Si Bon La France." Eddie was about to point out that he was singing on the beat, a cardinal sin for jazz singers, for any good singer, when he glanced at Carla brushing away tears. He shrugged a good Gallic shrug. You had to be French to appreciate Chevalier. At least white. Tonight was a reminder that he was lacking in both categories.

The casino was packed with damp-eyed women and dry-eyed Nazis, Pétainists, and Germans in uniform. The SS probably shared his opinion of Chevalier and had stayed away, but there were plenty of high-ranking officers from the Wehrmacht and other branches of the occupation army. The audience was comfortable with the Germans. Chevalier, mugging shamelessly, bowed and scraped before them. Expecting boos, Eddie watched the crowd eat it up.

Eddie called France home because he had no place else. The war wasn't his; neither was the defeat. As a guest he refused to criticize the nation that embraced him, but more than bad singing made him want to grab his trumpet and move on. But where would he go from here? For Eddie Piron in 1941, the streets of Paris delineated the parameters of his world as precisely as those of New Orleans and Chicago had in the past.

Chevalier eased into a lead-footed soft shoe. Carla didn't seem to care that he was a clod. Catching Eddie looking at her, she patted his hand, and then leaned over and kissed him on the cheek. Why was he worried that their child would turn out to be black? The tragedy would be if it was like its mother.

The Germans talked over the performers, laughed in the wrong places. They would enjoy themselves more serenaded with the rousing anthems of the bierstubes, Eddie decided, or martial music to send them marching over the next hill. Germans advertised themselves as the countrymen of Beethoven and Brahms, but closer to their heart were the torch songs of Marlene Dietrich and the cloying melodies of the Comedian Harmonists. No, that wasn't right either. Dietrich was in exile in Hollywood, the Harmonists disbanded because half their members were Jews. Chevalier was a cut or two above what you would find in the Berlin music halls today. In Berlin now, there was no place for Kurt Weill or Bertolt Brecht. No place for Eddie Piron.

At intermission, Eddie strolled to the men's room. A line stretching back to the lobby caused him to wonder if Chevalier had unsettled everyone's stomach. He stood at the end, advancing slowly when someone said to him, "Great show, ain't it?" It was Simone tugging at his elbow. "Ol' liver lips sure knows how to put a number across."

"I thought," Eddie said, "you were a jazz fan."

"Crazy for all good music." Simone nudged him ahead. "Line's movin'."

Eddie took a half step. He wanted to get away from Simone but needed the toilet.

"I was thinking," Simone said, "'bout the conversation we had when I told you I seen you play in New Orleans, and you pointed out, you mentioned it was a Negro club, and what would you be doing there? Gave it a lot of thought. Want to know something?"

"What's that?"

"You were right. The Dog Pound is a Negro club. But I was right too. Tried to figure out how we both could be. Give it all the thought I had, and come to the only conclusion."

Eddie waited. "Going to tell me what it is?"

"It'd be impolite."

"You've got a rotten memory—"

"So I have," Simone said. "Which is why I made some calls to the U.S. to double-check. They put in these new trans-Atlantic phone lines, sounds like you are in the same room with the person you're talkin' to three thousand miles away. I mention it so you'll know there's no mistake. I was told the New Orleans police've got a strong interest in you about an altercation in the French Quarter some years back. I'd be surprised they are actively lookin' for you.

Nevertheless, here you are in Paris in these tryin' times. Started me thinkin', who else is after you in the States, what other stuff you have pulled. Black man passin' for white here under the Nazi Germans."

"What do you want?" Eddie said.

"What've you got I might want?"

Eddie turned his back.

"Don't worry your head, you'll come up with somethin' nice, or everybody in Paris'll know their ace trumpet player is a spade."

"Do you think that would be bad for my career?"

"Ain't talkin' 'bout your career. Talkin' 'bout your future. Your life. These Germans, they got primitive ideas 'bout the colored."

"Go ahead, tell everyone in Paris I'm not white," Eddie said. "See if anyone believes it. The truth is, you're wrong. I just might sue you for slander."

"I doubt," Simone said, "you'd be happy with the attention. 'Specially after the verdict comes in."

Eddie was proud of the light skin and straight hair that allowed him to carve a niche for himself between the races. On occasions when someone suggested that he was other than the white man he claimed to be, he dropped the guise, often with raised fists. This was the first time he'd denied having Negro blood. After years in this city that had opened its arms to him, it was crazy to be in a situation where it seemed necessary. He really did need to use the toilet.

The curtain was up when he returned to his seat, Chevalier oilier and more oafish as he launched into his specialty number, "La Chanson du Macon." Carla said, "You were gone so long, I was beginning to think you weren't coming back."

"Where would I go?"

She shushed him, pulled him down beside her.

"No, I mean it," he said.

"Mean what?"

"Where would I go?"

⊰◇⊱

Mavis said, "You were gone so long, I thought I was never going to see you again."

"Ran into an old friend of mine by the john. We got to talkin', and I forgot the time."

"You didn't forget to pee?"

Simone snapped his fingers. Grabbing the balcony railing, he hoisted himself out of his seat looking at Mavis, and then he sat down again.

"An old friend from New Orleans?"

"I didn't know him there," Simone said. "Met him for the first time a few nights ago at a club on Place Pigalle."

"You lost me," she said. "Care to tell me who this old friend that you didn't know before is?"

Simone leaned forward, pointing down into the orchestra. "In the front row by the band. Next to the woman in the black dress. That's him."

"The tall fellow? He must be awful good-looking."

"All I can see of him up here is the back of his head. It don't look more good-lookin' than the back of most heads. Why do you say that?"

"While you were at the gents I couldn't help noticing the girl he's with, and she is one of the most beautiful I've seen in Paris. You expect one of these Frenchies that look like they were sawed off at the knees, that's how short they are, to be her husband?"

"She ain't his wife either, I bet."

"Without seeing his face, it still makes me happy to hear."

Several rows behind them someone said, "Silence!" Simone whipped around, but no one looked back.

"Know something, Mavis, you might have the right idea. Good-lookin' single fellow like Eddie Piron, you and him were made for each other. Want to romance him I won't stand in the way."

"You know I'm only teasing you," she said. "Keep your shirt on."

A man who didn't look like he was sawed off at the knees shouted "Faire taire!" Simone leaned close to Mavis. "A head turner such as yourself, you'd be first-rate competition for that gal he's got. Everybody can stand a little competition, even her."

"What's the catch?"

"Ain't no catch," Simone said. "Oh, did I mention he's a nigger?"

Mavis shaded her eyes, and stared down into the orchestra. "He doesn't look like one."

"Not all of 'em do where we come from."

"I always wondered what it would be like being with one," she said.

"You did?"

"Sure, as long as somebody had to point out that was what he was."

"Be quiet, damn it," someone said in English.

Simone kept quiet. There was nothing left to say anyway.

In the cab taking them back to the hotel, Mavis said, "You were kidding, right, about what you said about wanting me to sleep with a colored fellow?"

"Did it sound like I was kiddin'?"

"Not too much. That's why I am asking. If you aren't, why would you? You know they have all got cooties."

"Same reason I wanted you with that engineer from Germany."

"For his secrets?"

"That's right."

"This fellow has military secrets, too? What does he do?"

"Plays trumpet at that club."

"You're pulling my leg," Mavis said. "What kind of secrets could he have?"

"That's what I want you to find out. They wouldn't be secrets if I already knew."

"A trumpet player? The German, he knew about planes."

"Yeah, and you did a good job on him."

"I would say that he did it on me. But never mind. I did what you wanted me to, more or less. Where is the money from it?"

"He must've figured he could live without you. He took a powder," Simone said. "I'm not holdin' it against you. You'll do better with Piron."

"I'll say it again," she said. "A trumpet player?"

"There were plenty of SS in his club the time I dropped in. They run this burg, and they love jazz. You'll get some dirt on them, and maybe a few secrets about himself. He must have some racket, or what he be doing here?" To the driver he said, "Eyes on the road, Bud, you just run a red light.

"Still with me?" he said to Mavis. "You ain't said a word."

"I was thinking, how do I go up against a woman like the one he has now?"

"You got me."

Mavis started to laugh, to laugh at him.

"I mean, you got me."

CHAPTER SEVEN

The drunken Nazi wanted "Shine." Gert Weskers said, "I am sorry, I cannot play this tune."

"You call yourself a jazz musician?"

Eddie often had the same question. It didn't make things better, being in agreement with a Nazi.

"I . . . I have never played it before," Weskers said. "I don't know the part."

The Nazi, an SS Captain Krauss in Paris as part of a mission to facilitate the transfer of Jewish property to the Fatherland, said to Roquentin "Lock the doors. No one leaves until we hear 'Shine.'"

It was past 3:00, and Eddie was exhausted. Pounding the drums like the hopped-up viper the audience expected to see did that to you. The Nazi was soused more than a bit. A drummer himself, he tapped his fingers against a shiny holster on his hip as Eddie walked offstage, continued to the office, and returned with his trumpet, saying to Weskers, "Take my place at the drums."

"What do I know about them?"

"You know the Heinie may kill you if he doesn't like your playing."

Weskers picked up the sticks, examined them in his hands looking puzzled, and then swiped at the tom toms and snare, hammered the pedal against the bass drum. The piano player struck a few chords, and Eddie raised his horn to his lips.

It was good to be front and center under the lights again, even while risking the displeasure of an SS man with a load on. The song was a bravura piece by the great Armstrong, and he hit a few clams in the opening cadenza. His lip stung when he blew hard, and the verse was ragged. The chorus was better as he slowed the tempo, improvising on the melancholy theme, developing it until the guitar stole a canny, single-string solo that lifted the mood. The gold standard was how Satchmo had recorded it with his orchestra, but that was beyond the Angels' capabilities on their best day. And this wasn't one of them. Eddie wasn't playing for posterity, but for Nazis.

A handful of Germans were scattered around the bandstand, most of them uniformed. A woman sat by herself at a banquette, good-looking in an unrestrained, American way. The SS invited her to their table, but she waved them off to devote herself to her drink.

At the coda the SS broke into rhythmic clapping. Captain Krauss demanded to hear the tune again. Eddie didn't have another bar left in his lip. The captain pounded his glass against the table, a Katzenjammer kid run amuck. Eddie put down the trumpet, letting Philippe carry the melody, and then he began to sing.

"Oh, chocolate drop that's me,"

Krauss bellowed while his companions egged him on. Eddie fingered the valves, but didn't lift the instrument to his face. He loved the melody as much as he hated the lyrics written for a Negro road show. Armstrong had made it the tragic anthem of a beleaguered race, or a coon song—take your pick—and his version was how it was known best. Mouthing Armstrong's words, Eddie felt transparent, a black man impersonating a white man pretending to be colored.

"Just because my hair is curly
Because my teeth are pearly
Just because I always wear a smile,
Like to dress up in the latest style."

Lacking Armstrong's gravel in his voice, he compensated with rawness as he tried not to choke on the words.

"Just because I'm glad I'm living
Take troubles grinning, never whine
Just because my color's shady,
Slightly different maybe
That's why they call me Shine."

He finished covered in sweat, also Armstrong's trademark. Captain Krauss's companions hoisted him by the shoulders and walked him to the sidewalk under protest. Eddie told the other customers that he hoped to see them again soon. Everyone got up to go, all but the woman, who said to him, "Thank you from the bottom of my heart."

It wasn't unusual for Eddie to receive effusive praise from his fans. This was something else.

"I'm flattered," he said, "that you enjoyed my playing so much."

"That wasn't too shabby either," the woman said. "I'm talking about how you handled the Hun. He'd've started shooting if he didn't get to hear what he wanted."

"Shooting at me."

"Just the same," she said, "it wasn't something I care to be around."

The lights flashed on and off, and then they dimmed.

"No time?" she raised her glass toward Roquentin, who shook his head, tilted it at Eddie. "Not even for a quickie?"

Eddie went to the bar. He was also relieved that the Germans hadn't squeezed the trigger. It wouldn't have been the first time they had done that for a song.

"You're a hero," she said when he came back with a bottle.

He poured for both of them, drank off most of his watching the band file out of La Caverne.

"A real angel."

"During working hours only," he said.

"You don't sound like a Frenchman."

"My playing?"

"Your playing, your talking, how you don't go down on your knees in front of Nazis. There's nothing French about you."

Eddie didn't answer.

"I meant it as a compliment," she said. "As three, actually. You're American. Where are you from?"

"The South."

"We have something in common."

"You're a Southerner yourself?"

"I have no use for Germans."

Looking at her, Eddie looked at his watch. She didn't take the hint.

"I'm Mavis," she said. "You're—?"

"Dog-tired. I need to go home."

"Paris has changed," she said. "People are afraid to be friendly. It's no fun being in a foreign city without a friend."

Her eyes lingered against his, turned them away. Was that a blush on his cheek? She had never seen a colored man blush, but he didn't look colored at all. Much too fair, not to mention good-looking, and how could he be colored if she found him attractive? She wouldn't put it past Simone to lie about him to put a bug in her head about sleeping with him. She wondered why it was okay with Simone for her to jump into the sack with a Nazi, but to have second thoughts about a light-skinned musician who even the SS regarded with respect, the answer no doubt in the handsome face looking away from hers. She was dying to find out if he really was colored. More than whatever Simone had sent her to get, she wanted that question answered.

"What did you say your name was?"

"Piron."

"What brings you to Paris, Mr. Piron?"

"This, that, and the other thing."

"Aside from those?"

"The music."

"There isn't enough back home?" she asked.

"Too much of the kind I don't enjoy playing."

Simone hadn't sent her to get his ideas about the jazz scene, but she wouldn't learn anything about him here. Screwing was more productive than administering the third degree. Where she shined was in getting a man in bed and keeping quiet while he provided answers to questions she'd never think to ask. She said, "It's late. I'm a little tight. Tired, too. Will you see me back to my place?"

"Paris is safer than it's ever been. The militias chase everyone off the streets at night."

"Empty streets terrify me," she said. "So do militias."

"I'll call a cab."

She put down her glass, looked at him squarely. "You know," she said, "I'm not looking for a ride."

"Aren't you?"

She would tell Simone that Piron was fresh. It might be the music that brought him to Paris, but he also liked talking dirty. No, dirty wasn't the right word. What did the Frenchies call it? Oh yeah, *double entendre*. Wising off to white women.

"If it gets me where I want to go," she said. "When I take a ride with a stranger, that doesn't always happen." She checked to see if he was up to speed. He was nodding, going along with it up to a point, but not smiling. "If you won't take me home, let me stay with you. It's your fault I'm in the fix I'm in."

"How's that?" he said.

"I wouldn't be stuck here past my bedtime if I hadn't hung around to hear you play."

"What will my girlfriend say?"

"Not a thing," she said. "Unless you mention it. I don't recommend that."

"She knows everything I do."

"I don't recommend that either."

It was frustrating being unable to get him to open up, the frustration part of a larger feeling of anxiousness that she couldn't properly explain. Hard to figure why a trumpet player should have secrets that Simone could turn into cash. Yet there was an undeniable mystery about Piron. Even if there would be no payday down the road, she wanted those secrets for herself.

In the meantime, she had a job to do. "Tell me about her," she said.

"My girl? What for?"

"Maybe I can come up with a good story."

"She doesn't need a story."

"For you. About why you invited me to spend the night."

"It was past five when he put me in the taxi," she told Simone at the hotel.

"This was after you steam-cleaned him? You were with him so long, I was beginning to think you two had eloped."

"Where could we run off to with military patrols on all the roads?" she said. "We stayed in the club till I couldn't keep my eyes open."

"What did you get?"

"Conversation," she said.

"You should've slept with him."

"Yeah," she said. "I should have."

Simone gave her a sour look. Usually she would pout when he did that, demand to know what she had done that was so terrible. Tonight she enjoyed his discomfort, knowing the reason for it. She had fallen for Piron in a small way. Simone's tough luck. If it bothered him, he shouldn't have sent her to do a job on a colored man.

"Why didn't you?" he said. "On account of he's a nigger?"

"He wasn't all that interested. You saw what his girl looks like. What chance did I stand against her?"

"At three, four in the morning I ain't met the man that'd roll you out of bed, Mavis."

"He never let me get him near a bed."

Simone plumped the pillows behind his head, settled back against the headboard. He patted the covers, but Mavis remained in her clothes in the hard chair on the other side of the room.

"Thanks, but no thanks." She crossed her legs. "At least till you stop looking at me like that."

She watched him go through various facial contortions, ending up where he'd started.

"He must've let something slip about himself."

"He'd rather talk about his girl," she said. "Me and him, we're brother and sister."

Now Simone had the hairy eyeball for her.

"You don't want to hear what he told me? Yes or no?"

"As long as you're not comin' to bed, what else've I got to do?"

"Never mind that. His girl's trying to make an honest man out of him. He hinted that he got her knocked up, although it could just be he wants me to think he did 'cause what will cool off a woman faster than a man who is going to be some baby's daddy?" She paused while Simone lit a cigar. He tossed the match, and she saw it put a scorch mark in the rug. "I don't suppose it's something we can take to the payout window."

"It might be, if the woman isn't someone he picked up in an alley."

"Does she look like something you would find in an alley?"

"No, I will give you that," Simone said. "Most days neither do you."

Mavis pouted. She had been holding back, and it got away from her.

He continued. "From what I saw, she looked like a real lady. Elegant the way some frogs can be. Which raises the question of what she's doin' with a horn player."

"This is Paris, you're forgetting," Mavis said. "There's more women chasing after artists and musicians than there's artists and musicians to go around. It's a seller's market."

"Not for a nigger, I wouldn't think."

"You can't tell by looking even up close. I couldn't see one thing about him that isn't white."

"He either is colored, or he ain't. There's no in-between."

"She might think there is."

"Why? Because you do?" Simone said. "You ain't carryin' his kid. Think you'd be so broad-minded if a pickaninny was growin' inside your belly?"

Mavis didn't answer. Simone had won the argument. It was time to drop it, but she knew he wouldn't. He never did when he had her on the ropes.

"You tell me you didn't lay him 'cause he wouldn't go for it. If he was a German, one of these master race specimens they have got here now, or even a Frenchie, his clothes would've been in a pile on the floor before he knew he was out of 'em. It's the first time I sent you to do a job on a fellow, and not all of 'em exactly like Clark Gable, that you didn't clinch the deal. If you want to know, I don't believe you, the excuses you're makin'."

"You have a better idea about what I've got in here—" Mavis tapped her finger against her head, "than I do myself."

"It's between you and him," Simone said.

"Nothing is."

"It wouldn't hurt if you'd got his girlfriend's name so we can get her opinion about hatchin' a nigger baby," Simone said. "We'll bring it up with Piron and find out what he's ready to pay for our advice."

"You have it all figured out. What do you even need with me?"

He patted the bed again. Mavis uncrossed her legs and kicked off her shoes. Then she recrossed them.

"Say," she said, "did I tell you that boy can really play?"

The room shook twice as Eddie was wakened by the sound of an explosion. Lifting his head, he considered whether he'd been dreaming until a faint echo rolling across the city rattled the shutters. He had listened to enough artillery fire during the invasion to sort out the distant rumble of big 150mm German cannons from larger French 155s, which in any case rarely were fired. This was something else, closer, bringing the caustic flavor of cordite. He went to the window and raised the louvers, but the smell was gone. In the street, people were going about their business. Probably it had been a dream. Or not.

Sleep was a lost cause, the explosion just a part of what was keeping him awake. The woman from the night before had attached herself to him almost till dawn. Women like her were fringe benefits of the jazz scene. Those he didn't bring home, he sent away three sheets to the wind. Last night he'd done neither, because he wanted to talk. Normally he laid off his troubles on Carla, who was a repository for them without being crushed by their weight. He couldn't do that when Carla was their cause, she and the baby, his baby, the black baby that was going to get him killed.

There was something in the paper about Nazi fanatics proposing to institute the laws of *Rassenschande* in France. Rassenschande meant racial scandal and brought deadly punishment to violators, who sought to water down Aryan bloodlines by mixing with lower orders. He was a living, breathing example of Rassenschande, Rassenschande in the flesh, defying anyone to suggest that he should never have been born. Until today, when he would make of himself the last in the line of Piron mongrels, the price to be paid for staying out of trouble, and having the life that was off-limits to him back home.

CHAPTER EIGHT

The explosion blew in the windows, showering Weiler in glass. Thrown out of his chair, blinded, unable to breathe or move, he realized that he had been fatally injured. A blast of dry heat convinced him that he was being delivered prematurely to the gates of hell. Satan wasn't there to welcome him, no one more remarkable than Pfluge, his adjutant, who stood over him anxiously, dripping blood from his eyes, asking, "Are you alive, Major? We have been attacked. Are you alive?"

Weiler concentrated on Pfluge's voice, the bloody face blurred by smoke and dust. He wanted to get to his feet but was unable to move, sadly accepting that he had been rendered a paraplegic before Pfluge lifted the desk that had toppled across his hips. As the weight came off, Weiler picked himself up, piece by piece as it were, checking each part to determine if it remained and how well it functioned, until he was arranged nearly upright with one hand on the desk for balance. The other stirred the cloud in front of his eyes. Pfluge came into focus, along with a couple of junior officers who were also there to see about him.

"Attacked by whom?"

"We don't know. You are all right?"

Weiler filled his lungs, coughed, spit gritty phlegm. "How can I be—?"

He was starting to sound like Maier with his damn questions. Shepherding the colonel everywhere would do that to you. Plucking glass out of his scalp and the back of his neck, he unplugged a gout of blood that ran down his shoulders. He was fishing for his hand-kerchief when Pfluge took his own bloodsoaked rag from his face and pressed it to the wound.

"See to your injuries," Weiler said, "and those of the others."

"You are sure you are well, Major?"

"Do it."

Weiler stumbled through the wreckage of his office to a bank of file cabinets. A bottle of Albert de Montaubert Cognac from the exquisite 1912 vintage, 750 ml, worth half a month's pay, was stashed in the bottom drawer for a special occasion, and what was more special than that he was alive? He felt inside for it and immediately withdrew the hand, gushing blood from the thumb, the most disturbing of his injuries. Dipping the handkerchief into the puddle in the drawer, he pressed it to the back of his head. Cognac made a fine disinfectant.

Approaching sirens overwhelmed groans in the corridor. He went to the window, hobbled by pain in his hips. Fire trucks converged on the Tuileries, and men in raincoats and leather helmets linked together lengths of hose and snaked them through the foliage. Grass fires burned alongside the gravel lanes. The firemen squelched every one, but seemed puzzled about where to concentrate the flow of water. The smoke was thickest over a grove of chestnut trees. Weiler couldn't see through the leaves, but that was where the firemen were busiest.

Steam rose in threadbare billows and was dispersed with the smoke by a wet breeze. There was little in the way of flames. Weiler went downstairs gingerly as more *pompiers* arrived. A frenzy of preparation petered out with nothing much for them to do. A knot of spectators tightened around them, buzzing with speculation. As they packed close, a man was left standing alone at their edge. Weiler limped to his side and saluted.

"Are you all right?" Weiler asked him. "I nearly was killed."

"Were you?" Colonel Maier said. "I, myself, escaped unscathed."

Weiler was waiting for the colonel to inquire sympathetically into the extent of his injuries. He blinked several times but, with the blood, smoke, and dirt in his eyes, couldn't pull them into focus. Rubbing them until he cleared them cleared up nothing.

"How—?"

"I had left my desk to go to the toilet," Maier said, "and must have flushed at the instant the blast went off, because I didn't hear it. I was unaware anything had happened until I returned to my office and found a duststorm swirling inside."

Weiler started in the direction of the crowd. Maier held him back.

"Aside from a large hole in the ground close to the wreckage of a drinking fountain and some benches that have been rendered into excellent firewood, there is nothing to see."

"A very deep hole?" Weiler asked. "Did an underground gas line explode, as was the case—as we thought was the case at the apartment house on the Rue du Faubourg Saint-Honore?"

"Do you smell gas?" Maier said. "Who would be so crazy as to stand over a broken main? The damage was done by an explosive, dynamite I should say, or a less stable compound. Nitroglycerin, or material fabricated with amatol."

"That was used in the explosion which brought down the apartment building."

"It would be a remarkable coincidence, wouldn't it, if the same material was responsible for both blasts?"

"Why set it off in a park?" Weiler said. "Did the bomber have a gripe against the squirrels?"

"They are not at the top of his list of enemies. The explosion occurred along the broad path bringing walkers to the portico of the former museum. Sherlock Holmes isn't required to deduce that our enemies intended to deliver a surprise to those working inside—to leave it and quickly disappear, as a stork might deposit a bastard—when the bomb went off ahead of time."

"It makes sense," Weiler said.

Maier looked at him with a measure of annoyance. If it didn't make sense, would he have said it?

"You are welcome to suggest another set of circumstances to better explain what happened."

"Who would do such a thing?"

"What is the population of Paris, Major?"

"I don't know. Several mil—Oh," he said. "I see what you are getting at."

"A better question would be who is capable, and who has the wherewithal, courage, and determination."

Weiler mopped blood from his neck. He didn't have the answer.

"Very few of those several million." Maier coughed softly into his fist. Weiler thought he was being sarcastic, but then he coughed again and spit into the grass. "Those qualities are not characteristic of the French."

An ambulance arrived ahead of several others, and attendants brought out canvas litters and carried them through the crowd.

"Let's have the first look at what they find for the morgue," Maier said.

They dogged the attendants to the edge of a depression a couple of meters in depth, where the firefighters played hoses on smoldering ash. The water saturated the earth, formed rivulets that collected in a brown pool at the bottom. Two men skittered down the steep sides and tramped through the water, probing it with their feet. Back and forth they waded, then side to side, bumping shoulders as they passed in the middle. It was a small boy gazing up at the clouds while everyone else focused on the ground who spotted gray pants in the crotch of a plane tree. Brought back to earth, they were found to contain the lower part of a human body. The spectators scanned the treetops for the rest until a fireman also glancing the wrong way discovered the upper torso under a rose bush. The mob, pushing close, retreated after a quick look. A man vomited, and Weiler saw one or two others in a sudden hurry to get to where they'd been going when they were sidetracked by the blast.

The body parts were shredded, scorched, burned beyond immediate recognition. Weiler determined with certainty only that he was looking at the remains of a man, at least someone dressed in a man's clothes, twill trousers and a blue pea coat. A beret snagged on another bush was clean and undamaged and might have been left by a spectator who had fled. The body was missing both arms, a leg, the head.

"Find it," Maier said. "The head."

"It isn't in the pit," a fireman said.

"Look further," Maier said. "It can't have gone far without legs."

"Look for it yourself," the firefighter said. Then he spun around, saw Germans in uniform, and said, "Of course, Monsieur, yes sir, that's what we will do, sir."

The ambulance attendants placed the halves of the torso onto stretchers and carried them to their vehicles. Would they use one vehicle, or two, Weiler wondered. What was the protocol? Maier intercepted them and lifted the sheets from the remains.

"What do you expect to see?" Weiler asked. "I can barely stand to be around it."

Maier ignored him.

"I'm surprised," Weiler said, looking away, "that the bomber would attempt to bring down the building in the daytime. The Musee du Jeu de Paume was erected in the previous century when civic structures were as sturdy as the monuments of antiquity, built to last as long. In the daylight hours it's well guarded. At night it would be more vulnerable."

"Daytime is best if your aim is to murder the people working inside." Maier spit into the ruined corpse. "That is what this son of a bitch was trying to do, to murder us." He wagged a finger at the medics, who replaced the sheet and took the body away. "The building wasn't the target. Frenchmen harbor a fondness for the old pile. It detracts from the glory of France to injure it merely to evict German military intelligence."

"Who do you suppose he was?"

"Other than from desperate Jews and communists, where would the motivation come?" Maier said. "In Czechoslovakia we encountered opposition from large segments of the civilian population. We are breaking it with harsh reprisals until no one has the stomach to take action against us or to shield our enemies. The same will happen here, but faster. These are the French, after all."

"Even a man blowing himself up in an attempt to get at us sets the wrong example," Weiler said. "Let's hope it was a one-man operation."

"One man, but in several parts," Maier said.

Weiler laughed, but Maier didn't laugh back. It had struck the captain as a humorous remark, but for Maier it was an observation. The humor in the situation eluded Maier as completely as it eluded the man plucked out of the tree and bush.

A firefighter came off the lane with a cloth sack that he placed at Maier's feet, backing away as Maier tugged at the drawstring. A flock of pigeons flew by, and Weiler decided that it was imperative to track their flight across the sky, to see the birds safely to their roost in the eaves of the museum, looking back too soon as Maier still fiddled with the drawstring. The bag opened at last, and Maier peered inside and thrust his hand to the bottom, drew it out clutching an object caked in wet mud—a single brown shoe, the scuffed leather cracked over the instep.

"We have to keep searching," Maier said.

"Yes, we must have the head," Weiler said. "When we do, we may learn—"

"That its owner is dead?" Maier said. "I was thinking of the mate for this shoe."

Maier's smile was pleasant and good-natured, not ghoulish in light of the circumstances. Feeling an urge to say something about misjudging him, Weiler held back when he noticed a speck of pulp on the colonel's sleeve, and the smile remained as Maier spotted it, too, and flicked it away.

"Additional protection must be ordered," Maier said. "It is disturbing that an attacker came as close as he did without being stopped."

"I, myself, am shocked at his boldness. By the grace of God tragedy was averted."

"Without access to bombs the boldest bomber is harmless. When explosives are at hand even a docile Frenchman may turn his anger on us if he finds himself at odds with diktat, or after arguing with his wife, or when a German occupies his seat on the Metro. Where I would begin is in keeping explosives out of the hands of our opponents."

"I will institute a tighter watch at construction sites where dynamite is in use. An advisory will be posted to arsenals and military bases. This will be the last we hear of bombers."

"Unless they already have replaced what was lost here and on the Rue du Faubourg Saint-Honoré," Maier said.

"What . . . ?" Weiler was looking away again. "Some flesh, I believe, is stuck to your chin."

⬥

It was blazing hot inside the apartment when Eddie returned. Even with coal in short supply, the landlord sent too much steam heat upstairs. When Eddie complained, elderly Monsieur Drapeau explained that his boiler burned hot or not at all. He advised keeping a window open until the coal ran out, when Eddie could complain about the chill. Eddie never left without opening all the windows so the apartment would be less hellish when he came back.

Tonight it was close to unbearable. Eddie berated himself for not having seen to the windows despite feeling that he had done that, double-checking the last thing before he went out. Apparently he was mistaken. Now he opened them along with the louvers. The early sun would be in his eyes, which meant getting up at an hour when he should still be sound asleep. What choice was there? He couldn't go to bed in a sauna.

He unlaced his shoes and kicked them off beside one of the music texts he was studying to become a better sight reader. Because space was tight, Eddie's bookcase was the area under the bed. He hadn't opened the book since his day off, yet there it was in the middle of the floor. Had an earthquake rocked the place while he was at the club, sloshing his stuff? Burglary seemed a better explanation. But what would a burglar want here? Aside from the trumpet that never left his side, what of any value did he own?

An inventory of his possessions with special attention to his pile of records was over in seconds. Nothing seemed to be missing. The apartment was an unlikely target for a burglar who understood that the first rule of burgling was to burgle a place where there was something to steal. The Germans might have been back for a second look. But Germans weren't shy, didn't do their dirty work without observers. The snickerer and his friend, or their Gestapo colleagues, would have wanted him to be here, probably after softening him up with a beating, softening him up again when they didn't find anything.

Questions remained: The identity of the burglar. What he wanted. Why he thought Eddie Piron would have it. It was too much to think about, not enough to keep him awake. But when he slipped between the sheets, he couldn't get comfortable. He got up again and tore apart the bedding, replaced it with linen untouched by strangers.

CHAPTER NINE

"**S**o I quit following him and went back to her place," Mavis said.

"The girlfriend's?"

"Cor-rect. She wasn't receiving. The doorman said nobody was allowed up there she didn't tell him in advance she is expecting. I stood at the curb deciding what to try next, when I saw him again, the doorman, holding the door open, and then she stepped out. You know what you are looking for, you can see where she has got a tiny bump, and I don't think it's from too much strudel. I came over, all smiles, and said didn't I know her from such-and-such a place. She highhatted me, but started paying attention when I told her the gentleman who had gotten her in the condition she was in, he was, you know, tossing it to me on the side."

"Lower your voice," Simone said. "We're in church."

"That so?" she said. "I thought Notre Dame was a football team in Indiana."

"Very funny."

She looked up at the choir and the great rose windows, and into the vaults of the Romanesque arches high overhead. "Where do you suppose that hunchback keeps himself when he isn't ringing bells?"

"You're a regular Gracie Allen," he said. "How did she take it?"

"With a harumph. And a snort, in case I didn't get the harumph. Cracks were beginning to show in that stone kisser."

"Or else you're seein' things."

"It could also be that." Mavis led him into a side chapel. "It's peaceful here, makes me feel, I don't know, holy. A cathedral was not one of the tourist attractions I wanted to visit in Paris, but coming here is worth every penny."

"They don't charge to let you in a church," Simone said. "You know that."

"Yeah, sport, I do."

She surprised him by dropping to her knees before a crèche and genuflecting. She got up straightening her hem and said, "I spent four of the longest years of my life at St. Elizabeth's in Altoona, Pennsylvania. It isn't a reformatory, don't get the wrong idea. Where was I?"

"About Piron's skirt."

"I asked if he put her up in her swell digs, and should I count on moving in next door. She looked like she was going to drop her foal on the sidewalk. As it was nothing I cared to see, I scrammed."

"You're sayin' she was lookin' for a cop."

"It may have crossed her mind," Mavis said. "Since I was in the neighborhood, I went around asking about her."

"You don't speak the language."

"Point one in my favor. In that part of town only the peasants speak French. English is the language of the upper crust. English and German. I told people I was new and needed a little help in tracking down an old school friend."

"Learn anything?"

"All I had to do was describe what she looked like, and everybody wanted to be my friend. She was educated in Switzerland at one of these finishing schools where the better class of kings and queens send their brats."

"Why would a gal with money, looks, and connections, not to mention a family that is probably on the same wavelength as these Nazis, why would she be sharin' a bed with a nigger?"

"Nobody has a good opinion of her boyfriend. They all mentioned he plays jazz on Place Pigalle. No one said he's colored. I can't tell you she knows it's a black baby she's carrying around in her belly."

"Bet she don't," Simone said. "It's time we catch Piron, and I don't mean by his toe."

"I don't get you."

"When you were a kid, you never sang that song about catchin' a nigger by the toe?"

"What of it?"

"You had it wrong," Simone said. "The louder he hollers, the tighter I'm gonna squeeze. I ain't ever gonna let him go."

CHAPTER TEN

The man with the greasy chin had an urgent matter to report. Officer Bastien Landry of the Sûreté looked up wearily from the newspaper he'd been studying since the start of his shift. Under the new realities, the police were the puppets of their German masters. Landry was bored constantly, vaguely ashamed.

"As a patriotic Frenchman, I wish to disclose the whereabouts of a foreign Jew," the man said.

Landry turned the page, uninterested. "Where can the Jew be found?"

"In my home," said the man, who was elderly and identified himself as Albert Champenois.

"You know the penalties for harboring him."

"It is not a he, but a woman who persuaded me to take her under my roof. It didn't occur to me that she was a Jew, let alone a foreign one, until—"

Landry heard it often, if not exactly word for word. An announcement in *Paris-Soir* from a fascist militia promised a handsome bounty for every non-resident Jew denounced to the authorities.

"Until I realized that was what she must be," Champenois said. "Listen closely to her, and it becomes apparent that French is not her native tongue. She keeps to a peculiar schedule, never going out in daytime or remaining indoors through the night. She has neither friends nor visitors. No one phones her, and she does not make calls. The bulletins warning of who we must guard against to preserve our security were written with her in mind."

"You could be right about everything," Landry said, "and still wrong."

"I could. Also the sun may rise in the west tomorrow morning. In these times, a woman rents a furnished room and moves in on the same day bringing nothing, not even a change of clothes, locks herself inside like she is hiding from . . . everybody, and I should ignore what is obvious?"

Landry had no opinion about foreign Jews, French Jews, Jews of any kind, but the parade of informants wouldn't end soon. He rolled a form and several carbons in his typewriter and began recording Champenois's story, disgusted now on top of everything else. "What's her name?"

Reports of fugitive Jews progressed routinely up the chain of command in the station in the eighth arrondissement without action being taken. Landry had adapted to the present situation in the preferred manner shared by nearly everyone. Let the Nazis hunt all the foreigners they cared to, but without their help. It was a German game, and for the Jews.

Corporal Bernard Parneix saw opportunity in his comrades' laxness. Examining every report, he took personal action on the low-hanging fruit. Close to midnight, accompanied by an Officer Drumont, he knocked at a tumbledown fieldstone home behind a sturdy doghouse in a grassless yard at the address for Albert Champenois. "Where is she?" Parneix asked the old man in robe and slippers barring the way inside.

"She is Dracula's daughter, who doesn't stir until dark," Champenois said. "When I returned from the police it was still light, and she was gone, however. I suspect she won't be back at any time tonight, any time at all."

"You gave some clue that you were going to denounce her?"

"Don't insult my intelligence. People like her, they have a sixth sense to warn them when trouble is on the way. Those who don't—"

"Yes?"

Champenois shook his head, dragging a finger across his throat.

"There is no sixth sense," Parneix said. "You probably chatter in your sleep."

"Good night, officers," Champenois said. "I am sorry you made a trip for nothing."

Parneix had his foot in the door. "Tell us what she looks like."

"With pleasure. She is young, slender, pretty, and rather dark, as I mentioned at the station. Not characteristically Semitic, but that is what she is. I won't forget her. Find a thousand like her, and I will pick her out of the mob."

"It won't be necessary. More!"

"Her way of speaking—"

"We know. How was she dressed?"

"She came with the clothes on her back, a simple skirt and chemise, and made no additions to her wardrobe. She said that her things were in storage, and would arrive any day."

"You believed her?"

"Up to a point."

"Which point is that?"

"When I came to understand there was nothing in it for me."

"How long did you have her here?"

"I can tell you to the day when she turned up," Champenois said. "It sticks in my memory, because it was the morning after the explosion on the Rue du Faubourg Saint-Honoré, when the apartment house was brought down. I remember that the utility company sent a worker to check my gas line. I had to bribe him to turn the gas back on after he said I needed a new pipe. It cost a pretty penny that I hadn't budgeted."

"Show us her room."

Champenois took them through a stale kitchen to a small, drab living room and a smaller, darker room behind it. He lit a lamp, which put minuscule light on rough walls, a cot wrapped in a thin blanket, a bowl, a pitcher, and two hand towels on a bruised stand. Empty hangers clattered together when Parneix opened the closet. A mouse ran out, causing Drumont to take a quick step back and Champenois to laugh softly into his hand. The air smelled of cat urine.

"As I said, she brought nothing."

Parneix got down on his knees and looked at the dust under the cot. In a corner the mouse was squeaking. Pressing his hand against the pillow as he raised himself, he nudged it aside, uncovering a handbill advertising a jazz show on Place Pigalle the previous month. He folded it carefully and placed it in his pocket, then took it out for a second reading. Crumpling it into a ball, he tossed it in the direction of the mouse.

The girl—Anne Cartier was the name she had given to Champenois, though it was believed to be fake—was not the easy pickings he had anticipated. Indeed, he had made the trip for nothing. These things happened, but he would inform the Germans of what he'd learned. If they got lucky, or if hers ran out, it might yet be possible to derive benefit from his tour of M. Champenois's basement.

Since the night of "Shine," Eddie had started every show on trumpet, trading off with Weskers when his lip tired. Tonight his form held deep into the late set. In a short time he'd reclaim the spotlight on a permanent basis. Weskers could take over on drums, if a teacher could be enlisted to give him lessons. Otherwise he had to go. There was no room for a second trumpet, a second-rate drummer, or a second archangel with Eddie et Ses Anges.

La Caverne was overrun with SS, as it often was for the late show, drunken officers shouting requests for favorite tunes. Some were songs Eddie had never heard of, a few with German titles. Many were swing numbers, which he had no desire to play. The swing virus had crossed the Atlantic, passing over France and infecting Germany, where he hoped it would prove fatal, not just to the music.

He led off with "I'm Coming Virginia," a virtuoso piece by Bix Beiderbecke, his favorite white trumpeter, and built a medley with "Clarinet Marmalade," which Bix had made his own. The long solo improvised originally for reeds put a strain on his lip; but, caught up in its sinuous beauty, he blew his heart out. By the last chorus he was out of gas. The audience didn't notice. Unless the applause that went on for minutes was charity.

A woman alone at one of the small tables didn't clap. She was pretty but somewhat withdrawn, one of those women he would see nursing a drink by herself at two and three A.M. before rushing out. The Germans hadn't spotted her, or they would be demanding that she join them. Her eyes never left Eddie, who noted a paradox. The SS, real fans of the music, rarely watched him except when they were calling for the next song, yet this woman listening with evident displeasure never looked away. He tried telling himself that he'd swept her off her feet and she was too embarrassed to show it. A better explanation was that it was past midnight and he was the one who didn't want to spend the night alone.

Syrupy ballads made women crazy to have him. Next on the playlist was "Dr. Jazz," an uptempo number. Without cueing the band, he switched to "Body and Soul," leaving the angels in the dust till his lip gave out in the second verse.

Making way for Weskers, Eddie took his place at the drums. He rapped the high hat till the sticks felt right in his hands, and then nodded to the piano player, who tickled the opening of "Alligator Crawl." Weskers stuffed the rubber tip of a toilet plunger into the bell of his horn and blew sixteen muted bars. Eddie provided a steady backbeat, taking a restrained solo before the coda.

Wrapped up in the music, he forgot the girl. When he saw her again, she was dabbing her cheek with a hankie. He could forget about making her fall in love. The trick was in preventing her from becoming hysterical.

She wasn't there the next time he looked. He checked the other tables, but she hadn't fallen in love with the SS either. It wasn't the first time a pretty girl had made eye contact, vanishing before he had a chance to make his move. Not every admirer was elusive. He searched for a replacement, but no promising candidates stood out from the crowd. It bothered him that he'd been wrong about her. Lately, he misread every woman. None more so than Carla.

Ten hours later, he was back at La Caverne to hear Roquentin sing his praises. Tourists wouldn't know if he'd stunk up the joint. The SS appreciated good jazz, but who gave a damn about what they thought? Only Roquentin was knowledgeable about fine playing, as well as a human being whose opinion Eddie valued. He grumbled when Eddie said "Good afternoon," and let him prepare breakfast for himself.

"I hope," Eddie said, "you're not commenting on my performance last night."

"What? No, you were okay." They were in the kitchen, Roquentin looking around as though he had come to get something and forgotten what it was. "Terrific, actually. It slipped my mind."

"That's a fine compliment. Where is the incentive to play well when my most important critic doesn't care?"

"Keep up the good work." Roquentin opened the pantry and looked inside.

Eddie said, "Something missing?"

"That's what I'm trying to figure out. Someone broke in early in the morning."

"What did they take, rationed goods? Coffee? Sugar? Chocolate?"

"As far as I can determine, they didn't take anything."

"That's good," Eddie said.

"Unless they took something, and I don't know what it is. That could be bad."

"Money?"

"I locked the receipts in the safe as I always do. They're still here. The safe wasn't touched."

"It must have been some poor, starving bastard looking for food." Roquentin shook his head.

"He was still here when I let myself in, and I got a quick look at him. He hadn't come for a meal, but to rob."

"Any idea who he was?"

"I'd say a teenager. I didn't see his face, but he was slim, not tall, didn't show a weapon or move aggressively. When he was aware he'd been discovered, he ran into the back and out a window."

"That's how he entered?"

"No, he had to force it to climb out," Roquentin said. "If I didn't have sixty-year-old knees, I would have caught him."

"Where did he get in?"

"Another puzzle. None of the doors or windows were tampered with, and I distinctly recall locking up before I went home. It's as if he hid here after the last show so that he could have the place to himself."

"It's a lot of trouble for some chocolate."

Roquentin put up a pot of coffee. "Not if you want it bad enough."

"There was a time," Eddie said, "when I felt that way about fame and success."

"Oh, when did it change?"

Everything had changed since the Germans arrived, but he refused to put all the blame on them. Carla had done her bit, and a sudden hunger for New Orleans that answered his fear of fatherhood and marriage to a woman with whom he hadn't counted on spending his life. Other things were different, too, but he couldn't say what they were. How could he, when he didn't realize anything had changed till he heard the words coming out of his mouth?

An independent French Gestapo with headquarters at 93 Rue Lauriston near the Bois de Boulogne enforced the Aryanization laws with enthusiasm that not even the Nazis matched. Criminals and thugs, many of them Muslims from the North African Brigade, they took license for plunder, preying on Jews whose property they confiscated before turning them over to the SS. Wealthy Jews were the prize. Every Jew was fair game.

A band from the physiognomy branch, students of Nazi racial science, and self-proclaimed experts in spotting Jewish types, converged on Belleville, a working-class neighborhood bordering the 19th and 20th arrondissements, and raided an apartment house where Polish and Austrian Jews were hiding. Two dozen men, women, and children were handed over to the Germans. French Jews swept up in the net were kept for ransom. Of these, one presented a unique complication. With an olive complexion, almond eyes, and black hair to go along with an unidentifiable accent, she appeared to be something other than her valid French passport proclaimed her to be. Lacking the skill for interrogation that didn't involve torture, which would make for bad publicity if she turned out to be a Frenchwoman, the Rue Lauriston Gestapo made a gift of her to their German counterparts. Incarcerated in the fifth-floor cells at the counterintelligence directorate at 84 Avenue Foch, she was summoned almost immediately for questioning.

"Your name," asked her interrogator, who did not give his own name, which was Schiller.

"You have it in your hand."

He opened her passport. "You are Anne Cartier?"

"That's right."

"A Jew."

"Do I look it?"

"I don't know," said the interrogator. "I don't know what all Jews look like."

"Not like me."

He tapped the passport against his knuckles.

"Is my passport not in order?" she asked him. "Return it, and I'll be on my way."

"It raises questions. Are you planning a trip?"

"Where would I go? I carry it in case I am stopped on the street and asked to prove who I am."

"Which raises this one: Why should you think that?"

Fear took over, leaving her unable to answer. She was a sharp-witted girl. In the smallest part of a second, the interrogator knew, she would come back at him with a clever remark, but he would make less of it than the troubled look already fading from her face.

"That I'm here. It shows that I was right."

"Where do you live?"

"My address is on the second page."

"Tell me anyway. Have you forgotten it?"

"Now I am accused of feeble-mindedness," she said. "You are being ridiculous."

"I never am," he said. "What is it?"

"Number 79 Rue des Tonneliers, Strasbourg, Alsace."

"What are you doing in Paris?"

"Visiting," she said.

"Visiting Jews in Belleville?"

"I didn't know they were Jews. You, yourself, admitted that you can't always tell who the Jews are, and recognizing Jews is your profession."

"What were you doing with them?"

"I had the misfortune to be on the same street when they were seized, and was taken too. Misfortune compounded into farce."

"Why were you there?"

"I was visiting my friend."

"Her name."

"It is a he—but can't we keep him out of it? We broke up last night. My boy—ex-boyfriend threw me out. I won't say I didn't deserve it. It was a brutal breakup. Where delicacy is advised, I am frank. That's why I was on the street alone in the early hours."

"You came to Paris to be with him?"

She shook her head. "It began and ended here."

"What brought you?"

"You'll take it personally."

"Everything is personal with me."

"As with me," she said. "After Alsace was returned to Germany, I did not want to remain. I am a Frenchwoman, France is my country. I have no desire to live under the Reich."

"You will have to travel farther than to Paris."

"Perhaps Germans won't be here long."

"Perhaps," the interrogator said, "we will pull up your skirt and get to the bottom of things."

It didn't make her squirm. The fear he'd noticed before was still there to be exploited. It had to be, but she'd gotten it under control.

"Aren't you overlooking one small detail?" she said.

"It will be revealing just the same."

Did she know he was under constraint not to rape? His superiors conceded that it was a valuable investigative tool, but argued that it was bad for morale. In most cases he agreed. He considered himself a humanitarian, susceptible to natural feelings, and these damn Jewesses used sentiment and every other trick to impede him in the performance of his duties.

Real Frenchwomen presented problems of a different stripe. He would be careful that no mistake was made with Anne Cartier. Violations of the guidelines were not unknown at 84 Avenue Foch. Heaven help him if he was found guilty of one.

"We will get to it later," he said, "or not. Convince me that you are who you say you are, and you can go."

"What more," she asked, "can I give you?"

She was flirting with him, a second meaning concealed in each innocent word. Warmth on his cheeks wasn't a blush. He never blushed, wouldn't have been promoted to senior interrogator and honored with commendations if he was easily embarrassed. He had been a student of religion at Freiburg University, regarded by classmates as cold and distant, a prig. It was impossible that this girl had caused him to blush. What he felt was a variation of what she had exhibited—fear. Sudden fear that he could be wrong about her.

"You say you are from Alsace, yet you speak with an accent that isn't German," he said.

"My family were colonials in North Africa; I was born in Algeria, in Oran. My father was the principal of the French high school, but things weren't good for us. The Arabs sense weakness and would like to slaughter all the French. Therefore my family returned to France, to their old home in Strasbourg. I am Alsatian by history but have no connections there. I was thinking of leaving before I arrived. Of course I came to Paris. Who would live in Strasbourg when Paris beckons?"

Not he. He'd left Freiburg specifically because Paris beckoned. Here was his first reason to believe the girl: They thought alike. A colonial background would account for her accent. It might also explain her coloration, something she would not wish to be forthcoming about, not only with him. He was certain she wasn't a Jew. Rather, he was certain that he didn't want her to be one. His dilemma was how to dispose of her case at his high standard of diligence when he didn't have one hundred percent of the evidence. She looked at him insouciantly while he settled on a solution. He would set her free. The next five suspects brought before him he would handle less generously, no matter how compelling their stories might be.

On the third floor, secretaries typed reports of the action in Belleville for distribution to investigative bureaus throughout occupied Paris. A copy transmitted to military intelligence was routed to the desk of Major Weiler, whose thoughts of lunch were interrupted. Moments later, they were disturbed again by martial music.

He looked out at a Wehrmacht band, all spit and polish, marching through the Tuileries. Sundays were days of entertainment for the high command, organ concerts for those who attended church, and the military serenading in the gardens. Paris made it easy to forget that he was posted here to do a job.

The list of arrestees contained no familiar names. Every Jew was a Shapiro, a Cohen or Kahane, a Levi, Levin, Levine, or Lewittes, and how was he to sort through that oriental stew? One name stood out. Anne Cartier. What a Frenchwoman from Strasbourg was doing on a roster of foreign Yids strained his imagination. An error must have been made, unless she was married to a Frenchman, and the error should be charged to her husband. Weiler was thinking of a *charcuterie* on the Île de la Cité when he was hit by another reason why the name stood out. Anne Cartier was the woman connected to the explosion on the Rue du Faubourg Saint-Honoré. Colonel Maier would want to know that she was under lock and key. He would, that is, if she was the right Anne Cartier. The French were also tasked with a shortage of memorable names.

Weiler fit his cap on his head, adjusted his uniform in the reflection of the window. Pleased with what he saw, he called for his driver and car.

Sunday traffic was light on the main avenues of Paris, although not much lighter than any other day. The occupying authority issued permits for only seven hundred civilian motor vehicles in the whole of the city. Millions of bicycles clogged the streets as a result, the cyclists as reckless as motorists, more prone to take risks. Half an hour went by before the car from military intelligence reached Avenue Foch.

The interrogator was out to lunch. A junior officer assured Weiler that all Jews turned over to the Gestapo in the last ninety-six hours remained locked up on the fifth floor. The interrogator would be back within the hour to answer questions. Weiler didn't have an hour, wouldn't spend it waiting if he had it. He demanded to be taken upstairs.

The Jews were a ragged bunch, thrown together in a cell unsegregated by sex, age, or social status, by any category other than Jewishness. Weiler barely could stand being near them. None of the women looked like an Anne Cartier, like anyone who could spend a single day on the Rue du Faubourg Saint-Honoré without drawing the attention of neighbors. He called her name. Everyone looked up. No one stepped forward. "Anne Cartier," he said again. Tired of the game, the Jews retreated into their cage. Before he could say the name again, the junior officer told him that the interrogator he wanted had returned.

He was a tall man in a shapeless suit, gray at the edges of a haircut done by a butcher, and ungainly, swinging his arms exaggeratedly as a counterbalance with each step. The Gestapo was made up of men like him, outwardly unappealing, mediocrities in civilian life who seized the one chance for position and power they would ever have. The secret police spied on everyone, enemies of the Reich, loyal Germans, even the military. Even on each other. Weiler despised him on sight.

"You have an Anne Cartier," Weiler said, "sought in an investigation of the utmost sensitivity. Release her to me." He pulled him close to the bars. "Which one is she?"

"She isn't here."

"Bring her. I want her now."

"She was freed ninety minutes ago."

Weiler wanted to kill him. "This was your decision?"

"After a consideration of the facts, yes. The woman isn't a Jew. As she had been arrested in error, there was no cause to keep her."

"I'll see to it personally that you take her place," Weiler said. "Where did she go?"

"I don't know."

"Where was she arrested? Who are her associates? She will go back there, to warn them to go more deeply into hiding. I will send men immediately to return her."

"She was living with a boyfriend," the interrogator said. "He threw her out, and she was picked up on the street. She has no one, no place to go back to. I know where her family lives, though."

"Where?" Weiler shouted.

"In Strasbourg. It isn't as though we have lost touch completely."

"I could murder you with my bare hands," Weiler said.

"Had you been here during the interview, you would have seen that she is an innocent Frenchwoman. I did the correct thing. There is no purpose in keeping her with these cursed Jews. She is not like them."

"She's beautiful?" Weiler said.

The interrogator started to answer, but, catching himself, he shrugged instead.

"That's different," Weiler said.

"She is."

"You fell in love," Weiler said. "I would torture you before I killed you."

The interrogator had had enough, and said so to Weiler's back. Weiler was thinking of how best to tell Colonel Maier of the near-miss in having Anne Cartier, and what could be done to the fool who'd freed her. Probably nothing—the Gestapo looked after their own. What Weiler had in mind, Maier would want to do to all of France.

CHAPTER ELEVEN

At the Librairie du Jazz on the left bank Eddie was lost in the stacks of old records. U-boat attacks on shipping in the North Atlantic prevented American goods from reaching France, and there was nothing new on the shelves. It was just as well. Eddie had no fondness for the syrupy big-band arrangements that were the rage back home and threatened to displace him from the bandstand where he was king.

He selected several sides by Jelly Roll Morton's Red Hot Peppers. Eddie wasn't a fan of the Peppers' cornetist, George Mitchell, but Jelly had gotten brilliant playing out of him, and Eddie was still stealing from it. He'd discovered the records when they were cut fifteen years ago and had brought them to France and played them till there was nothing in the grooves but hisses and scratches. Replacements were available for a few sous in the bargain bins at the Librairie du Jazz.

He was taking them to the listening booth that was furnished with a better phonograph than the old Victrola in his room when he was bumped from behind. The records slipped from his grasp. Bumped again as he made a grab for them, he watched helplessly as they crashed to the floor.

"You break 'em, you buy 'em," someone said in English. Eddie turned his head, and Simone smiled back.

Eddie had a sick feeling in his stomach. It wasn't the cost of the records, which was negligible; more like he'd been carrying the Mona Lisa and dropped it in a sewer.

"What the hell?" Simone said. "It's just shellac."

Eddie got down on his knees to gather the pieces. "Steamboat Stomp" and "Sidewalk Blues" had survived intact, and he took them carefully in both hands and put them aside. A store employee wearing an indifferent expression came by with a broom and steered the mess toward a corner. Fatal crashes happened all the time at the Librairie du Jazz.

"I'm terribly sorry," Eddie said to him. "Tell your boss I'll pay for everything."

"You can afford it," Simone said. "You can afford to break every record in the store. Hell, you can buy the place out from under his boss."

"I wish—"

"Boo hoo," said Simone. "You got the jack. I seen your girlfriend at the Casino de Paris, and she is a luxury item. You can afford her on what you bring home from blowin' a horn, it makes me sorry I didn't listen to my mama and take music lessons."

Eddie grabbed the records he wanted and started for the cash register.

"You don't mean to say you ain't payin' for her, she's payin' for you?" Simone stepped quickly around him. "Gigoloin' is a step up from what you were doin' on Decatur Street in the old days."

Eddie was ready to lay him out flat. But with his hands full of records, there was nothing he could do but try to squeeze by. Simone didn't let him pass.

"French woman keepin' you in clover don't seem right. Strikes me as a violation of natural law, a colored boy from New Orleans livin' high on the hog in Paris, France, better'n most white folk. I would like to discuss it with her. How you got the job spongin' off of her. What you do to earn your pay."

"This isn't New Orleans," Eddie said. "Get out of my way, or I'll—"

"You could try. Might land a lucky punch. One thing you will definitely accomplish is loosenin' my tongue."

Eddie put the records down without thinking about what he was going to do. There was time for that later, when he would be forced to consider the consequences.

"I know who your people are, what they are," Simone said, "'xactly what happened in the Quarter that has police all over the world duty-bound to send you back. Lucky for you I ain't a chatterbox that's gonna devalue your precious secrets by givin' 'em away. But it's a heavy responsibility keepin' 'em, for which I expect to be recompensed. What's it worth to you, havin' me seal my lips so folks here don't know the man you are?"

Eddie drew back his fists.

"Lay a hand on me, I'll go straight to your gal. From what I observed, she is not a prime candidate to be growin' a baby inside her that has a fine chance of comin' out black as the ace of spades. You're fitter'n me. I ain't much of a fighter, but it'll be the costliest punch you throw in your entire life."

Eddie lowered his fists as several customers stepped between them on their way to the cheap records in back.

Simone lowered his voice. "This don't have to be the melodrama you're makin' it into. I'm gonna protect your secrets like a goose settin' on the golden egg that won't let harm come to it, so set your heart at ease. How much you fancy this valuable protection I'm providin' is worth? Your peace of mind."

Eddie didn't answer, let him go on.

"Woman like her has got more bucks'n she knows what to do with. She ain't givin' you none don't excuse the fact you ain't gettin' it. Ask her for it. Fine-lookin' fellow like yourself don't come cheap. Not askin' don't speak well for the product, encourages her to think she is gettin' second-rate goods."

Eddie shook his head. It was all he had to say.

"Don't be bashful," Simone said. "Once you get the hang of it, you won't ever want to quit. Not even if I am struck by lightnin', and off your back."

Eddie couldn't remain quiet hoping Simone would go away. He was being blackmailed, but he refused to allow the blackmailer to set the rules. He said, "She doesn't have her own money. It comes from family."

"You'll ask her. She'll ask them. She loves you, don't she? Why's she carryin' your baby if she don't."

"It's a great scheme you figured out," Eddie said. "But it won't work."

"Get yourself a positive attitude," Simone said. "We ain't arrived at step one, and you tellin' me it is doomed to failure. Put some of that charm I seen on display at your club into it. You'll get results."

Eddie shoved him away. Simone bounced back with clenched fists. For a man who wasn't a fighter, he wasn't a stranger behind them, circling cautiously to his left, his head bobbing constantly, an elusive target.

Eddie saw a punch coming and reached to block it. Simone answered with a jab. Eddie turned his head to protect his lip, and the punch glanced the side of his head. He hit back at Simone with an uppercut landing under his jaw. When Simone didn't go down, Eddie wrapped him up in a bear hug.

The shelves tottered, releasing an avalanche of records that shattered against shoulders, and backs, and were ground to shards under the feet of the battling men. Eddie wanted to break off to stop the destruction, but Simone was winging kidney shots non-stop in the clinch. Eddie went punch for punch fueled by anger he didn't know possessed him. A roundhouse right caught Simone high on the bridge of his nose. A spurt of blood from both nostrils made a fine target to enlarge the damage.

Simone fell back against shelves standing almost to the ceiling. They groaned, Eddie heard wood crack and splinter, and thousands of records rained down. The man with the broom stood by, looking miserable. There was a loser in every fight. Already he'd lost this one.

It was hard to throw a solid punch struggling for footing in the debris, and so Eddie and Simone grappled. Simone wasn't a bad dirty fighter, murderous in the clinches where knees and elbows came into play, and he could stomp on Eddie's feet. Eddie was fearful of head butts to his lips and teeth. He didn't want the brawl prolonged, or to let it end without landing one more hard blow.

In Simone he saw tormentors he'd held back from striking out at in places where that was impossible for him to do. A looping punch that caught Simone flush on his broken nose raised a howl, and he threw himself on Eddie, smothering his punches as they waltzed like exhausted lovers waiting to be torn apart.

The man with the broom declined in favor of the manager, a silver-haired woman who placed a hand on each man's chest and spread her arms.

Simone blew blood bubbles out his nose and said to Eddie, "You'll pay for this."

The woman, a Madame Combelle, said, "Someone will. You imbeciles have destroyed my stock. I have no way of replacing it, not a single record."

Pain lurking in Eddie's cheek and around his left eye while he'd pumped adrenalin cried out now. What hurt worse was the devastation he'd caused. He'd liked to fantasize that one day every record in the Librairie du Jazz would be his. Now he would be charged for them without taking any home.

"I'm sorry, Madame."

"A lot of good it does," she said.

Her hankie was in her hand, and she was about to give it to Eddie when she looked again at Simone and awarded it to him. He balled it under his nose and took it away sopped with blood. "I've just started with you," he said to Eddie. "The price—for everything—is goin' up."

"What is your name?" Madame Combelle said to him. "He I know. He will pay his share. Who are you?"

"Anything I owe, he'll take care of," Simone said. "He's good at makin' messes. Makin' 'em his whole life. He can learn to clean 'em up."

Kicking through the wreckage, he started for the door. Only the man with the broom didn't get out of the way.

Roquentin said, "Not again! What happened this time?"

Eddie said, "It's nothing. My lip is okay. I can play."

"Your face will scare the customers."

"I'll wear a hat and pull it low, the old derby I sometimes use for a mute. You'll keep the lights down, and I'll stay out of them. It won't be a big deal."

"Only for you. You'll have to go back on drums. Gert will play trumpet."

"Only for a night or two. I'm a quick healer," Eddie said.

"Is that what you call it? What's wrong with you, Eddie? Why can't you stay out of trouble?"

It's my luck, it wasn't good even before I was born. It wasn't. It's so bad that I can't even use it as an excuse.

A short, erect man in a gray business suit and with a weathered briefcase bouncing against his thigh came into the club as the early show wound down. Eddie pulled the derby lower over his face. The man ignored the music, drank mineral water, looked uncomfortable, bored, and somewhat haughty. During the intermission he trailed Eddie to the office, snapped open the briefcase, handed him a business card, and introduced himself as the attorney for the record store. The owners wanted money for the damage Eddie had caused. They'd located the other party to the fight, who insisted that he had none, and would fight the action. He claimed to be blameless, had been minding his own business when he was attacked without provocation by Eddie, and might bring a civil suit against the Librairie du Jazz. The owners were sorry, but were left with no choice but to come after Eddie to pay for the broken records. It was a tragedy all around.

Eddie reacted with anger, most of it for Simone, but in proportion to the amount of destruction for which he believed he was being overbilled. Simone was right about one thing, he should go to Carla. It was distasteful, but they had to talk about many things. The money might never even come up.

The pain in Carla's face was as great as his own, revealed in sighs and one long groan.

"Oh no, why do you keep doing this, do you hate yourself and are trying to get killed? You look horrible."

"Not as bad as I feel."

"You are suffering?"

"Not how you think."

"What happened?"

"I was at the Librairie du Jazz. A fellow made insulting remarks. Next thing you know is what you see."

"He objected to your playing?"

"To my family."

"He knows them?"

"Not really."

"He was spoiling for a fight," she said, "and you were there. Was he the winner?"

"I'm being sued by the store for damages caused by both of us. I suppose that makes me the loser."

"You can't get blood from a stone, as they say."

"I've already bled. Blood is easy."

"How much money are they asking for?"

"I don't have the number. More than I've got."

"I can help," she said.

"Why should you? You didn't break anything, or have the pleasure of hitting him. I got into this trouble without you. I'll get out the same way."

"How?"

Eddie shrugged.

"I will give you the money. You never come to me for a single franc, no matter how hard up you are, and knowing I can give you whatever you need."

It was what he was afraid of. He'd rehearsed a loud demand that she foot the entire bill, assuming that like Simone she would tell him to clean up after himself. Having opened a corrosive breach, he would let the affair disintegrate until she gave up her claims on him. Instead he'd allowed his pride—such as it was—to interfere, coming off as a lost lamb, and she the mother ewe with infinite resources of love.

"You don't have it," he said.

"I will ask my parents."

"You'll tell them what it's for?"

"When I am about to introduce you as the man I'm going to marry, the father of their grandchild? I'll say I need it for myself."

Simone was right. There was no trick to getting money out of her. He would have her picking up after him for the rest of his life. Who could ask for more? While wanting less.

"You look so unhappy," she said. "What could that bastard have told you that required you to take a poke at him?"

"He called me a nigger."

"He might as well have said Eskimo. Why let it bother you?"

"If I were one, would I have your approval to knock his block off?"

"The subject is distasteful," she said. "Please change it."

"Would I?"

"He could say any damn thing about me, since I have no regard for anyone's opinion but yours. It's because you are a man that you take offense. Boys are brought up to fight over the slightest threat to their honor."

"It has little to do with masculinity."

"Well, then what? A stranger makes a ridiculous remark, and you let it get under your skin. I didn't know it's so thin."

"It's not," he said. "It's black."

She looked at him gravely. "I don't see black skin, except around the eyes, where it's black and blue. You were hit in the head and don't realize it." She attempted to embrace him, caught him by the wrist, pushed up his sleeve, and thrust her bare arm alongside his. "I am darker than you. If I'm not a nigger, how can you be one?"

"It isn't in the color," he said. "But in the blood."

She threw down his arm. "My brain must be scrambled like yours, for allowing this absurd conversation to go on."

"What if one of us were black," he said, "for argument's sake?"

"If it were me," she said, "I would kill myself. As I'm not, I won't."

"And if I were?"

Her bemusement gave way to frustration and dismay, and then something that seemed to him to be alarm. "What are you telling me?"

"Do I have to spell it out?" he said.

"Yes, and write a book about it, too, because I cannot understand how it can be possible. Even then I won't."

"Under the laws of Louisiana, where I'm from, I'm a black man."

"How, when you don't look it in the least?"

"An ancestor before my great-grandfather's time was from Africa. Legally, that makes me black. It's called the one-drop theory. For all practical purposes I am black."

"This is France," she said defiantly.

Her generosity rubbed him the wrong way. Making his secret into nothing, she would relieve him of the peculiarities that were at the heart of who he was.

"Under the Germans," he said, "it's more like Louisiana each day."

"Who made this law?" she said. "Why do you let them decide who you are? I will decide."

"All right, what do you say?"

"You are a white man. End of story."

Out of kindness she offered absolution from being the awful thing that the law in Louisiana said he was. Who would make a better mother for his child?

Maybe if he was a nigger he'd feel different. He was something else, though, a New Orleans Creole of color, a pure mongrel who looked down his nose at black and white. Possessed of the most exquisite French culture, he disparaged Carla's haute Parisians from the vantage point of superior refinement. Take away the racial laws and he would vanish, mongrelization dead-ending in assimilation. How did you explain snobbery born of suffering to an aristocrat?

"You don't agree?" she said. "You don't want to."

"What I am's not something to be ashamed of. Where it's lacking is in the quality of the enemies it makes where I come from."

"It doesn't bother me," she said. "You are lighter than I. As long as the child looks like either of us, it will be beautiful."

"If it comes out black?" he said.

"The chance is small."

"You've been impregnated before by a black man?"

"I just know."

"Give me a better answer," Eddie said. "After, we'll fix the odds."

"It can't come out looking like a Negro," she said. "I still don't believe you really are. You don't look like one. It can't be."

"I had a brother who was nothing like me. There's a chance the child will be as dark as Tom, or darker. In New Orleans I know people who look white and have black parents, and Negroes from light-skinned families."

"You've concocted these scenarios to torture me."

"Better a sadist," he said, "than the father of your black baby?"

"You put your vanity above everything. I, on the other hand, worry for the child."

"Love it, and it won't require as much worrying."

"Are you forgetting the Germans will consider it less than human? And what they've promised for those they deem subservient to the master race? I, for one, don't doubt their sincerity."

"My trust is in the French," Eddie said, "in their open-mindedness. Liberté. Égalité. Fraternité."

He listened to her laughter, reluctant to call it that. He'd never heard a sadder sound. When he told her it was time to stop, she added tears to the sorry show.

He couldn't have said it better himself.

CHAPTER TWELVE

The interrogator considered himself among the luckiest of men alive. As proof, he was alive, when Major Weiler could have had him put aboard one of the transports removing Jews from the city to pay for his mistake. Unluckiest were the Jews. Although he'd never been told—nor had he asked—where they ended up, he knew that none returned. Better to devote himself to serving up more of them to the appetite of that terrifying place than to speculate about what it would be like there for himself.

Fearful of another blunder that would bring down Weiler's wrath, he took pains during interviews with the remainder of the Belleville roundup. Their stories were all the same. Polish Jews driven from their homeland by the Wehrmacht, or by the Soviet invasion toward the end of 1939, they had fled to the country with the largest standing army in Europe, where Hitler would never reach them. Not welcomed with open arms, neither were they turned away. Those who could thread a needle, or buy for nineteen francs what they could sell for twenty, or, if they were young and attractive and willing to sell themselves, didn't starve. Their threat to the Reich, the interrogator determined, was contained in their genes. Soon they would be disarmed.

Fresh loads dumped regularly at his door built a backlog. All of expatriated Polish and Dutch Jewry might have been waiting to be processed through his office, but he refused to sacrifice thoroughness for dispatch. Major Weiler lurked in the background, and no one received a third chance from him.

After a week he was done with the mob from Belleville, and they were loaded into a truck that would take them to the transit camp in the old housing project of La Cité de la Muette, the City of Silence, at Drancy in the northeast suburbs. A new batch, doomed in advance, took their place. Rather than ask the tiresome questions, he preferred to shoot every one and be done with it. That would make him redundant, however, and he would be returned to Germany, to the back office of a casualty insurance company in Chemnitz where in eight years he had risen to assistant chief of the actuarial department. His situation in Paris was too precious to squander on shortcuts. If he lived to be one hundred, he'd never have a job as pleasant as the one he had here.

Around 1:00 A.M., following a three-hour wait in the back of the open truck, the Belleville Jews were driven from the city under the care of three gendarmes. There was no heater in the cab, and the driver and the officer riding alongside him were frozen almost as stiff as their cargo. A neon glow in a haze of woodsmoke beckoned from the side of the road. The men in front looked at each other at the same time. The truck pulled into the gravel lot of the Auberge Cochon Agile, and they went inside, leaving the other gendarme, a nineteen-year-old rookie, in charge of the Jews with the promise of a cup of hot chocolate when they returned.

Many beers later, the gendarmes went back out into the cold, spilling cocoa and fumbling for their weapons when they saw the Jews clustered at the side of the truck. Ordering them to back away, they advanced on a pool of blood in the gravel, and its source, the teenage officer sprawled on his belly. Brain matter was caked against the back of his head. His rifle, unfired, remained within reach. The terrified Jews stood by to continue the journey. The driver, also terrified, fled immediately. It was left to the third man to call in the report of what had happened, and he was long gone when help arrived.

A head count revealed four passengers missing. Pressed to identify the political faction behind the cowardly attack, the Jews gestured with upturned palms. One man was responsible. In Yiddish he had announced under the guard's nose what he planned to do, and called for the others to join him. While they argued against it, he worked loose a piece of metal from the back of the truck and used it to stave in the teenager's skull. A few arguers went with him when he ran.

Soldiers came with motorcycles, dogs, and searchlights to assist the police. Militia volunteers were told that the escapees probably would attempt to infiltrate back into the city where they had hidden before. Footprints in a centimeter of new snow pointed in that general direction before branching off, and hunters were commanded to run down each set of tracks.

The militiamen discovered the most promising leads already assigned. Worse, they were instructed not to shoot, but to capture the fugitives for questioning. They had abandoned cozy beds in the middle of the night in anticipation of good sport, and were unable to conceal their frustration. Rather than chase after nothing, a squad retired to the auberge to drink themselves into oblivion.

The innkeeper ushered them back into the night at a little before 3:00. Leaning on each other for support, two of them broke off from the main group in the parking lot and continued into some trees. They were zipping up when they spied a stranger in the shadows dressed poorly for the cold in a thin shirt and no coat. When they called to him, he took off.

Under orders not to shoot, the militiamen made a quick calculation. If they were reproached for killing him, they could protest that they were heroes who had prevented a murderer's escape. If they held fire, and he was rearrested elsewhere and recounted how he slipped away from them, they would be mocked as toy soldiers. In their condition it wasn't easy to hit a zigzagging target in darkness. Three dozen rounds were fired into the woods before a slug glancing off a stump brought him down. The innkeeper, running to see what the gunfire was about, slipped off his apron and used the strings to fashion a tourniquet around the fugitive's thigh before he bled to death on his property. Newspapers were spread in the trunk of a militia car, and he was arrayed around a load of political tracts. Within forty-five minutes he was back at 84 Avenue Foch.

He was shivering uncontrollably when the interrogator was called in for a look at him. The room wasn't cold. He didn't seem afraid. Didn't, for that matter, seem Jewish. Jews didn't fight back. Few even ran to save their neck. Here was one who fought, ran, killed. A gift for the interrogator to bestow on Major Weiler, to redeem himself in his eyes.

"Your name?"

"You've already forgotten?" said the man. "It's just a few days since we chatted."

"You Jews are all of a type. Nothing sticks out in my mind. Nevertheless, we must get to know one another, and I like to begin by being cordial." A sudden blow to the side of the head knocked the man out of his chair. "We are done with cordiality," the interrogator said. "Who are you?"

"Moshe Pipik."

The interrogator had picked up enough Yiddish to know the name meant Moses Bellybutton. Other Jews who thought they were comedians had called themselves that until they learned that he was not to be trifled with. He picked up the Jew and reseated him, adjusting a slumping shoulder as though posing him for a portrait, and when the composition was to his liking, hit him again, putting him back on the floor.

A puddle from the Jews's leg wound spread over old stains in the carpet. The interrogator, a deliberate man, had plenty of time. The Jew, already slipping into shock, did not. "Get up," the interrogator said. "You are making a mess."

The Jew rose to his knees, grabbed the chair, and clawed back onto it. The prosecutor kicked at his shoulder, and he toppled back onto the rug.

"Didn't I say to get off the floor?"

The Jew dragged himself to his feet, tottered, and fell down on the chair.

"Your name," the interrogator said. "I didn't get it."

"Rogers," the Jew said. "First name Mark."

"You are too creative by half."

"Take it or leave it."

The interrogator raised his leg again, used his toe to prop him upright.

"Jews don't fight," the interrogator said. "It isn't in them. Yet you killed the soldier in the truck. How do you explain it?"

"What's in it for me if I tell you?"

"Less pain before we're done."

"I'm not afraid of pain."

"We will teach you."

Rogers, who knew he was dying, shrugged.

He presented a rare case to the prosecutor, who complained that his work was dull. The Jews, a meek lot, offered no challenges. There was nothing to do with them but to record the same answers to the same questions and put them on the trucks. Confronted by a Jew who acted unpredictably, he missed the other kind. The interrogator wasn't a monster. There were enough of those on hand at 84 Avenue Foch when the occasion called for one. He was a manipulator who valued subtlety over brute force. He was only human, though. If the Jew refused to cooperate, heaven help the Jew for making it personal between them.

He picked at the tourniquet until the knot came undone, stepping back as Rogers's femoral artery released large pulses of blood through his pants. He would need a bucket to clean up. Expecting fear from Rogers, he was disconcerted by a brief expression of triumph before the Jew's eyes rolled back and he dropped off the chair.

"Rogers?" the interrogator said. "Rogers!"

Blood disgusted him, Jewish blood—the cheapest kind—in particular. But he placed his hand over the wound and clamped it as well as he could, shouting for help.

A doctor was always on call at Avenue Foch to tend to the prisoners as a medical practitioner/torturer. It was one of these, Dr. Furtwangler, who had interrupted a residency as a neonatalist to come to France, who ran in in his pajamas and retied the tourniquet. When he was finished and both he and the interrogator were drenched in blood, he said, "Don't think you will get anything out of him. He is barely alive. Throw him on the trash heap and start on another."

"You call yourself a doctor?" The interrogator broke off as the prisoner began to mutter. "Rogers," he said. "Rogers, do you hear me?" Lifting the slumping head, he put his ear close to the Jew's lips.

"He is delirious, death will follow shortly," Furtwangler said.

"Save him."

"His life is worthless. He is. I am going back to sleep."

"Save it, or I swear I will have yours."

The interrogator shook the dying man's shoulder, listened to him babble as Furtwangler went out and returned, bringing a jar and rubber tubing. Furtwangler rolled up the Jew's sleeve, made an incision in his arm, and started an intravenous flow. Rogers's color didn't change. He did not appear to be stronger. His words remained indistinct.

"You haven't accomplished a damn thing," the interrogator said.

"Do you want to save him? Let him be. He needs rest now."

"I want his secrets. Those are what I want."

Furtwangler loaded a hypodermic needle from a glass ampule and gave Rogers a shot. Almost immediately his eyes fluttered open.

"What is that?" the interrogator said.

"Adrenaline."

"What will it do?"

"In his condition it will kill him," Furtwangler said. "He will have moments of near lucidity first."

"Rogers," the interrogator said, "we want to help you, but you must cooperate. Do you wish to live?"

The dying man groaned. The interrogator thought he heard a yes.

"Who are you?" he asked. "Where are you from? Why are you in Paris?"

The Jew's eyes snapped open, pink and glassy. Now the interrogator thought he heard a laugh. Furtwangler adjusted the knot on his thigh, and more blood ran out. To the interrogator it seemed the doctor was fine-tuning a device that he, himself, had been trying to operate in mittens. Rogers's head drooped, and he babbled again. The interrogator had a hundred questions, a few answers before the Jew fell silent.

"Transfuse him again," he shouted at Furtwangler. "Give him another shot."

"Blood is precious. We can't afford to waste any on a Jew."

"This is a special case," the interrogator said. "I demand that you do it."

Furtwangler yawned, started back to bed. "A dead Jew in particular."

When Major Weiler arrived for work that morning, the inter-rogator was waiting outside his office. Weiler's impression was of a brawler who had been up all night in a bar room in one of the working-class arrondissements, fighting for Germany's honor and his own. He didn't look like a winner. His hair was a clotted nest. Pale blue eyes were slits in bluer pouches. There was blood on his clothes, in the wild hair, on the back of his hands, and under his nails. "I have excellent news, Major, wonderful news," he announced, so eager to dispense it that he followed Weiler to the toilet.

"You have rearrested the woman, what was her name—Cartier—whom you allowed to play you for a fool?"

"Not her, but—"

Weiler ran water in the sink, and held a pocket comb under the tap. Either he had lost the knack for disparagement, or the inter-rogator was utterly obtuse. His good humor was undiminished.

". . . but an associate from whom we obtained the gist of their plans. You were right about her. She was—"

Weiler pulled the comb across his head, refashioning a straight part on the left side. He plucked individual hairs from between the teeth of the comb, counted them before washing them down the drain, and pushing others still rooted in his scalp to the needy place that had lost them. Where did a minor functionary—an amateur—come off telling him that he was right about a criminal matter? Could he have been wrong?

". . . involved in an intricate conspiracy against the occupation. The plotter we captured was a highly placed member of her gang. There isn't much we don't know about them."

"Dispense with the preamble. What did you learn?"

"It begins—"

"I can listen just as well in my office. Do you intend to remain in the toilet all morning?"

"If I may have a moment to freshen myself," the interrogator said. "His blood is all over me."

In ten minutes he returned to Weiler's office, looking the same. Weiler pointed to a chair. He pulled it close to the major's desk, uninvited.

"The man we captured was a Jew calling himself Mark Rogers, a *nom de guerre,* as the French say. The woman also assumed an Aryan name."

"You have their real identities?"

"They didn't reveal them even to each other," the interrogator said. "They were illegals in the occupied zone, and before that in Britain, where they were recruited by the Special Operations Executive and trained in the use of explosives."

"It's no secret that we've been hit with train derailments caused by bombs, and factories blown up by anti-German elements."

"They were after larger game," the interrogator said, "less in the way of military targets than with political value. They hoped to stir the populace, and boost morale, build . . . resistance, I would call it, to the occupation."

"The attack on the Musee du Jeu de Paume was theirs?"

"Rogers admitted direct involvement."

"How did they enter the country?"

"They were flown across the Channel and dropped by parachute."

Weiler snorted. The way to keep an ambitious subordinate in his place was to treat him as an incompetent and tighten the screws when he was on to something. Ask Colonel Maier.

"Rogers may have been lying," the interrogator said. "Under the circumstances, I doubt it."

"How many in the cell?"

"Four, at least. Perhaps as many as six."

"All of them French Jews?"

"A Danish communist, Janssen, doesn't seem to have been Jewish. He operated under the cover of a professional musician."

"Janssen was killed, his murder arranged to look like suicide," Weiler said.

"I'm aware of that. He was resident here when the others were landed. He found places for them to live. More than that I wasn't told. Rogers was wounded during capture and unable to speak at length."

"Who killed Janssen? Was there a falling-out among the group? A mutiny? Conflict with a rival subversive faction? I must have answers."

"Rogers was in very bad shape," the interrogator said. "There was no opportunity to develop a comprehensive line of questioning."

"Who was their leader? Did you learn that much?"

"There was another musician, a piano player, a Dutchman, Dutch Jew, who Rogers held in high regard. Possibly him."

"Goudsmit? Was that his name?"

"I'm sorry. I don't know more."

Weiler gazed away. How did he tell Maier that the Dutch Jew at the heart of the conspiracy had been in his hands, and disposed of without being drained of secrets?

"As the gang members are dead or dispersed, we have nullified their threat," the interrogator volunteered.

"I will make that judgment when I know more. Ask Rogers about the pianist, and about Janssen's death, and who the others are, and where they have gone to ground. Whatever it takes to obtain good answers, do it."

"I . . . I already have."

"Obviously not," Weiler said. "I'll draw up a list of questions for you to put to him."

"Under the circumstances, that's impossible."

"I will conduct the interview myself. You will see what is not impossible."

"Rogers is dead."

Weiler said, "What?" Then, at the top of his lungs: "You killed him."

He was done shouting, his thoughts in too many places for the full show of outrage that was called for. He had underestimated the dimensions of this disaster, and its repercussions. Maier would have to be told that no fewer than three of the criminals had slipped through his net, two of them executed summarily without being squeezed dry.

"He was too far gone," the interrogator answered finally. "We did what we could to keep him going longer, but he resisted all efforts. He was determined to die."

Weiler knew the feeling.

CHAPTER THIRTEEN

Five days had gone by without a word from Carla, a record. After the biggest fight they'd ever had, when she insisted that he quit the band and move in with her, essentially give up his career to be her pet, she'd cold-shouldered him for less than seventy-two hours before turning up at the club as though nothing had come between them. He'd gone along with the charade rather than rub her nose in it, but didn't think she would surrender her pride a second time. The first move was up to him.

He got no answer when he called, tried again every hour till it was time to leave for work, picturing her beside the phone, listening to it ring, knowing it would drive him nuts. His own pride was on the line, although he had a way around it. Everyone would agree that in her condition something could have gone seriously wrong. As he started for Boulevard Victor Massé, he almost wished it had.

The concierge didn't seem unhappy to see him. Carla hadn't declared him persona non grata.

"I haven't heard from her in days," Eddie said to him. "It's got me worried. Do you know if she's been well?"

The concierge rang her apartment. "You aren't the only one who is concerned," he said, holding the intercom to his ear. "Her parents came by yesterday, very upset, and went away more so when she didn't come to the door. They told me they would be back until they caught her at home."

"I'm not going without a look inside."

The concierge had coached other tenants through lovers' quarrels and was an authority on when they had gone on too long. Grabbing his keyring, he accompanied Eddie to the fourth floor. Eddie knocked on Carla's door, pounded it while the concierge tried wrong keys until the fifth was a charm. A bad smell rushed out on stale air. Stepping around the concierge, Eddie was first inside.

"Carla," he called out, "Carla, it's me. Where have you been keeping yourself?"

There was no sound but the ticking of her Louis XVI mantel clock in the foyer.

"Mlle de Villiers?" the concierge said. "Is anybody home?"

She'd left the city without letting him know, Eddie told himself, nothing more ominous than that. But she never went anywhere without telling her parents. He was in the bedroom, pressing his fingers against the tight covers on the bed, when the concierge called out, "Monsieur Piron, don't come in here."

Eddie ran toward the voice. The concierge stepped out of the bathroom to stop him, but Eddie pushed through his arms, brought up short by the body dangling from clothesline looped through a ceiling pipe above an overturned chair. The bad smell was concentrated here. It had been building since shortly after the last time he and Carla spoke.

The pain etched in her face was replicated in his heart. A hanging resulting in quick death from a broken neck was not something she would have known to do. Carla had died agonizingly by strangulation, but he couldn't say that hadn't been her intent.

The body had begun to deteriorate, the beautiful features losing the sharpness by which he'd read her moods so clearly that he knew them before she did. Her blouse was unbuttoned, her lower abdomen crosshatched with scratch marks deep enough to have drawn blood. A kitchen knife in the basin could only mean that she had tried to cut the baby out of her belly before stepping onto the chair. The concierge pushed him away. He didn't resist or go home to wait for the police to call as he was admonished to do, but remained by the door like a dog standing guard over his mistress's body till gendarmes arrived.

One was gray, the other very young, and they were interested more in the rich appointments of the apartment than in the corpse hanging from the bathroom ceiling. They spun it like it was a book rack with the same old story on every side. The gray one said to Eddie, "Don't touch anything," and the young one asked, "Where is the phone?"

They went out, and Eddie heard from one of them the long, lilting whistle that begins low and rises in pitch before tapering off breathlessly and means, well, will you look at this? Left alone with Carla, he set the chair upright and climbed onto it, imagining her final step. Then he took her around the waist, lifting her slightly as he pulled the loop over her head, the full meaning of dead weight brought home suddenly as the chair tottered, and he would have dropped her if he hadn't caught the shower curtain rod and come down on his feet. The gendarmes returned, and the older one asked, "Who gave you permission to do that? We said not to." Eddie brushed past them, saying "I need to make a call," and dialed Roquentin.

"Tell Weskers he's in the spotlight tonight," he said. "I won't be coming in."

"What is it this time? You miss so many shows, I might as well turn over the band to him and bill him as the star."

"It doesn't matter what it is. I can't make the first set. Even if I could, I'm not in any shape to play."

"I have no idea what you are getting at," Roquentin said.

"You can read about it in tomorrow's paper."

He went back to the living room and stared into space while the gendarmes made themselves comfortable on the sofa. It didn't seem possible that his sorrow would lift and he'd be anything like he was before. Seized by the idea that Carla had done him a favor in eliminating the threat hanging over his head, he decided that he was the worst person in the world for even contemplating such a notion, a bout of self-hatred interrupted by the arrival of the coroner, a man perfumed in chemical vapors, who looked at the body on the bed and bellowed, "Who took her down?" and when Eddie answered, "I did," said to him, "You are the boyfriend? It was the human thing to do. I can't fault you."

Why bother, thought Eddie, when he was doing an excellent job himself.

"What has happened is obvious," the coroner said before remembering to introduce himself as Dr. Doucet, "but I am required to ask of you questions of an intimate nature. Give me, first, the full name of the deceased, her age, the date and location of her birth? I assume this is her permanent residence, and that she had been living here at the time of the unfortunate—"

The questions came one on top of the other until Eddie wasn't thinking before he responded, a realization that stopped him cold.

Was it this sweet-natured doctor's job to lull him into lowering his guard and giving information that could be turned against him? What could be laid at his feet that was more sinister than being the inspiration for tragedy? There was no law in France that prohibited driving the woman you love to suicide.

He avoided mentioning that Carla had been pregnant. The coroner would find out in the morgue. By then he would know whether to pretend the baby was news to him. In the meantime, he'd keep his answers short, his secrets to himself.

He had a question for the coroner, but couldn't ask it. Would the autopsy reveal whether the baby would have looked black? If not, Carla had killed herself for nothing. Otherwise the largest part of her shame would be posthumous, and all the worse for how she handled it. In his grief was a great deal of anger. She had committed crimes against five people, herself, her parents, the baby, and him. It seemed unjust that none of that was in the statutes.

The coroner didn't let up. Eddie was answering by rote again when he was asked, "Do you want me to give you an injection?"

"What for?"

"To settle your nerves. We can't have you going into hysterics."

He would have laughed in the coroner's face if he hadn't seen Doucet closely observing his reaction. What clearer indication of hysteria was there than inappropriate mirth? He fastened a lugubrious stare, fearful that what Dr. Doucet had in store was not a sedative but a drug that would destroy his inhibitions, leaving him to babble defensively. The stare prompted another intense look, a shake of his satchel full of goodies before the coroner put it down.

Next were bland requests for information that could be obtained just as well from papers in Carla's purse. Eddie was braced for invasion when the coroner announced that he was done with him, which produced a soothing effect better than medication. He was free to go, but not to travel. The police would want a word. Home by 11:00, he was amazed at how well he slept until it occurred to him that he was thinking about it half awake in the middle of the night. Alert, his nightmares were more vivid, and he couldn't focus on anything else. When he opened the shutters, more darkness seemed to pour inside the room. The phone rang, and although he knew it was nothing good—no call before the sun came up ever was—he was glad not to be alone with his thoughts.

The Sûreté requested his presence to discuss the unfortunate death of Mlle de Villiers. He shaved and went out for a hard time.

The investigator assigned to the case was quick to mention that he had been at Le Bal Tabarin a year before when Eddie had performed at a benefit concert for war relief. He'd never cared for jazz and had to be dragged by his wife, who had received complimentary tickets, but he was pleasantly surprised by the music, which wasn't all that bad. Concerning the suicide, he expressed his condolences and counseled Eddie not to eat his heart out over something that probably could not have been prevented.

"Have you a realistic idea of why a woman with a promising future would have acted as she did?" he asked, and said, "These things happen. She was something of a Bohemian, a hyperemotional type, wouldn't you say? That may be all we ever know. All that we have to."

Eddie's only discomfort was razor burn from the hurried shave. The kid-gloves treatment mystified him until the investigator said, "I am Inspector François Bernard. Don't forget to extend my sympathies to Monsieur and Madame de Villiers."

There he had it. He was sheltered by the de Villiers mystique. Scandal in a family with a lesser name would be bathed in bright light instead of swept into the shadows at every turn. Carla hadn't exaggerated her father's power and influence.

A serious investigation would be conducted at some time. The de Villiers needed to know what had brought about their daughter's horrible death. It would be handled discreetly by officers whose loyalty had been bought by the family and whose silence was guaranteed. For now Eddie had nothing to fear. The single lie he'd told was to Roquentin, who would find nothing in the papers.

Someone else had questions, he was told. It didn't alarm him. Under the de Villiers umbrella, nothing did. His immediate concern was in getting back the lost sleep he needed to stay sharp through the late show tonight. Expecting to be traded off to another prober like Bernard, who would tap-dance around sensitive areas, he was hustled out the rear of the building, where a black Mercedes-Benz was idling. That he didn't go weak in the knees, he attributed later to his morning fog. Instead he yawned. His only visible reaction, it didn't reflect what he felt inside.

A Wehrmacht officer, a lieutenant, sat with him on the back seat, saying nothing. Not even the limousine that Carla occasionally borrowed from her parents was as luxurious or ran as smooth. He wouldn't speculate as to where he was being taken, though he had an idea that he wasn't being summoned for a command performance. A shameful fact he'd discovered about himself: Without his horn to cling to in uncertain situations, he was as anxious as a five-year-old deprived of her doll.

Too soon, the ride ended in a slow sweep around the Tuileries. Marched inside the musee at the northwest corner, he lost the rhythm of his footsteps in the martial clatter. Upstairs, a Nazi major squinted at him through a veil of cigarette smoke. Eddie borrowed a Gitane and sent up a smokescreen of his own.

"I am Major Weiler."

Eddie was put off by his lightly accented Parisian French. German francophiles with ambitions to remake France under the Reich were more doctrinaire than the bureaucrats and careerists force-fed the language after the takeover.

"You know who I am," Eddie said.

"The trumpet player. Tell me why your girlfriend killed herself in the gruesome manner that she did."

"I can't."

Weiler exhaled more smoke and blew it away. "Two lies in one breath are not an auspicious way to start. Let us place our cards on the table. You don't wish to give me what I want, though you can. That is your hand. Here is mine, which trumps it. You will."

Scratching at the rash on his jaw, Eddie struck a thoughtful pose. Weiler frowned.

"Mlle de Villiers was not emotionally disturbed, as many suicides are," Weiler said. "To her horror, she had been impregnated by a Negro and feared her child would be born with African traits and coloring and the other unfortunate aspects that go along with that. As the scion of aristocrats, she could not endure the humiliation and revulsion that would cling to her for the rest of her life, and chose to end it." He paused to study Eddie through the smoke. "True or false?"

"Since you believe you know everything," Eddie said, "perhaps you can tell me what she's thinking even where she is now."

"I doubt you would wish to hear it," Weiler said, "or to know what her last thoughts and words about you were."

He told himself the Nazi was the best bluffer he'd run up against. But poker wasn't a German game, and how did Weiler have so much intimate detail? Certainly Carla hadn't made her confession to her parents, or to the Nazi, and then gone ahead and killed herself. Simone knew his secret, at least in part. But if he gave it up, what did he have left to trade?

"Mlle de Villiers is a sympathetic figure, hardly deserving of her fate," Weiler said. "Typically, in instances of fornication with the lower orders, the victim is aware of what she is letting herself in for, or, with the truly depraved, invites it. Here the opposite is true. The young woman was an innocent exploited by a seducer. If my daughters were to find themselves in a similar situation, God forbid, I hope that they would act as heroically. What is your comment?"

"You don't need my opinion."

"This is the second honest thing you've said. The de Villiers are the finest exemplars of modern France, proud patriots who loved their daughter deeply. They are demanding severe punishment for the criminal who destroyed their family. They have great influence and prestige. A judge will take their wishes into account when hearing your case."

"What am I charged with?"

"In Germany, the crime would be Rassenschande, meriting the penalty of death. France is not so progressive, yet something in the existing legislation may be found to give the same result. As of the moment, I have not recommended a formal charge."

Good news, except that nothing having to do with Germans ever was. Since when did the absence of a provable crime interfere with Nazi justice? A bluffer himself, Eddie said, "I'll just go, then."

"If only it were that simple," Weiler said. "I am doing what I can to save you. For that I need your cooperation."

"Since I'm not charged, I can save myself."

"If you were to disappear, who would ask about the charge? Do you think your fame protects you? Aside from your fans on Place Pigalle, would anyone notice that you were gone? The de Villiers want your head. Literally. I am all you have to keep it on your shoulders."

"What have I done to deserve such tender care?"

"Nothing," Weiler said. "That is to say, you haven't done it yet. We are interested in a number of jazz musicians in Paris."

"I don't suppose you're asking about club dates."

"Joke at your peril," Weiler said. "They've been linked to anti-German activity. You are acquainted with them and can give us the information we want."

"I won't be your spy."

"Did you know that everyone expresses the same lofty sentiment when we approach them to work for us? In the end, they all do. Consider this: If you refuse, we will cut off that precious lip of yours and suture it to the tip of your nose where you can observe your error closely. How does that appeal to you?"

Eddie shivered. He couldn't help it.

"That's what I thought," Weiler said. "The first musician we wish to learn about is Anton Goudsmit."

"Who?"

"I should remove your lip now. You performed with him."

"I did?"

"It was at your nightclub. At the request of the SS, I took him there myself."

"I don't remember—"

"A piano player."

"I still don't know who—"

"The Dutchman."

"That was you up on the bandstand that night," Eddie said.

Weiler stubbed out his cigarette.

"It was the only time I met him," Eddie said. "We didn't say two words to each other besides calling out the numbers we were going to play. You saw—"

"What did you hear about him?"

"Nothing."

"None of the other players said anything?"

"All of them did," Eddie said. "They agreed that the officer who smashed his fingers must be a monster."

"Oh, and what are their names?" Weiler lit another cigarette. "Never mind. Do you now deny knowing Borge Janssen?"

"He was my drummer."

"You played with him every night?"

"Six nights a week, yes."

"You must have discussed other topics besides the music."

"If we did, I don't recall."

"You deny knowing that he was active against the occupation?"

"All I know about him is that he had problems keeping three quarters time."

"He was also a suicide. Your acquaintances have a proclivity for killing themselves. What is it about you?"

Whatever it was had followed him from New Orleans and didn't end with suicide. Janssen hadn't taken his own life, but it had been made to look like it. If he hadn't forgotten, then neither had Weiler, who fashioned a hard stare intended to provoke answers that weren't well thought out.

"Goudsmit and Janssen are gone," Eddie said. "How can I get you what you want?"

"Begin with Janssen's friends."

"I don't know that he had any."

"The other members of your band. Try them."

"They had even less to do with him than I did. How can Goudsmit and Janssen harm Germany now?"

"Their deaths create a false impression that they were heroes in opposing us. France doesn't need new heroes. She has St. Joan, who is enough. You must help to bring out the truth about them. As they are already dead, you cannot injure them."

"I'm a trumpet player," Eddie said, "not a detective."

"Now you are both. Prove your ambidextrousness," Weiler said, "or I will prove mine by making a present of your head for the de Villiers, while keeping your lip as a souvenir."

"Do I know him?" Colonel Maier asked when Weiler briefed him about his interview with Eddie.

"The American sought by Interpol."

"Why haven't I heard of him before?"

Weiler knew better than to contradict the colonel. Playing dumb was Maier's way, one of them, of challenging him to weave disparate elements into the framework of the larger case.

"Piron is the Negro trumpeter in a jazz band on Place Pigalle sought for attempted murder in the United States."

"Does Interpol headquarters in Berlin know you found him? After they've been apprised, you won't be bothered with him again."

"I have more ambitious plans for him."

Maier cupped a hand behind his ear. Weiler had made a bold statement. He would have to back it up.

"The information came from our wiretap on the other American, Simone," he said, "from which we concluded that Piron had impregnated the de Villiers girl."

"What has this got to do with my investigation here?"

"She was a trollop. Her parents should be flogged in the public square for raising her without morals, and will have the rest of their lives to regret it."

"There's no rush to tell them what awful people they are," Maier said. "Some of their business activities necessitate German participation."

"By establishing Piron's blame for her death, I was able to instill the fear of God in him," Weiler said.

"Why should I care if he is afraid of God?"

"The bomb-maker found in the Seine—Janssen—played in Piron's band. Goudsmit, who was head of Janssen's organization, operated under the cover of a jazz musician. I will increase the pressure on Piron until he exposes their plot, and his role in it, and gives up the Cartier woman and the rest."

"Why didn't you threaten him with torture, give him a taste of it, and skip all of this fancy footwork?"

Weiler had no qualms against torture, other than that it was also Maier's way, but he was determined to show his ways more effective. His brains were being wasted playing second fiddle to the doctrinaire colonel—unless he'd misjudged Piron, in which case he had none, and was begging for a posting on the eastern front.

"Let us try subtlety," he said. "If it doesn't yield better results, then we will break him physically."

Maier didn't appear to be listening, but held up one finger, wagging it. "Don't we always?"

CHAPTER FOURTEEN

German architects scouting locations for permanent Gestapo headquarters in Paris were drawn to the Second Temple Israelite near the Hotel de Ville. The massive, century-old Moorish synagogue was a remnant of an era when the promise of the European enlightenment inspired French Jews to construct houses of worship that rivaled their Christian counterparts in grandeur and elegance. The congregation had disbanded under the occupation, its members dispersed throughout the capital or else relocated to the unoccupied zone, those who hadn't fled Europe altogether. One of the prime organs of Nazi power wasn't a natural fit for a Jewish showcase; the interior would have to be scraped down to the bare walls. The ark, the pews, torah scrolls, and eternal light were at a trash dump when laborers gutting the interior were halted by a directive from Berlin calling for the entire structure to be demolished and rebuilt from the ground up.

The wrecking ball was no match for the thick walls. The synagogue had been constructed of Jerusalem stone by Italian masons whose work was meant to endure at least as long as the monuments of antiquity. The project would be delayed months by the time crews chiseled down to the bedrock. For the building to be destroyed in a timely manner, it would have to be blown up.

The impending explosion was a continuing story in *Paris-Soir*, which played it as a festive occasion. Citizens starved for entertainment crowded the area to observe the preliminaries. Among them were some who helped themselves to the pickaxes, shovels, crowbars, and other implements strewn over the site. The work was slowed further until the demolition firm posted watchmen to keep trespassers at bay.

In the hours before the structure was due to come down, the night watchman noticed a small truck idling under an unlit street lamp across the street. In the gloom it was impossible to see who was behind the wheel. After stopping there for half an hour, the truck moved away. Ninety minutes later, it was back.

Three figures all in black scurried out. Keeping to the shadows, they approached a steel shed where dynamite was stored. A blinding flash that set the watchman's heart racing wasn't followed by an explosion. An oxyacetylene torch was being used to cut the locks. It was a reckless act, inviting catastrophe, and he welcomed the excuse to quit his post in search of a phone. The truck was still there when he returned. He started toward the shed with the idea that the gang was inside and he would cage them, and then he stopped. For what he was being paid, it was insanity to risk his neck. What was keeping the damn flics?

The truck doors opened, catching him by surprise as the three-some made another run at the shed. A car from the Sûreté rattled down the block. He ran to intercept it, waving his arms, pointing it toward the curb. The driver cut the lights and officers took up positions around the shed.

The metallic walls, blast-proof and soundproof, contained what noise was being made. Then the watchman picked out the three-some slump-shouldered and moving slowly. Twenty meters from the truck, they were spotlighted in the glare of headlamps. An officer shouted "Don't move."

They surrendered to the light, turned into the face of it like black sunflowers. A couple of flics were almost on them when a gun went off. The officer half a step ahead of the other clutched at his throat. A second shot dropped him. The watchman noticed canvas sacks bulging in two of the gang's fists as they stood under the protection of the shooter, who was in the lead, slightly apart from them. The other flics held fire while the caravan to the truck resumed.

The police car wheeled away from the curb, and as it swerved around the fallen officer the watchman heard two bullets strike. Sweet steam shrieking from the radiator sprayed the air. The vehicle plowed into the shooter, scooping him onto the hood and delivering him to the truck, where he tumbled off. Another gang member lost his satchel sprinting for the sidewalk. The car jumped the curb and pinned him against the side of the building, then backed away from the body glued to the bricks.

The car put down a trail of rubber behind a fugitive running flat-footed down the middle of the street, the bumper practically grazing the runner's heels when the engine seized. The driver was on the running board with his gun out before the car rolled to a stop, but was unable to get off a shot. He kicked the door shut, cracking the window glass. The runner didn't look back.

Of the three men lying in the street, only the flic seemed to be alive. Blood bubbled in a 10-centime-size hole above his Adam's apple. The watchman knelt beside him and held his hand till the last bubble burst. Then he went to see about the others.

The man beside the truck didn't look like anyone he expected to find stealing dynamite from a construction site, clean-cut with an intelligent face that was rather handsome. War and the occupation had created dislocation at every level of French society. Sober-minded individuals routinely acted out of character to keep afloat. All of this was in the back of his mind as he went to check the body crushed against the wall. The briefest glance, and he started back to the truck. It was better not to look closely.

A wool blanket was draped over the passenger's seat. Underneath it was a pyramid of satchels. He unzipped the one on top, let his flashlight play over sticks of dynamite, coiled fuse, and a detonator. The flics pulled him away as he opened another. The pyramid wobbled and would have crashed onto the floor if he hadn't smothered it in the blanket and nudged it back into place. He was a hero tonight for the second time, but neither officer commended him. He had acted well while they made a hash of things. There was a chance they would lose their jobs.

"What about the other one?" he asked.

"There were only two," one officer said. "I was chasing shadows."

"I definitely saw a third."

"You are in error."

"Not at all."

"Think hard. You are making a mistake in believing that we didn't get them all."

It was three in the morning, and he was exhausted and a little slow on the uptake. If there were three, and one got away, he wasn't the same hero he'd be if there were two and they'd been foiled.

The flics could be heroes now, too. Why insist on three and make trouble? Even thieves had to eat.

Maier turned away from the window as the ground spanked the plane. The landing strip was laid out on a high meadow out of the sight of the camp he'd come to visit, twenty kilometers from Munich, the closest big city. He'd never been to this lonely part of Bavaria before, but he felt at home. All of Germany was his home, as all the world was his oyster. His and Hitler's.

The car waiting at the edge of the tarmacadam was one of the powerful Mercedes Benzes always at his disposal. They were excellent machines, posh yet reliable, the envy of junior officers who rarely got to see them from the inside. Maier had no appetite for luxury. His cherished places were the overlit rooms and unheated cells where he was called to do his special work. Crucial as the work was, he couldn't say that it gave fullness to his life. Before joining the party in its earliest days while a graduate instructor in philosophy at the University of Frankfurt, already the stepfather of three small girls and with a boy of his own, he wasn't tormented by a lack of fullness. The party had given him something he hadn't been aware that he was missing—significance—and what could be more precious? There was nothing he wouldn't do for Germany, but question it.

Like the airfield and the modern highway that delivered him from there, the camp had been carved out of pastureland. Nothing grew well at these altitudes but softwoods and grass and the cattle that fed off the grass. The thin soil was expendable to the planners in Berlin who decided how much milk and cheese the country needed to produce, and enormous tracts were given over to the camp. He had underestimated its scale. He had seen only the smallest part of one section. Not far away were satellite camps of the "school for violence" that was the Dachau complex, but it was too soon for him to fit the pieces together. The gorgeous mountain landscapes, the giant imperial German eagle cast in stone above the main gate, made for a perfect picture. All that was missing was . . . nothing.

The commandant, SS Sturmbannführer Alex Piorkowski, invited him to his residence, where lunch was being prepared by an orderly, a former chef at a three-star Cologne hotel, but Maier declined. He had an aversion to these professional mediocrities, nothings before the war, who were living high at the public trough. He reminded Piorkowski that he wasn't here to be entertained but to interview one of his prisoners, and time was essential. Seeing the commandant's disappointment, he mentioned that he wasn't hungry.

"I will have him brought immediately," Piorkowski said.

"Why don't I go to him?"

"It's dangerous. Typhus is rampant among the inmates, who are the dregs of Europe, and wouldn't hesitate to kill you if they could."

"Can they?" Maier said.

The Sturmbannführer wouldn't allow an important visitor on the yard protected only by the standard escort. Maier was surrounded by a small army, which didn't permit the candid perspectives he wanted. Thousands of men wandered about, as aimless as the herds they had displaced. Most wore striped pajamas unsuited for winter temperatures in the mountains. Two distinct kinds became apparent: hard cases with green tags on their pajamas, and their opposites tagged red. The latter, many of them, had faces showing Jewishness to be their crime, which indicated those in green to be the thieves and killers also housed at the camp. He could imagine what it was like at night when the greens feasted on the reds out of sight of the guards, or with their connivance, and what it was like in sight of Piorkowski, a shark who feasted on everyone.

The man he wanted was in a barracks a kilometer from the administrative unit. Deep inside the camp, a notion that he was a visitor at a human zoo gave way to a feeling that he was the rare beast brought here for the edification of the men in striped pajamas gazing at him in wonder. What was more exotic than a healthy, well-fed man dressed in everyday clothes, absent the smell of death that was the distinguishing characteristic of their species? He was trying to put himself in their place—up to a point—when he spotted a familiar face.

Familiar only as a caricature of the man in photos he'd studied, the features twisted and shrunken, made narrow by hunger and dulled by malnutrition, aged by worry, saddened, crazed, and deformed by pain in the manner of life here.

He announced to his escort that he'd found the prisoner he wanted, so they should return wherever they could be of use.

"We are not to leave you alone," a lieutenant, the senior officer, said.

"Then leave me in peace."

The soldiers stepped away, not far. "Professor?" Maier said. "Professor Smits?"

The inmate concentrated on the ground. Among the pebbles and cinders Maier noticed an infinitesimal cigarette butt in the dirt. The man pounced on it, but too little was left to hold together, and it fell apart as he tried to fit it between his lips.

"One of you," Maier said to his escort, "give him a cigarette."

"It's against the rules," said the lieutenant.

"Give it to me."

The lieutenant stood stiffly as Maier patted him down for a pack, which he placed in the inmate's hand with a book of matches. "Now something to eat."

"It is also ag—"

"My lunch is growing cold at the Sturmbannführer's. Inform him that I will be picnicking on the yard." Maier turned to the inmate, watched him light up and draw deep, contain the smoke greedily in his lungs before releasing it in an ecstatic sigh. "Professor," he said.

The inmate scarcely acknowledged him, intent on his smoke.

"I've traveled a good distance for a word with you," Maier said.

"To free me from this hell on earth? Is that what you said?"

"You know better."

"The price for my word is my freedom. If it is beyond your means, I have nothing for you."

"You haven't heard what I want."

"A word, you said. For which you're not prepared to pay." He started away. "I don't do business like that."

"It's up to you," Maier said. "But you know what Piorkowski will do when these men—" He glanced toward his escort. "When they inform him that you sent me away."

"In coming here, you've already awarded me my freedom," Smits said. "Whether I receive it in exchange for conversation, or Piorkowski turns me over to his torturers, I'm not long for this place."

"My report will state that I need to talk to you again. Nothing will change for you except the calendar. Don't be stubborn, and things will go better for you here."

"There is no better here."

"An excellent rejoinder," Maier said. "I wouldn't stand a chance against you in the public forum. However, Dachau is not a debating society. Words are abstract. Pain, and hunger, cold, and suffering, as you know better than I, are not. There can be better here, just as there can be worse. Better food, warmer clothes. I can ensure that you have them. I'm not Piorkowski; I have nothing against you personally."

"Why, then, are you one of them?"

"Times changed. It isn't a comment on my humanity that I adapted handily."

"Foolish me," Smits said, "for believing otherwise."

Maier conceded the debate, but Smits wouldn't win the argument. He squeezed the professor's shoulder softly. Smits cringed as he increased the pressure. Well below the threshold of pain Smits looked like a beaten dog. Yes, pain, and even its promise, was real, and words were abstract, which didn't make them cheap.

"The information I want harms no one," Maier said. "You are doing yourself an injustice in not letting me have it."

"I will decide."

"Certainly," Maier said. "How can I compel you, when you have me over the proverbial barrel? Look, here is my lunch. Please, share it with me. There's plenty for two."

Smits watched the lieutenant coming toward them with a tray cloaked in a linen cloth. His expression hardened, but Maier heard his stomach growl. He took the professor behind a barracks and hunkered down with him out of the wind.

"You are from Utrecht?" Maier said. "Am I correct?"

"Rotterdam, originally. As a teenager I was awarded a scholarship to the University of Utrecht. Things worked out well. I was offered a teaching fellowship, named an assistant professor before I was thirty, a full professor by thirty-five, and never found reason to leave. And would still be there, if I hadn't been brought here."

"What are you accused of?"

"Don't you know?" Smits said.

"I should point out the rules of our discussion. I supply the cigarettes. You smoke them. I supply the food. You get to eat it. I ask the questions. You provide answers. It's an arrangement from which both of us benefit."

Smits revealed a measure of disgust with himself that Maier hadn't seen before. He was about to walk away when Maier instructed the lieutenant to place the tray on the ground, and he watched, paralyzed, as the officer spread a tablecloth, anchoring one corner with a coffee pot and another with a decanter of red wine. A silver platter was placed near him, and Maier lifted the lid on a bowl of pasta in a red sauce that gave the flavors of tomatoes, and spices, and the sea. There was a loaf of bread, and butter, and a meat dish, which Maier pushed toward Smits's side of the cloth. "Have it all. Like Hitler, I am a vegetarian. Killing animals is a crime."

Smits appeared as a dog of a particular breed, one of Pavlov's, Maier thought, watching him drool.

"My crime," Smits said, "is membership in the Dutch communist party."

"Not an ordinary hack. You are the chief ideologist."

"It's no secret. But I won't divulge the names of my comrades. For the privilege of turning all of this fine food into shit, I refuse to surrender what self-respect I possess."

"My concern is not the party," Maier said, "but one of your students."

"I won't—"

"There's nothing either of us can do that will harm him, as he is already dead."

Smits tore a large chunk of bread and stuffed it in his mouth, crammed in more until he began to cough and choke. After prolonged near-starvation, too much to eat could lead to sudden death as a weakened body was overwhelmed in processing it. But Maier let him have all he wanted until he looked up as though it was time to settle the bill, and he realized he'd left his wallet at home.

"You haven't mentioned what your discipline was," Maier said.

Smits pointed to bulging cheeks that were too full to allow him to speak.

"I'm told it was chemistry. That you are a brilliant scientist who sometimes takes on difficult experiments for the Dutch chemical industries."

Smits nodded. It was less compromising than speech.

"Anton Goudsmit was your student?"

"Anton is dead?" Smits spit food down the front of his shirt and on the tablecloth.

"Was he special?" Maier gave him a napkin to wipe himself. "A promising chemist you took under your wing?"

"Not at all; another of thousands of undergraduates passing through my lecture hall through the years. I'd almost forgotten him. A C student."

"Yet you do recall him."

Smits dug a fork into the spaghetti, was shoveling it into his mouth when Maier caught his hand.

"He was a musician. It's the only thing about him that sticks out."

"A pianist, wasn't he?" Maier said. "Tell me about him."

"He was a prodigy at the keyboard. A genius with little understanding of how good he could be."

"And you would know because you are also a—?"

"Strictly an amateur. I couldn't hold a light to him."

"But also the preeminent jazz critic in the Netherlands."

"Some would say I was."

"Here you had this brilliant player in your class, whose talent only you recognized. You would have done something to nurture it."

"I bought him the latest records from Britain and the States, and introduced him to the biggest jazz names in Holland. He was light years ahead of them. There was nothing he could learn from them. It was rather the other way around."

"What else?"

"I told him to stop wasting his time on chemistry. As advanced as he was at the keyboard, that's what an oaf he was in the laboratory."

"Go on."

"He was a Jew, you know, and the situation in the Netherlands was deteriorating. He had no future there, or on the Continent. I had counseled other young men, promising chemists, to get out. None did. Goudsmit, however, was eager to resettle. I advised him to try the States. He'd learn more about the music in six months than he would in a lifetime in Europe. As his family had to remain in Holland, he didn't want to go that far."

"Where did he land?"

"I don't know. He quit school. We lost touch."

"He was an ingrate?"

"I don't understand."

"He didn't come to make his good-byes, and to thank you for all you did for him?"

"He . . . yes, he might have."

"Without mentioning where he was going?"

"France?" Smits said. "That's right, he said France."

"According to the registrar, Anton Goudsmit left the University of Utrecht in April of last year, days before the invasion of the low countries. It seems peculiar a Jew would flee the Netherlands for France, escape from the fire to go only as far as the frying pan."

"How could he know the French wouldn't fight? He was fortunate to make it out of Holland."

"Not so fortunate, seeing how he ended up," Maier said. "France isn't the safest place for a Jew on the run."

"No place is," Smits said.

"There's Palestine."

"Palestine is closed to the Jews. A few thousand at most are allowed by the British to enter each year."

"It wouldn't be difficult if he had the right papers."

Smits shrugged. "What do I know about that?"

"You reds have forgers to aid the flight of the brilliant protégé of an important comrade."

"We are firmly opposed to the Zionist enterprise," Smits said. "The Jews will not solve their problem as neocolonialist lackeys of

British imperialism, or in bourgeois nationalism, but in the international brotherhood of the toiling cl—"

"Spare me," Maier said. "I'm to believe you wouldn't have bent the party line for him?"

"I wrote the party line. Other countries would gladly have taken him in."

"Which countries are these?"

"We lost touch. I can't say."

"Which brings us back to Palestine," Maier said. "He wasn't happy there? The weather didn't agree with him? The food? The quality of the music? What went wrong?"

"What do you mean?"

"Why did he leave the Jewish paradise to end his life among French anti-Semites?"

"I can't tell you that he reached Palestine, let alone what it was like."

"You didn't know he was back on the Continent doing party work? He was your protégé in every sense."

Smits scrambled to his feet. As Maier pulled him back, his eyes overflowed with tears. Credit Piorkowski, thought Maier, that the professor couldn't endure being manhandled, despite his confident front.

Smits grabbed the tablecloth and snapped it with both hands. Maier pushed away as food went everywhere and wine and coffee splashed him. Smits took the cigarettes from his pocket, flung down the pack, and mashed it under his heel.

Maier called to the lieutenant standing by with his men. "Put Professor Smits out of his misery."

"I'm not authorized to execute—"

"Give me your weapon." Maier lifted the flap on the officer's holster, removed a Luger Black Widow revolver, and pointed it at Smits, who stood motionless as moisture seeped across the front of his pants.

"Do I have your word as a gentleman that Anton really is dead?" Smits blubbered.

"He is, whatever you want to think I am."

"All right, then," Smits said. "He parachuted into France."

"Just like that? The wind gathered him up in Palestine, and blew him over France?"

"The British flew him. The SOE, Special Operations Executive, charged with clandestine activities in occupied Europe."

"Flew him from where?"

"The eastern coast of England. I don't know exactly where the airfield was."

Maier cocked his head.

"I don't."

"How did he get there from Palestine?"

"He was recruited by the British to take on a special mission."

"Jazz musicians are recommended for those?"

"Chemists are," Smits said. "Even an oaf can mix explosives into a bomb. Anton was valued in that he had lived in Paris after escaping from Holland, and before escaping again to Palestine. He agreed to return, and was airlifted along with several young Palestinians."

"We've picked up other Jews the British inserted into France— why didn't we learn sooner about Goudsmit?"

"I don't know everything," Smits said.

Maier shot him in the foot.

Smits collapsed onto his side, howling. The lieutenant stepped forward to retrieve his gun, but Maier brushed him off. Smits unlaced his shoe, gingerly rolled back the tongue. Maier batted his hands away. "Answer, or I'll put a bullet in the other one."

"I can't, I am in immense pain."

Maier drew back the hammer. Smits said, "Anton knew the British are bumblers with no regard for Jewish lives, and probably he would be captured and summarily killed like the others. He had friends in Paris, loyal comrades, and the names of a few who infiltrated after he left and were waiting for someone like him. They needed him."

"For what?"

Smits clutched his foot and moaned, one eye on Maier, who was unmoved by the performance.

"I don't know why. Really, I don't. The British have plans for rousing the French from their torpor. Fools' plans, as all British plans are. We . . . the fighting communist underground hit the occupation where it hurts."

"Where is that?"

"It varies. Targets are not decided by the central committee in Holland, or in France, or Moscow."

"Who does?"

"Agents on the ground know best, and do whatever is in their power to accomplish."

Smits pulled off his shoe. His sock was wringing wet with blood. He peeled it away, and Maier saw a ragged hole where the ankle met the heel. If the professor were a horse, he'd be put out of his misery without delay.

"One more point of information, and I will be out of your hair."

Smits winced as he investigated the wound.

"Without Goudsmit could the group continue their activities?"

"How can I tell you what is happening there when I'm here?"

"What if you were there, professor?"

"I wish I were."

"Certainly every heroic communist does. Would you continue your activities as your group fell apart around you?"

"Absolutely."

"To the last man?"

"We are never down to the last. We recruit more."

"Frenchmen?" Maier smiled. It was something he found counterproductive during questioning, and most other occasions, but he couldn't help it.

"More men," Smits said.

"Communists?"

"Not all. Some never find out they are working for us."

"Useful idiots, you mean."

"Useful," Smits said. "What about my foot?"

"You will receive proper treatment shortly."

His escort gathered around Maier, and he marched back to the administrative wing for a word with the commandant.

"Did you get what you wanted from the prisoner?" Piorkowski asked.

"He was useful."

"Will you need him for further interviews?"

"For nothing."

"I see. We will review his situation appropriately in due course."

"As he has already eaten his last meal," Maier said, "I see no justification for delay."

CHAPTER FIFTEEN

Eddie slept badly, wasn't entirely awake, and ran out without his hat. He was too far from the house to go back for it when the skies convulsed, and freezing rain collected in his hair and ran down his collar, sending him chasing after the first bus that went by. The squall, passing quickly, laid down a glaze to which the city surrendered abjectly, as had become its habit, and he arrived at Place Pigalle fifty minutes late. The woman waiting there was half-frozen.

"Monsieur Piron," she said, "I was beginning to think I'd missed you."

Blue lips and a cherry red nose didn't detract from her dark prettiness. He was all but certain he didn't know her. If he did, then he wasn't awake yet. Hers wasn't a face a sensible man would forget in any arrangement of colors. His guess was that she was one of the women who lay in wait for him more typically after the late show to be taken back to his place, or in the case of the unattractive ones to hint strenuously and to no avail that that was where they wanted to go.

"I'm Mrs. Goudsmit," she said.

It undercut why he thought she was here. Maybe not. Her teeth never stopped chattering while he decided how to handle her.

"You played with my husband."

One thing he could do was to turn her over to the Germans and get them off his back. But he wouldn't do that to his worst enemy. Not even to a dog. Well, maybe to his enemy.

"Did I?" Dumb was good. Dumb was how to continue living with himself. Hadn't he established that with Carla? "I don't recall—"

"Briefly." She fell in alongside as he stepped onto the curb. "He was a piano player. A Dutchman. He was arrested for being in Paris without papers. The SS took him to your club, and you jammed together. Then they took him away."

"I remember now."

The woman nodded in the empty way of eyewitnesses to tragedy overwhelmed by sadness and unable to describe what they felt.

"He was a fine player," Eddie said, "influenced mainly by Earl Hines, I'd say, and some of Teddy Wilson."

"He idolized them," she said. "He could sound like either one and combined their styles."

"I thought I knew all the best players in Paris. It surprised me that I wasn't acquainted with him. I had a ball."

"You're kind," she said. "He held you in the highest regard. That is why he had his arrangements sent to you after his arrest. Of all the musicians working in the city, he believed you would make the best use of them."

Eddie thought for a while before he remembered the envelope with the book of music inside that had arrived mysteriously at the club. How did he tell this young widow burdened with sentimental attachment that her late husband's writing had no practical value for him? He didn't use charts, favoring head arrangements that afforded his musicians leeway to improvise.

"They're brilliant," he said.

"I'd like them back. Anton didn't leave me much, and I've found someone with an interest in purchasing them."

"Another jazzman?" He didn't know anyone who performed the music as Goudsmit notated it. "I'll have to hunt for it."

"You don't know where it is?"

"My apartment is a mess."

"I really must have it right away."

"Give me your phone number."

"It can't wait," she said adamantly. "I'll help you look after the show."

Which brought him back to what he had speculated about her originally. "Where did your husband learn to play?"

"I . . . I don't know. He was self-taught."

"He must have had excellent teachers at some time."

"He picked up everything from records," she said. "He wasn't taking lessons when we were together."

A faint accent that he had puzzled over seemed to be German. Again he revised his opinion. He had thought she must be involved in whatever about her late husband intrigued Major Weiler. It was as plausible that she was an agent of Weiler's on a mission to entrap him, and that he could be rid of her almost at no cost to his conscience.

"How did his music book come to me?"

"After he was taken away, I went to the police station and was told that a book belonging to him had been found in the cell. He had mentioned that he wanted you to have it if anything ever happened to him. I asked that it be sent to you after the inspectors released it."

Roquentin's head poked out of La Caverne, searching up and down the street. "Where the hell were you?" he said. "I told Weskers he was fronting the band tonight." He looked at the woman and rolled his eyes at Eddie. "Never mind, you're here now. No harm done."

Eddie took the bandstand while she found a table out of reach of the footlights. Almost immediately the houselights dimmed, and he signaled the downbeat for "Memories of You."

Inserting a straight mute in the bell of his horn, he blew one chorus with a romantic, nasal tone before taking the verse in a rough growl made bluesier by the cold he felt coming on. He played to the woman, who was not moved by the music, undecided what to make of her. Had she come for the book as she said, for the Germans as he feared, or for him? Carla would forgive him for backing the longshot. Hadn't she forgiven him everything aside from the one thing that was unforgiveable till the day she died?

The woman nursed a kir that Roquentin topped off throughout the first show without opening a tab. Eddie led off the second set with "Nobody Knows You When You're Down and Out," draining the tragic lyric of pity. The SS stormed in during the refrain, Weiler trailing a mob to the front, displacing ringside customers who scurried to the sides of the room. Eddie made way for a mournful duet by Philippe on the piano backed up by drums before the clarinet brought relief. The woman also had scurried. He checked the other tables, the line for the ladies' room, and at the bar, but she was gone without her late husband's precious book. Without him. The Germans weren't enjoying the show. They banged their glasses on the tables, drowning out the music as they called the titles of songs he had no intention of playing.

Icy rain stalled over the city in the hours after the buses stopped running. He returned to the apartment soaked to the skin. A pot of water was whistling on the stove when he stopped sneezing long enough to fill a teacup and to hunt for Goudsmit's book. He looked first in the bureau and bookcase, the likely places where it was unlikely to be, and then tore the place apart, not so desperate to find it as glad to have something to do at four in the morning when the prospect of sleep was vague. After half an hour he was convinced he'd been mistaken when he said that he still had it. He stopped searching, and immediately noticed a pile of old newspapers beside the door, and picking through them discovered the tattered accordion envelope, its torn seams and edges repaired with tape and fastened with brown string.

He untied the knot and slipped out the unbound book of charts, big-band swing song arrangements that were all wrong for him. Goudsmit was a competent arranger and knowledgeable musician who must have known that there was no place for swing in the repertoire of one of the last stalwarts of old-fashioned New Orleans jazz. Crabbed notes in the margins were scribbled in a language he didn't recognize and took to be Dutch. He quit trying to decipher them, shoved the book inside the envelope again, and kicked it all the way under the bed. If the woman came for it, it was hers, no questions asked. Something was going on that was beyond his understanding. The safe, wise, only thing to do was to keep his distance.

He walked in again reeking of camphor and eucalyptus oil from the cold remedy he'd picked up at an herbalist in the Latin Quarter. Roquentin held his nose, and said, "Have you gone to war against the customers? You'll drive them all away."

"I can't play if I can't breathe," Eddie said.

"Wash it off. I'll put up a pot of chicken soup."

"For my cold? It's an old wives' tale."

"For your breakfast."

Eddie stepped into the toilet to scrub the balm off his chest. When he came out smelling nearly as bad, Roquentin was in an apron standing over the stove in a chicken-and-celery-flavored cloud. "How do you know Janssen's girl?"

"I don't," Eddie said.

"The woman you brought into the club yesterday, wasn't she Borge Janssen's girlfriend?"

"You're confused. She's Goudsmit's widow."

"What Goudsmit? Who's Goudsmit?"

"The piano player the SS hauled in one night. You remember, he played a set, and they smashed his fingers and took him away. She was his wife."

"Watch your step," Roquentin said. "Her hobby is driving jazz musicians to their grave."

"I'll take my ch—okay, I will," Eddie said. "Why do you say she was Janssen's girl?"

"I ran into them together in the Marais not once but twice, shortly before he died. With those dark good looks of hers, she isn't a woman I'd forget. Evidently, you did."

"What do you mean?"

"She dropped by not long ago and sat alone crying into a hankie. I remembered her with Janssen, and thought she must have warm feelings for the place. Didn't you notice her?"

"It's hard to see the customers' faces with the lights in my eyes."

"Then you didn't see those warm feelings. They were for you. What gave you the idea she was the piano player's widow?"

"She told me she was."

"No law says she can't be both," Roquentin said, "Janssen's girl, and Goudsmit's widow, and with her cap already set for you. It could get messy."

"What did you really know about Janssen before you hired him?"

"You hired him, I paid him," Roquentin said. "He could play. I didn't demand a résumé."

"That's it?"

"What do I know about you?" Roquentin said. "What's behind this belated interest in our late drummer?"

"The Germans put me on the hot seat after Carla died, but what they really want to know about is Janssen."

"He hated them. That much I can say."

"He hated everyone," Eddie said. "He hated me for hating America more than he hated it himself."

"God bless his soul. I hate the Germans, too."

"What do they want from you?"

"Nothing—besides the club."

"What?"

"We're barely scraping by. I'm not making money, nor am I losing any. I can go on for a while, but they are pressing me to sell at an absurd price, or take on a partner with connections to the SS."

"If you go, I go."

"What makes you think they'll let you? You're the draw. Without you, the business is worth nothing."

"What'll you do?" Eddie said.

"I'll know when my back is to the wall."

"Mine's there."

"Stall the bastards. Act indecisive. That's my advice."

"It's not hard."

"Don't tell them you might be able to find out what they want. They'll demand more. Of course, if you lie unconvincingly, that's no good either."

"What is good?"

"Before they called us in for talks was good. Before they became your biggest fans was better. Before the invasion, that was paradise. Didn't you know?"

Mavis opened the bag from Galeries Lafayette and waved beige stockings under Simone's nose. "Genuine silk," she said. "You can hardly find these back home. I'd buy up every pair in France if I had the money."

"When we're sittin' on a pile, you'll sink your end into stockings, corner the market like Jim Fisk done with gold."

She rubbed them against her cheek, and then she pulled one on. Simone was in the bathroom lathering his face when he heard her say, "Oh, crap," and tilted the medicine cabinet mirror for a look.

"What's the matter now?"

"They're no good. I caught a run."

"Must be the silkworms ain't eatin' their Wheaties."

At a knock on the door she tossed them in the trash and went to answer it.

"What're you doin'?" Simone said.

"Somebody's here."

"We don't know nobody here."

She was knocked aside as the door flew open, and two men rushed in. Simone was toweling shaving cream off his cheek as they forced him back against the tub, on him so fast that he was thinking how ridiculous he looked with half his face shaved when he was caught flush on the other half with a punch.

Since the fight with Piron, he'd carried a sap. It was in his jacket on a hook behind the door. As he put a hand inside the pocket, a blow he didn't see coming dropped him to all fours. He was flipped over onto his back, and they went to work on him with feet and fists, stomped so hard over his heart that he felt it stop, and pain was all that was left of him. He grabbed at their legs. When he caught a foot, three others came down on him till he let go.

Few of his fights were fair fights. He'd stack the odds in his favor or else back down, not ashamed to run rather than risk a beating. In a tiny hotel bathroom against a couple of goons, those strategies were no good. He stopped fighting back, covered his head in his arms, rolled into a ball. It made it easy to haul him back onto his feet and for one of them to pin his arms while the other hammered him.

He hadn't noticed the goddamn cat that had Mavis's tongue. She was a noise machine much of the time, a chatterbox, a loud snorer and a moaner in the sack, a shrieker at scary movies, a sobber at tearjerkers, a grunter on the toilet, and the outstanding wailer at a burial they'd happened to walk by at Cimitiere du Montparnasse. Instead of putting up a racket where it might do some good, she'd been struck dumb. It made him want to scream himself, but the goons were pounding his belly and it was a struggle to suck air into his lungs.

He'd given up on her when she let out a shout, an ear-splitter straight out of the opera house she was always trying to get him to take her to, a pure, perfect note with a gorgeous vibrato, a high C, or maybe a high F over C rising in intensity until one of the goons pointed a finger like the barrel of a gun, and it quieted her just the same as if he'd fired. In the fresh silence he pummeled Simone with renewed vigor, made him pay for Mavis.

The goons weren't amateurs. Destroying his body methodically, they dropped him to his knees again and winged punches non-stop, every part of him a target. Then they settled on his kidneys, pounding so hard that if he survived—a big if—he'd be pissing blood for weeks.

Of the lessons they had come to teach him, there wasn't one that he didn't already know: It wasn't smart to get mixed up with Nazis, or to scam one, or to be in France in wartime. To have gotten out of bed this morning. To have been born. The agony he'd been put through in five minutes outweighed all the good times he'd had in forty years, with sufficient pain left over to balance against any pleasure that might come later.

He must have lost consciousness then, because the next thing he knew he was staring into the bathtub drain inches from his face as cold water poured down the back of his head. Another punch left him limp at the bottom of the tub. The goons realized he'd absorbed all the punishment he could stand, or else were arm-weary. A final blow, and they were done with him. One of them picked up his hat from the floor. He straightened the crease with the side of his hand, adjusted the bend in the brim, brushed the felt against his sleeve, and then he nodded to his partner and they left without a word, although Mavis said later that they smiled and tipped their hats.

Simone came to again with water spilling over his forehead, warm water wrung from a washcloth, looking up into Mavis's frightened eyes as she admonished him, "Don't die on me, please don't, I'm begging you—"

He got a hand on her shoulder and pushed with all the strength he had left. She didn't notice it. She dragged him onto the wet tiles, sat him with his back against the tub, and washed his wounds.

"Ow," he said, "you're killin' me."

"They didn't?" She put her face near his. He thought she was looking for a place to kiss him where he wasn't bruised, but decided that she was double-checking. "You'll be okay?"

He didn't say anything. It frightened her. "Who were they?"

"I didn't get their names."

"You know what I mean. What did they want?"

"It ain't obvious?" He took away the washcloth, flattened it over his jaw, and wrung the blood out of it. Then he touched his nose, which made a clicking sound as it drifted to the side. Just when it had begun to heal, they'd busted it again. He tried his shoulders, his ribs, his back, gritting his teeth. Probably he could find a spot between his toes their fists had missed, maybe not. "We overstayed our welcome."

"They couldn't have said something? They had to do this to you?"

"It's how they operate, these Nazis," he said.

"What did we ever do to them?"

"Start packin'," he said. "Anyplace has got to be better'n this."

"That's what you told me in Chicago. And in Milwaukee, I seem to remember. Not to mention Detroit and Cleveland. St. Lou, those other towns."

"You can't say we don't get around. You had a nice Paris vacation. We'll go back where we speak the language and can figure the angles. We'll make out fine."

"Go back with nothing?" She said it coldly, not caring that he suspected she wanted to pick up where the goons had left off, finish the job.

"With our lives."

"Thank you very much," she said. "You forgot those lies . . . excuse me, the promises, you made to me about cleaning up on the Frenchies? We come all the way to Europe, and what have I got to show for it besides a stamp on my passport, and having to listen to a schnozz you're never going to breathe through it right again?"

"Things'll get better again," he said. "They always do."

She laughed in his face. "What about that Piron character?"

"What about him?"

"He was going to be our meal ticket. You were pushing me in bed with him, a colored boy no less, and he got the last laugh."

"The nigger's too stupid to scare."

"I don't get you."

"I had the dirt on him. Told him I'd take it to the Germans if he didn't pay, but you can't scare anybody stupid as he is."

"You didn't go to the Germans."

"Blackmail's tricky. They'd've arrested him."

"You don't think he had that figured out?"

"I was gonna hit up his girl and her family. Who knew she'd kill herself and let him off the hook? Believe me, he wouldn't be laughin' if she didn't."

"Look at you," she said. "You don't believe you now."

"Mavis—"

"I believed you enough. It's time I took matters in my own hands."

"What can you do with those?"

"I can screw as well—" She stopped. It hadn't come out how she meant, but she didn't think Simone missed the point.

His head tilted back, and he slapped the washcloth over his forehead. "It ain't the answer. We got a boat to catch."

"I was trying to say I can screw Piron without screwing him. Screw him but good. He'll be lucky he doesn't get lynched."

"The absinthe you been drownin' in here, it poisoned your brains."

"Go back without me," Mavis said. "I'll catch up."

CHAPTER SIXTEEN

A fan at the late show had presented him with a hard-to-find
pressing of "Really the Blues," Tommy Ladnier's last leader date,
recorded months before the unfortunate trumpeter's death from a
heart attack at thirty-nine, and Eddie had stayed up playing the side
over and over. On four hours of sleep, he was improvising on Ladnier's
hot licks, transposing the spectacular clarinet duet by Sidney Bechet
and Mezz Mezzrow that was beyond the ability of the Angels' reedman
to mimic. Rehearsals were the order of the day. He would drill the band
until they made the number, a showstopper, their own.

Steady knocking that seemed to come through the walls threw
him off the beat. When the neighbors wanted to quiet him, they

hammered the heat riser, or else Madame Gilbert downstairs took a broomstick to the ceiling. He put down the horn and opened the door to Madame Gilbert's boy, fourteen-year-old Pierrot, shuffling his feet on the mat.

"A telephone call for you, Monsieur Eddie," he said.

Eddie dug in his pocket for a coin. "Tell maman I'll be right down."

Madame Gilbert was a blowsy redhead in an immaculate apron looking half as old as the mother of a boy as big as Pierrot had a right to look. A war widow, she let her hand linger against Eddie's as she gave him the phone. She was not lacking in intuition that some mornings, when the boy was at school, she was this close to an invitation upstairs.

"Hello."

"Did you find it yet? This is Anne Goudsmit."

She was trouble. Not the lackadaisical sort that was Madame Gilbert. Eddie's instinct was to hang up and make the trouble go away. But trouble didn't take no for an answer. "Call tomorrow," he said. "I'll have it for you."

Madame Gilbert smiled wryly as he pressed his thumb against the cradle. It wasn't out of the question that she had had a word with Anne Goudsmit, advising her not to invest her affections in a flighty young man. She held a rag under the faucet and washed his germs off her phone, advertising the fastidious homemaker some lucky stiff was going to snatch off the market if he didn't move fast.

Clutching his collar, chin against his chest, Eddie left La Caverne in the face of a wet north wind. His shoes were taking on water, the dampness already in his socks, when someone came out of the shadows and marched beside him. He shifted his trumpet case to his left hand and walked faster, then slowed. Fast again as the stranger kept pace. Tired of the game, he put his foot out and stopped short. His companion tripped over it and whirled around.

"You again," he said. "Why aren't I surprised?"

"I need my book now," she said. "I'll help you look."

"It's three in the morning. I'm bone-tired."

"Yes, you can use help."

Her opinion of him meant nothing, but he didn't relish bringing her to search for the book in plain sight on his sofa. It wasn't as though he didn't have sympathy for her. Who could be that cold-hearted after what had happened to her husband and boyfriend—whatever they really were to her—and with Germans breathing down her neck? But she was poison.

"You're up late for nothing. No book is more important than sleep. I'll have it for you soon. I'm sorry, but—" He yawned, faking it only a little. "You understand."

"Perfectly well," she said, and continued alongside him.

Before he could point out that obviously she didn't understand, he saw a gun, not a small one, angled at him. A ridiculous move on her part. How would she get back her precious book if she shot him? He'd never have peace till it was in her hands.

"That isn't necessary," he said.

"Just the same. . . ."

On the stairs he heard a sound behind the Gilberts' door. This wouldn't be the first time he'd wakened Madame Gilbert coming back from the club with a new friend to spend the night. He knew what she would think, seeing him with a gun at his back. He'd be hard-pressed to argue that he hadn't bargained for something like it, though not from Mrs. Goudsmit.

He hit the light as he came inside the apartment. It startled the woman, who froze on the doorstep. Easy to kick the door shut in her face, but he wanted to be done with her once and for all. If she were to change her mind and ask him to hold on to the book a little longer, he'd insist that she take it away.

He looked at the brown envelope on the sofa till she was looking at it, too, without seeming to recognize what it was. "The book you're prepared to shoot me for," he said; "you'll find it inside."

She switched on his reading lamp. "If you don't mind," she said, and sat down with the book in her lap, examined the pages and covers, inside and out, flipped through it a second time. Then she looked in the envelope, turned it upside down, and shook it, angry and disappointed as she squeezed her hand inside and poked her fingers in the corners. "This isn't all," she said. "You're holding back some of the pages. Let me have them."

"You've got everything."

"I have nothing. This is worthless."

"Hardly," he said.

"What do you know?"

"I took the liberty of reading the scores. I thought there might be something in Goudsmit's writing I could borrow. These arrangements aren't right for my band, but they're not bad. Some other musician will be happy to use them."

"Do you think I'd put myself in danger for musical scores?" she said. "Where's the rest? Don't lie."

"They're complete arrangements, there are no gaps. See for yourself."

"I'm not a musician. I don't read music."

"I can show you."

"Let's say I believe you," she said. "Can it be a cipher?"

"A what?"

"A code. Some elaborate musical code. Can't it be?" She adjusted the lamp and buried her nose inside the pages, as if what she wanted was perhaps not to be found in the musical notation but contained microscopically in the ink, or the fibers of the paper, or the cloth cover. "The notes," she said, "the musical staff, they can't stand for something else?"

"It's jazz," he said. "Just jazz. Who are you?"

"I'm sure I told you several times. Do you need a formal introduction?"

He caught her arm before she could heave the book at the wall. "What did you think you'd find?"

"That's none of your business."

"The Germans have made it theirs. They're asking about Goudsmit and Borge Janssen."

"You'll tell them about me?"

"I told them I'd keep my eyes open," he said. "They're open. I didn't promise more."

"There's something we're missing." She opened the book again, making room for him beside her. "Take a second look."

"As you said, it isn't my business."

"I spoke rashly. It's everyone's."

"You sound like Janssen."

"I take that as a compliment."

"Take it any way you like. Take it and go."

A hard rap on the door had her reaching inside her bag. "Lower your voice," she said. "You woke the neighbors."

The knob turned, and the door rattled in the frame. "It isn't the neighbors," Eddie said.

He went across the room on his toes. His eye was at the peephole when the door shook again, and someone who didn't care if he woke everyone in the building shouted "Open up. Police."

She sat tight, showing the gun. He grabbed her other arm and pulled her to the window, and she broke free, gathered up the book, and slipped it back inside the envelope while he boosted her onto the sill. "It's three stories to the ground," she said. "Do you expect me to jump?"

Reaching around her legs, he reeled in a couple of rungs from a rope ladder.

"You make so many quick exits—?"

"I would have burned to death in a hotel fire in Chicago if it weren't for the fire escape. There are no fire escapes in Paris. I don't take chances. Not with fire."

"What is a fire escape?"

"Some other time," he said. "You'll come down in an alley behind the building. Stay there till it's safe to go out to the street."

"What about you?"

He eased the window shut behind her. The door hadn't stopped rattling. "Hold on," he shouted. "You'll tear it off the hinges."

Two men were waiting. Not the pair who had ransacked the apartment after Janssen's death, but cut from the same drab cloth. One ran past him as he was pulled into the corridor and he was prodded downstairs, listening to his place being torn apart. On the landing, Madame Gilbert reached out to him in a torn bathrobe in a yellow floral pattern over a flannel nightgown. Pierrot was with her in pajamas and slippers. A stranger, a six-footer, stood between them.

"I'm sorry," Madame Gilbert cried. "They forced me to let them in. I wouldn't have, but they threatened to arrest the boy. I'm sorry—"

The stranger clapped a hand over her mouth. Eddie was sorry, too.

They put him in a car without markings. "What do you want with me?" he asked them.

Noisy a minute ago, they had nothing more to say. He was almost relieved when they parked at a police station. A sweeper with handcuffs dangling from one wrist pushed his broom the length of a corridor, redistributing the dirt. In a room stinking of cigarettes and anxiety, an Inspector Goulart asked him if he was the Eddie

Piron born in the United States and employed as a musician at La Caverne Negre on Place Pigalle.

"Yes to all of that. What do you say I did?"

"You are accused of criminal assault upon a young woman."

He didn't comprehend. In his New Orleans Creole French, the words meant one thing. In Paris, something else. They had to. How else to understand what he seemed to have been told?

"You mean rape?"

"This is what the victim says. What do you say for yourself?"

"I have no idea of what you're talking about."

"Of course you would not." Goulart placed a cigarette pack in his lap. Without lighting up, he leaned his head back and inhaled deeply, as if he could obtain the nicotine he craved as easily from the air.

"When am I supposed to have—Where did it happen?"

"At this time last night. In the kitchen of your jazz club."

"Who is she?"

"Are there so many?"

"Not even one," Eddie said.

"You don't know who would bring the charge?"

"No clue."

"You will be informed of the accuser's name along with the details of the crime in due course."

"I'd like them now."

"Now it is five o'clock in the morning. What else have you to say for yourself?"

Was he being goaded into talking about the Goudsmit woman? The police weren't shy. If they knew about her, they wouldn't have knocked or invited him to discuss a rape that hadn't happened.

He was lodged in a pen with a couple of dozen mecs like those he rubbed shoulders with on a daily basis on Place Pigalle. No one stopped snoring, or rolled over to make room. It could have been worse. There wasn't anyplace where he would rather be charged with rape than Paris, France. Where he came from, a mob already would be gathered outside the jail, braiding a noose and slinging it over the bough of a tree while a fire was stoked underneath it. He squeezed into a spot near the bars and sat with his back against them, closed his eyes trying for sleep. Yes, it could be worse. Instead of sheep, he counted his blessings.

A prisoner farthest from the bars stirred, and a tidal wave of motion swept over the sleeping pile, catching him in its drowsy currents. The men found their shoes and laced them, combed their hair with their fingers, demanded breakfast, which arrived on a trolley cart that he declined to go near. The only appetite he had was for his freedom.

One of the men checked the time on a Bulova diamond wristwatch. Every few minutes Eddie grabbed his arm and pushed his sleeve above his wrist. The expensive watch didn't keep time well. Days, weeks seemed to go by before the prisoners were called for questioning and to meet with attorneys and relatives. Many had returned to the pen by the time Eddie heard his name, and a turnkey led him in handcuffs to a room identical to the one in which he had been questioned the night before. A new investigator, also identical to the previous one, was there. Eddie didn't ask his name. Getting out was all that interested him. He said, "You'll inform me of everything now?"

The new man shook his head. "You will inform us."

The investigator stepped out and in a moment was back with a woman whose face was buried against his shoulder while she wept. He stood over Eddie, glaring as if to say, Bastard, look what you've done to her. Then came actual words: "She wants to talk to you

first. I will be outside." He tugged at Eddie's cuffs to satisfy himself
that they were secure. "You are not to try to touch her. Keep your
hands on the table."

Was this how rape was prosecuted in France? By leaving the
alleged victim alone with the rapist? A strange practice, thought
Eddie, unless the police were attempting to reduce a backlog of
cases by encouraging forgiveness and reconciliation. Even marriage. His accuser was well-built, dressed stylishly. If he were ever
to consider rape—

He'd been locked up too long, listening to a bad element, and
pretending to be like them in order to get along. Soon he wouldn't
be pretending. Being here was affecting his mind.

Eddie recognized her right away. He didn't remember her name,
then remembered that she hadn't given it to him. She said in English, "Don't pretend you don't know me."

"Not the way you claim I do."

"I say otherwise," Mavis said.

"We've never been more intimate than now."

"That's your story."

"What's yours?"

"You're going to Devil's Island, or like there, for a long stretch
unless you come up with ten thousand in cash, American money,
to make me . . . make this go away."

He tilted his head, looked at her from various angles.

"Think it's funny?"

"Am I laughing?"

"On the inside," she said, "which is not where last laughs come
from. If I was in your shoes, I'd be telling me right off the bat that
I could raise the money but fast."

"Even though I can't?"

"A famous entertainer such as yourself? Please."

"Fairly famous," he said. "Not rich. There's little money in jazz."

"There's going to be plenty in crying rape."

She began to sob, banging her head on the table. He didn't know what to make of her. Then he heard a click, the door being shut all the way. Mavis looked up-dry-eyed.

"You're screwed, buddy." She raised her voice so they could hear her outside, in particular the English-speaking detective who had rehearsed her in how to get her assailant to incriminate himself. "Did you enjoy yourself doing those disgusting things to me? I bet you—what's this? You say I've got the wrong gent? You were the right one, all sweetness and smiles, when you invited me backstage for drinks. Funny, you don't know what I'm talking about when so many people saw us together."

"None of them saw you attacked."

"Thank God," she said. "What could be more humiliating than being seen in that, those compromising positions?" She leaned across the table, seductive again, but businesslike in her tone. "I don't need eyewitnesses. With your criminal record in the States, who's everybody going to believe? Yeah, yeah, I know, you're a regular Paris institution. And me, who am I, just a tourist. After they find out you're colored, been lying about that, it'll be another story."

"It's different here," Eddie said. "The French don't care what I am."

"They'll care that you're a liar. Nobody likes their kind."

If anyone had been raped, Eddie would tell the judges, it was him.

"Know how many years they hand out for rape in France?"

"Not offhand, no."

"You're gonna," she said. "Oh, are you ever gonna."

Maybe he'd ask her to marry him. A wife couldn't testify against her husband under French law. Could she? Probably Mavis could tell him. She had all the answers.

The tears began again, and she began to wail. He knew what was coming, but could only sit tight as the door flew open and he was surrounded by flics who held him as she was helped from her chair and escorted out while he waited to be hauled back to the pen.

The holding pen emptied and was refilled with sad characters indistinguishable from those they replaced. He was the veteran, but with none of the honor accorded to old-timers in more venerable institutions. The food trolley came and went. Better to starve than to be made of the foul stuff served up here. The inmate with the Bulova surrendered it to a hard case, and then both were gone. Eddie hadn't any sense of the hour when his name was called, and he elbowed some men out of the way and trampled others to get to the bars. Already he fit in.

He was cuffed again and taken to another floor. Expecting a fresh round of questioning, he was marched to a two-man cell. A prisoner with zodiac tattoos on his hands and arms, his Adam's apple in the pincers of crab, told him to keep quiet or he'd kill him. Alone with his thoughts, Eddie wanted him for a friend anyway. A depressing commentary on his situation.

A turnkey was at the bars when he looked up. Given papers, and no time to read them, he put his name everywhere he was instructed. If he were signing a confession that led directly to the guillotine, he had no complaint. It beat one minute more in a cell.

Roquentin was waiting on a bench with two umbrellas, his pants legs plastered against his thighs. He gave one to Eddie, and they unfurled them walking out into a driving rain.

"How did you know where I was?" Eddie said.

"One of my mecs saw you in the pen."

"He didn't say anything."

"Claude LeGare. He had throat cancer. Evidently you don't speak sign language."

"Who did you bribe to get me out?"

"You know I haven't any money for bribes."

"How—?"

"I posted your bond."

"For that you have money?"

"I put up La Caverne."

"You must be nuts," Eddie said. "What if I scram?"

He'd meant it as a joke, but Roquentin looked at him gravely. Before he could assure him that he wasn't going anywhere but back to work, Roquentin put a hand on his shoulder and said "I wish you would."

"You are really going too far. I will appear in court at the proper time. You'll have the money back."

"If you run, it will be the SS's loss. Not mine."

"You changed your mind?" Eddie said. "You took them in as a partner?"

"They changed it for me."

"Don't tell me. At the point of a gun."

"They were gentlemen," Roquentin said. "They told me that Frenchmen are needed in Germany, and asked how would I like to go there to work for them."

"To open another jazz cl—" Eddie slapped his forehead. "Jail makes me stupid, you know?"

"To work in a salt mine in Brega," Roquentin said, "digging my grave. Don't feel sorry for me. Don't blame yourself. They are getting nothing. It's I who put one over on them."

"You haven't asked me who I raped," Eddie said.

"Tell me after I tell you about the little green men I saw coming out of a spaceship on Place de la Concorde."

At a bus stop they waited ten minutes in the rain, and then Roquentin said "It seems they've stopped running, but I have a few francs for a taxi."

"Have the Germans taken over from you already?"

"The paperwork hasn't been started," Roquentin said. "You know how they are. They won't do anything till all the t's are crossed, the i's dotted. The club remains mine until their attorney notifies me it's theirs."

Every cab passing by was full. They fought the storm all the way to Place Pigalle. Eddie was surprised to see Pierrot Gilbert in front of La Caverne Negre, holding a trumpet case to his chest with both hands while he studied the garish neon.

"I apologize for burglarizing your apartment." He handed over Eddie's horn. "You need to lock your windows when you go out. Monsieur Roquentin said you will not call the police on me."

Eddie dug in his pocket. Every centime was gone for small favors at the jail.

"Pierrot works for me," Roquentin said.

With his hand on the boy's head, he steered him to a table up front to which he directed a steady flow of soft drinks and snacks. Pierrot led the applause as Eddie came on stage during the run-up to "Milenberg Joys."

Eddie's stomach growled as he put the trumpet to his lips, a sweeter sound than came from the horn. He surrendered the lead to Weskers and played weakly behind him. The boy was as embarrassed for Eddie as Eddie was himself, but waved his arms like a cheerleader when Eddie pulled off a neat four-bar solo after the drum break. A shame that Pierrot was hearing him for the first time fresh from jail. He rarely sounded this flat in his nightmares.

CHAPTER SEVENTEEN

In Weiler's arms was one of the elegant beauties common to the French capital who turned racial science on its ear. Dark-haired and petite, she was of a different species than the broad-hipped giantesses venerated in Berlin as the machinery to expand the Aryan population into the far corners of Europe. The superior species, in Weiler's estimation, although he kept the treasonous thought to himself. Ice maidens, if this one was typical, immune to flattery and gestures of affection. When the music stopped, she slipped from his embrace, her mechanical smile earning an immediate place in the arms of a new admirer. Weiler sat out the dance at the table where Colonel Maier was nursing a glass of Riesling from Rhenish cellars.

"I just had the most peculiar experience with a Frenchwoman," Weiler said to him.

"On the dance floor?"

"It went no further. We danced two numbers. In that time she didn't say two words while I whispered sweet nothings in her ear."

"Have you considered that she despises you?" Maier said.

"She doesn't know me. I gave her no reason for her negative attitude."

"Other than your uniform? The insignia on your collar? Not all these women are crazy for Germans."

"No one put a gun to her head and forced her to come."

"You asked?"

"I will now."

Maier lifted one finger from his glass. It kept Weiler in his chair until he was asked to move by a carpenter carrying an installation for Le Bolchevisme Contre L'Europe, the next exposition at the Salle Wagram. Tonight's affair was the first annual Paris-Berlin joint chamber of commerce dinner dance with entertainment provided by Les Bourgeois Gentilhommes, a society orchestra featuring French and German music-hall favorites put over with a leaden touch.

"Aside from the women, you are enjoying yourself?" Maier said.

"Aside from them, what is there to enjoy?" Weiler said. "Are you?"

"I'm not here to enjoy myself."

Weiler didn't have to be told.

"I've been speaking to some of the oligarchs favored to take control of Jewish businesses in the occupied zone under the Aryanization campaign."

"A few look rather Semitic themselves."

"For the right price, they can be whatever they say they are," Maier said, "until we say they are not. Here is one whose lineage isn't in doubt."

He tilted his glass toward a man in a tailored dinner jacket whose brilliantined silver hair framed a sad, handsome face.

"He looks familiar," Weiler said.

"He is the quintessential French aristocrat out of a portrait by Ingres," Maier said.

"Something more recent."

"He has been in the news. You may have seen his picture." Maier stood up as the man came over. "Major Weiler," he said, "I wish to introduce you to my new friend, Carl de Villiers."

Weiler glanced first at Maier, whose face gave nothing away. But then it never did. The newcomer's features, now that he had a name to go with them, confirmed what Weiler had been thinking, that there was a close physical resemblance to photos he'd seen of the young woman who had killed herself. A mourner's button was further evidence that he was right.

"Monsieur de Villiers represents a consortium of investors proposing to take over the Goldfadden cinema chain. After cancelling Goldfadden's contracts with the European distribution arm of Metro-Goldwyn-Mayer, they'll be granted exclusive rights to pictures made at the UFA studios in Berlin, which they will dub into French, absorbing the cost of the new prints themselves."

"And they say that we Germans are efficient," Weiler said. "This is an excellent plan that gets rid of two Jewish birds with one French stone."

De Villiers said, "You are the Major Weiler who promised an investigation of my daughter's death. We spoke several times over the phone."

"I am unable to prosecute the case," Weiler said, "as it doesn't touch upon matters of security. A tragedy nevertheless. I appreciate this opportunity to extend my condolences in person."

"You can do more. The bastard responsible for Carla's hanging herself assaulted another girl, and again was set free. This cannot stand. He is a danger to all Frenchwomen. I demand that he be jailed immediately."

"A case of rape falls under the jurisdiction of the Sûreté," Weiler said. "Trust them to see justice done."

"They haven't lost a daughter to a black animal. In Germany he would be prosecuted to the fullest extent with predictable results."

"This is France," Weiler said. "It isn't that easy."

"Don't make me laugh."

Weiler doubted that anyone ever would. He was ready to send de Villiers on his way, but Maier indulged his anger, encouraged it.

"Why has the Sûreté toyed with this miscreant time and again?" Maier said. "Might not a way be found to bring pressure to bear against him so that Monsieur de Villiers can sleep well?"

"I want more than pressure brought to bear, damn it," de Villiers said.

Weiler couldn't have heard right. No one, no Frenchman, no SS officer, not his wife if the colonel had one, dared to talk to Colonel Maier like that. He circled around until he was looking into de Villiers's face, and could also read his lips.

"I want the blade of the guillotine brought against him."

De Villiers moistened his throat from his glass and restated his case from page one. Weiler was afraid that he would go on all night when Maier excused himself to make way for the carpenters.

"The trumpet player committed a rape?" Maier said. "Why wasn't I informed?"

"Heads will roll first at the Sûreté for not letting us know," Weiler said.

"You spoke to him after the suicide. What is there to tell the old man?"

"The apple doesn't fall far from the tree. His daughter was also a blind fool who couldn't see two moves ahead. He wants racial justice of the kind we have at home? A pity that he can't have it.

Under the Rassenschande statutes, the girl's crime was no less than her black lover's."

"You didn't bring in her boyfriend for screwing a white girl. What did you get from him?"

"I got nothing."

"Not less?" Maier said. "Arrest him again. De Villiers can be a valuable asset. If we are able to offer a kindness, then we should. It's a Negro head that he wants. Who will miss it?"

Overnight the run of lousy days ended, the sun in full possession of a hard blue sky, and dry breezes out of the south. A gorgeous day that forced Eddie's cold into remission for an early dose of spring fever. The recommended treatment was a leisurely walk to work.

With no warning, the wind shifted to the north. Clouds screened the sun, and the temperature dropped. Hatless, Eddie coughed and sneezed. His trumpet case weighed a ton. Dragging his feet still several blocks from Place Pigalle, he heard his name and saw Roquentin waving to him where he usually got off the bus across the street. They stepped into the gutter at the same time and shook hands on the center stripe, where they would have died together if Eddie hadn't given Roquentin a quick shove out of the path of a Wehrmacht truck.

"A close call," Eddie said, watching the truck roar down the avenue without slowing.

"It isn't the only one," Roquentin said. "I almost missed you. You can't come to the club. The SS is looking for you."

"Who do they say I raped?"

"We didn't get that far. I hate to be the messenger of bad news, but better that you learn it from me. The SS don't just bring bad news. They inflict it."

"They're still there?"

"They don't intend to leave without you," Roquentin said. "You've got to hide."

Eddie laughed, stopped to shake his head, laughed some more.

"I can use a good joke," Roquentin said.

"It's not very funny."

"An unfunny one will do. Never mind—if you want to keep it to yourself."

"I came to Paris, you might say, so that I wouldn't have to hide. Now I'm told to go into hiding here. There's nowhere in this world, it seems, where I can show my face. Is it so ugly?"

"It's the world that's ugly," Roquentin said. "But this is no time for easy philosophizing. We need to get you off the street. Who would take you in?"

"Carla."

"You still have the key to her apartment? That might not be too bad."

"I mean where she is now," Eddie said.

"No one else?"

"I'd be asking them to risk their neck to save mine. Considering what mine is worth, it's a hard sell."

"I was afraid you'd say that," Roquentin said. "I have a place."

"What did I do to deserve it?"

"You think too highly of yourself. The business is lost. I'm already being squeezed out. Keeping you out of the hands of the SS is the one way I have of hitting back at them. You're doing me the favor."

"Let me think about it."

"Your opinion doesn't count. They say you were complicit in Carla's suicide. I won't contribute to yours."

"Where do you plan to put me?"

Roquentin stepped on Eddie's toes, shielding him from the sidewalk. Out of the corner of an eye Eddie saw a couple of flics walk by, holding down their kepis against the wind.

"At the club," Roquentin said

"There's a funny joke."

"We'll play it on the SS. They won't look for you there."

"They're looking for me there now."

"Yes, and you would appreciate how efficient they are. After they haven't found you, you can move in upstairs. I use the attic as a liquor closet. You'll make up a pallet on the floor. There's all the booze you can drink."

"Man doesn't live by booze alone."

"Come downstairs when the customers go home and help yourself to what is in the kitchen."

"Just for a little while," Eddie said. "Until something better comes along."

Roquentin took away his trumpet and gave him an umbrella. "When in our entire lives did something better come along?"

It was too wet to sit in a park. Too public. It had always bothered Eddie that he wasn't more famous. He'd never really been accepted here. The French didn't take fully to artists who weren't native sons. Ask Django, born close by in Belgium and never allowed to forget that he was a Gypsy. Even to serious fans of the music, Eddie Piron was at most the American trumpeter at La Caverne Negre. It would have been best if no one had ever heard him play, or heard of him, seen a face that nothing could be done about other than to hide it in the dark.

He rode a bus to the Avenue des Italiens near the Paris Opera. At the huge Cinema Berlitz Palais, a hook-nosed ogre looking down from the marquee turned him away. The doors were thrown open for good Frenchmen who had come to learn about the Jews living among them. Le Juif et La France, an exhibit assembled by the Institute for the Study of the Jewish Question, had displaced the movies for the time being.

He ducked inside a neighborhood cinema without looking to see what was playing, sat through four showings of *Remorques*, with Jean Gabin and Michèle Morgan, before the lights came on and the ushers kicked him out. He had plenty of time left to kill. La Caverne didn't come alive until the rest of Paris shut down for the night. Thank God the rains had stopped. Soon, he suspected, he would thank God for even smaller miracles, if he had anything to thank Him for at all.

At a cab driver's café, he lingered for hours over coffee with his nose buried in a book. The manual for the Paris hack exam was a riveting masterpiece of French literature which he was unable to put down. They were sweeping around him, stacking the chairs on the tables, when he finally trailed the last cabbie to the street.

La Caverne was empty now. Roquentin tossed the drunks onto the sidewalk no later than 5:00. The buses had stopped running. Eddie had a long walk back to Place Pigalle. Though the rain had let up, he kept his umbrella open in front of his face. Not the craziest person on the avenues at an hour when everyone had a load on.

In Montmartre, all the night people knew him. Whores and dips were his biggest fans, along with the bums who loved a soft touch. Tonight he crashed through their outstretched hands. Someone running after him shouting his name caught up and blocked him against a wall.

"You're a genius," he said, "greater than Armstrong. Where were you tonight? We missed you—"

Disheartening to meet his number one admirer and discover a musical ignoramus. Jabbing the point of the umbrella at the stranger's belt buckle, he made his escape.

La Caverne was dark, the savage on the neon sign rigid and color-less without his electric charge. Eddie tapped the umbrella handle against the window, and again on the door. He wouldn't blame

Roquentin for changing his mind about helping. Not too much. Hobnail soles scuffed the sidewalk over the German lyrics to "Lili Marlene" in drunken, three-part harmony. Soldiers arm in arm staggered into him, bouncing him against the window. Waiting to be cut to shreds, he felt a hand displace the shudder on his spine. It crept to his shoulder, his neck, grabbed him by the collar, and pulled him inside the door.

"What kept you?" Eddie said. "I knocked, and knocked—"

"I was in the crapper. What's your excuse? It's almost six." Roquentin bolted the door, took Eddie away from the windows.

"Weskers was good?" Eddie said.

"What?"

"I asked how Weskers's playing was."

"This is what you worry about?"

In the darkness, Eddie nodded. The music always came first.

"Do you need the toilet?"

"No," Eddie said.

"You're sure? Once you go upstairs, I don't advise coming down till there's natural light. What about something to eat or drink?"

"I want to see my new digs."

"Shut your eyes. That's what you'll see."

Roquentin caught his wrist. Eddie knew every corner of the club but lost his bearings immediately. He stumbled over a stair and was led up a narrow flight that groaned under the weight of two men. A door opened on rusted hinges. Behind it the air was redolent, of dust and soured wine, with a soupçon of dead mouse. Roquentin let him go. Another step, and he was left stranded on an island of spongy footing.

"I dragged a mattress up here for you," Roquentin said. "It isn't the most comfortable, but you could do worse."

"Could I?"

He didn't mean it the way it sounded. He didn't mean anything. It was one of those remarks he routinely made that crashed like a lead dirigible. Roquentin was sticking his neck out for him and deserved an apology, but Eddie saved it for another time. If his situation became tense, the insults would come quicker and sharper with even less thought behind them. It was always like that with him. He thought it might explain why he'd never married.

"You know I like to stay over at the club when we close very late," Roquentin said. "I won't do that while you're here. You're on your own."

"You don't want to be around if the SS comes back and finds me," Eddie said. "I understand."

"I don't want to draw them to you with a light."

Eddie's cheek stung. Roquentin was pinching it hard. "Au revoir" was followed by footsteps and the hinges squeaking. Eddie dropped down on the mattress, pulled in his ankles, and sat Buddha-like in absolute darkness, the emperor of all he surveyed.

The door opened downstairs. He shouted "Wait," as the dead bolt snapped into place. He'd forgotten to ask for his trumpet. The hell with food, and drink, and going to the toilet, as long as he could have his horn. To sit in the dark silently fingering the valves, making music in his head. Otherwise he was on Death Row.

The world had turned against him. It had done the same thing before, and he'd bobbed and weaved, feinted the world into believing it had seen the last of him. A dozen years, and now a meaner world had set its hooks for him. Good luck to the world, because Eddie Piron wouldn't let down his guard again.

He was prepared to lose himself completely this time, to alter his appearance, become fluent in another language, to change his opinions, even drain his memory, if that's what it took for him to survive. There would be no Simone to link this new Eddie Piron to the old one. All that he'd keep from his present life was jazz, because without it he'd truly cease to exist. Having seen what his future would be, he needed to settle on a place to live it. One of the outer planets, perhaps. He was trying to be realistic.

He slept. He realized it as a knife edge of light sliced across his face, opening his eyes, and he watched it broaden on the floor. A filthy window shielded from the street by a shutter was its point of entry. He gave the crank a single turn, then dialed it back. The future had begun. Sunlight, and fresh air, and the sound of the city had no part in it.

He laid his head down again. Entering a dream, he heard sounds downstairs. Baffled by the long flight, and the attic door, they came softly, faded, and gradually died. Then he heard them again. He wasn't alone. He knew it as well as Robinson Crusoe did after spotting a naked footprint in the sand.

He leaned his upper body over the edge of the mattress, clung to it like a life raft as he pressed his ear against the bare floor. Listening hard, he imagined that he heard eggs sizzling in a pan. Certainly they were what he smelled. An omelette frying in sweet butter. Barefoot, on his toes, he crept down the stairs and through the empty nightclub to the kitchen. "Boo," he said.

Roquentin, standing at the oven with an apron over his pants, whirled around with a fierce look. "Get back upstairs."

"What harm—?"

"Now."

He retreated to the attic. Sure, he needed to be cautious—he and Roquentin did—but there were moments when they could relax a little.

But when he was settled again on his raft, he heard voices, Roquentin's provincial twang surrendering to guttural consonants and strangled vowels, sentences that went on forever before finding a verb. He held to the mattress eavesdropping on a conversation conducted through an interpreter. A short silence, and then there were footsteps on the stairs, and a knock, and though it had to be

Roquentin (the SS knocked heads, not doors), he couldn't pry himself loose till Roquentin came in with a tray under a linen napkin, not much different than room service at the Ritz.

"How did you sleep?"

"Like a baby," he said. "I cried all night."

A belly laugh from Roquentin wasn't what he expected. Roquentin's life was in show business, and he'd never heard that ancient gag? France needed new comedians to replace the clowns in gray uniforms, who weren't funny at all.

Roquentin placed the tray on the floor beside the mattress. Eddie gobbled a croissant, but eating like an animal embarrassed him. He tugged at Roquentin's cuff, didn't touch another morsel till they were sitting shoulder to shoulder.

"Who were you talking to?" Eddie asked him.

"They won't be back any time soon," Roquentin said. "Have you figured out where you'd like to go from here?"

"Yes, I'm going to live on the planet Jupiter."

Roquentin nodded gravely. "It's a long journey. You'll need money. I owe you a week's salary, and can lend you some more."

"Knowing you'll never see it again? That isn't a loan."

"You'll send what you can from the moon. How will you get out of France?"

"Switzerland is still neutral. What other way is there?"

"The Pyrenees. They say Franco isn't turning back refugees. You might consider Spain."

"I'll consider everything," Eddie said.

"I have to go downstairs," Roquentin said. "Sorry to leave you alone. But if someone else comes by to ask where you are—"

Eddie ate half of what was on the tray, saved the rest. There was no telling when Roquentin would be back. He emptied the coffee pot. Fifteen minutes later he refilled it. The coffee didn't allow for more sleep. Or maybe he'd slept enough. It was a unique experience for a jazzman, but he didn't recommend it. Better to be up all night making music till he was too tired to draw another breath.

The light climbed the walls and mounted a jumble of broken furniture in a corner. On the chair on top was a yellow Editions de la Pleiade paperback of Voltaire's *Candide*. He read a page and tossed the volume across the attic. What wouldn't he do to have a policier? For Simenon, or Sherlock Holmes, or any of the great crime solvers whose powers of deduction might even discover a way out of his predicament? He gave Voltaire a second chance, forcing it down like castor oil. The Paris taxi manual was more engrossing. With a better plot.

He didn't put it down until the light faded. He was hungry again. Thirsty and cold, although sometimes, when he felt the walls close in, he was hot. Bored crazy. Crazy to have a woman. Without one he dwelled on old girlfriends, a pornographic bedroom rotogravure, puzzled why sex should be foremost in his thoughts. A question with an obvious answer: When wasn't it? Wasn't the instinct for sex the last to go? Preservation of the species, and all that? He wasn't concerned about preserving an entire species, but only the smallest part, the single unit called Eddie Piron.

He closed his eyes again. Music woke him. A band—not any band, but his Angels—taking the "Livery Stable Blues" at breakneck tempo, a stampede. Eddie hated the number, cornball musical antics from the earliest Original Dixieland Jass Band recording sessions replete with barnyard sounds. Years ago, he'd stricken it from the Angels' playlist. Fans who tossed money at the stage demanding to hear it were out of luck. Weskers had announced that it was his favorite number, led a failed rebellion to bring it back as an encore specialty. Tonight Weskers was all over the melody, losing it during a choppy improvisation, and unable to find it again, leading the clarinet and piano to a dead end and abandoning them there. Eddie restrained himself from sneaking downstairs to hide behind the back curtain and play the notes while Weskers silently fingered his instrument up front. Forced to listen helplessly while Weskers butchered the music was real torture. The SS could take lessons from Gert Weskers.

"It's a good thing for you that I'm leaving," he said to Roquentin in the kitchen after the late show when the crowd and the staff had cleared out. "If I stayed, I'd hit you up for a huge raise. You'd pay, or listen to Weskers every night."

"Don't knock him. Gert's my revenge on the SS. They think they're getting a going concern, but he's chasing away customers."

Neither man laughed. What Roquentin had said was funny in a way, Eddie thought. Looking at it another way, that's the last thing it was.

"I'm going home to sleep in my own bed," Roquentin said. "I have an early appointment with the lawyer. You're on your own till noon. Do I have your word you'll keep out of trouble?"

"What trouble?"

Another gag line that fell flat. Why wasn't anyone laughing?

Eddie stood by the window out of sight of the street watching Roquentin walk to the end of the block. Then he turned on the lights, giving himself a minute to find his trumpet. He began in the office, in the file cabinet and closet, and the cardboard box under Roquentin's desk filled with umbrellas and sweaters, and at least two pairs of shoes that was the lost and found, moved to the kitchen and then the club, convinced that Holmes had nothing on him as he homed in on the stage and slid out the trumpet case from a tangle of light cable behind the drum kit. He hefted it to feel the weight of the horn inside, and then dashed to the attic, where he remembered the lights, and ran back to shut them off.

The next days were carbon copies of the last. Every so often he removed the trumpet from the case to fondle it, toying with the valves, putting the mouthpiece to his lips, and snugging it against his embouchure and holding it there like a baby with a pacifier. It killed him—he feared it really would—that he couldn't blow a note, and he played two full sets along with Weskers and the Angels without making a sound.

Time was a burden, the long hours with nothing to do so meaningless that he believed he'd lost his mind. But after losing it, it returned to torment him with knowledge gained in places he never wanted to visit. If he lost it again as the empty days repeated themselves, that was okay. Living like this, he had no use for it.

Wakened early by furniture skating against a bare floor, he shouted, "Hey, let a fellow sl—"

It was too much noise from a nightclub owner with an aversion to physical labor. He bit his tongue, hoping no one had heard him above the racket. His mind was in excellent working order, back from wherever it had been keeping itself, spinning off grim scenarios when he'd rather not think at all.

The sun made its appearance on the floor, and climbed the walls. Eddie knew it was noon when light topped the broken tables and chairs. The furniture stopped moving. The racket became the sounds of hammering and drilling, and of wood being sawed. Abruptly, the activity ceased. He was in blackness again when someone came in downstairs.

"Eddie? Eddie, are you still here?"

"Where else?"

The attic door opened. Roquentin struck a match and waved it under Eddie's nose as though to satisfy himself that he was at the right address. Then he laughed. When a bad situation became worse, it was hard to keep a straight face. That's how life was. Eddie's life now.

"You can't stay longer," Roquentin said. "My lawyer informed me that I have until the end of the week to vacate. I came by early to let you know, but the SS were already here with their carpenters and electricians. They are making La Caverne like . . . from the look of things, it will be as joyful as a hospital ward."

"You'll be able to buy it back for sous on the franc," Eddie said.

"I'd sooner burn it to the ground. Come—" Roquentin took him to the kitchen. "You need to eat, and to have good food to take on your journey."

Roquentin lit a candle, held it in the bread box, and the ice box, and then whipped together sandwiches using his finest cheeses. Eddie gobbled two. Roquentin made two more, and wrapped them in wax paper.

"You're too good to me," Eddie said.

"I almost forgot." Roquentin slipped a roll of bills from his pocket, and dropped it into Eddie's. "Promise me one thing. That you get out of France in one piece. I won't tolerate finding out you're dead."

"You have my word."

Roquentin grabbed him by the shoulders and kissed his cheeks. Eddie squirmed. If he lived in France for a hundred years, he would never get used to being kissed by a man. Kisses wet with tears were hardest to endure.

"I advise you to remain until midnight," Roquentin said. "I'll be leaving Paris soon myself, returning home to Toulouse in the south. If you change your mind about Spain, maybe I'll see you on the road. Who knows?"

The sandwiches went in the garbage with Roquentin's advice. Eddie didn't have the stomach for it. Being out in the middle of the night in a city under military occupation would call attention to himself. Besides, he needed all the sleep he could get before starting out for God knows where. He cranked open the shutter, pulled the mattress to where the first light of dawn would find it.

He was on the street five minutes after his eyes opened. A contractor's truck was at the curb, and he watched workmen in paint-spattered clothes collect their gear and carry it inside La Caverne. If he'd slept thirty seconds longer, he'd have had to spend another day in the attic waiting for them to knock off, or else shinny down the drainpipe.

At that hour of the morning Place Pigalle was terra incognita. His friends, the night people, were not to be seen again before dark. The sidewalks belonged to men and a few women marching glumly to their jobs. A paradox: In the harsh light of day, the City of Light showed its dark other side. The people, depressed and sullen, moved as though a hidden hand was pulling their strings. Some German officers swung by in a Wehrmacht staff car, the strings not well hidden. This wasn't the same city that had captured his heart with its vibrancy and openness. It was all a big hospital ward. A psychiatric ward.

At a bistro three steps below street level, unshaven laborers at a marble counter turned their head toward the stranger with the trumpet case. Eddie stared back until something in the newspaper demanded their immediate attention, and then he dropped a coin in a pay phone.

"Madame Gilbert, it's Eddie Piron," he said. "Did Pierrot leave for school yet? No, I'm fine. May I have a word with him?"

The woman was gone so long that he used up all his change waiting for her to return to the phone.

"Allo, Monsieur Eddie."

"Pierrot, has anyone been in my place since I've been gone?"

"Why would they, if you are not there?"

"That's an excellent question. Forget it. Answer mine."

"It is possible," the boy said. "I'm at school all day. Someone could have entered then."

"Is anyone there now?"

"Inside?"

"Inside or nearby. Keeping an eye out."

"I will find out."

"Be smart about it, and quick," Eddie said. "Don't be seen yourself."

At the other end, the receiver rattled around on its cord until the boy came back. "There's no one in the hall. I didn't hear anyone inside your apartment."

"One favor more," Eddie said, "and then you are off to class. Go to the window. Are any strange cars stopped on the block?"

"Police cars? Cars with license plates from the occupation administration?"

"Especially those."

The venetian blinds clattered, and Pierrot said, "I don't see any like that."

"Now be a good boy and get to school. If anyone asks if you've heard from me, tell them you haven't."

"You want me to lie? The priests say it's a sin."

"Till the occupation ends, the sins will be on me," Eddie said. "After, we'll see."

He walked back to his neighborhood against the glum tides. Did he stand out because he didn't appear miserable? In his heart there was sadness, but he didn't think it showed. How ironic that he was leaving the city he'd called home for years, and his was practically the only face that didn't appear suicidal. One thing he wouldn't miss was the occupation. He covered his mouth as it opened in a yawn. If he were fully awake, he would make smarter observations.

The apartment reeked. With the windows shut, it was a repository for stale air, sulfurous fumes from the basement boiler, and kitchen odors from the neighbors which turned fetid when they could not escape. Eddie opened all the windows before ducking into the shower. In the medicine-cabinet mirror he considered a disguise, a moustache and various beards. Maybe he would part his hair on the other side, or sweep it straight back, or color it. Preliminary experiments with razor and comb ended with him looking like someone trying desperately to appear other than who he was. Like the furtive refugees who were easy to pick out on the streets. He shaved, and combed his hair as he always had. Getting out of France in one piece, as Roquentin put it, would be accomplished with his wits rather than whiskers.

He didn't pack a suitcase, not wanting to be burdened with luggage, but his horn went everywhere with him. Over several layers of underwear went the suit which he had worn off the boat at La Havre. The mirror showed a dandy at the height of fashion of a dozen years ago. He exchanged the suit for something newer, not flashy.

As he transferred Roquentin's wad of bills from one pair of pants to another, he was aware of its thickness. To count it would seem he was measuring his friend's kindness. Still, he needed to know how much money he had. The amount was equal to close to two months' salary. A fortune. If he ever saw Roquentin again, he'd grit his teeth and return the kiss. He'd always liked the club owner. Today he loved him. In spite of his lousy advice.

The morning rush was over. He'd sit tight until the streets were busy again. He felt safest alone in a crowd. But every sound and footstep, each knock on a neighbor's door had him conjuring the police closing in. Even the fresh breeze that blew out the rankness portended disaster.

Unable to sit still, he set out immediately for the Gare de l'Est and the early train into the Alps, the time better spent reconnoitering at the Swiss border for a clandestine crossing.

At the top of the stairs, he turned back for something to read on the long ride. His policiers weren't on the shelves, but scattered with his music books on the floor. So the flics had already been here. They came so often that he should have left them the key.

On the third floor landing he was ambushed by Madame Gilbert, who took him in her arms and smothered him in kisses. Had she torn off his clothes, it wouldn't have been more unsettling. Pierrot hadn't told her that he was going away for good, because he hadn't told the boy. A troubling start for his secret journey.

A taxi stopped across the street went into motion as he came out of the building. It darted ahead, then lagged behind, drew even as he waited at the corner for a red light to change. The men who scrambled out were not prime physical specimens, but of the furtive breed trying to blend in where they always would be strangers. The gun shoved into his ribs felt more natural than Madame Gilbert's passionate embrace. Prodded toward the cab, he didn't resist. When wouldn't he rather ride than walk?

CHAPTER EIGHTEEN

Another day in the attic, a few hours longer upstairs, and they might have missed him. If it had snowed or rained, as it did almost constantly this unforgiving winter, if the railway workers had called another strike, or avalanches had buried the track, he would have put off his departure and avoided them. His life was the residue of what-should-have-beens, coincidences as improbable as running into Simone halfway around the world, missed opportunities, bad ju-ju. The unholy star he'd been born under shined brightest in New Orleans but cast its light everywhere he went. On his birthdays, his great-aunt Bertha used to take him to St. Louis Cemetery Number One to light candles and burn incense, and to chalk three X'es on the oven of Marie Laveau, invoking the voodoo priestess's intercession with the demons in her luckless nephew's behalf. Behind Bertha's back he'd roll his eyes, angering Marie Laveau unnecessarily and hardening her heart against Bertha's pleas.

The taxi took him through working-class neighborhoods into the slums. It was more bad ju-ju that he hadn't fallen into the hands of kidnappers like those in his policiers, who transported their victims in Packard limousines to penthouse hideaways where they were kept alive on pâté and Champagne. His captors hadn't said who they were, but their sullen grubbiness seemed to give them away as flics. Otherwise he hoped Germans had him, foreign Nazis preferable to being snatched by the Milice. These three were miscast as militiamen, subdued when they should have been boastful. Anxious, and grim. He took cold comfort in their lack of swagger. He disdained amateurism, apprehensive about falling into the hands of first-timers, whether kidnappers or surgeons.

They circled a block twice before regaining their bearings. A series of sharp turns took them away from the Seine embankment on industrial avenues, a shadowy part of the City of Light. It had been a long time since a military patrol went by. The filthy streets were under the occupation of pigeons and rats.

The cab pulled up behind a factory building a shade darker than the pearl-gray cobblestones. He was dragged from the back seat, and his trumpet was taken away. Chicago gangsters concealed tommy guns in violin cases. Didn't all Americans know their tricks? In every sense he'd been disarmed.

A freight elevator took him up past smells of dried fish, coffee, and exotic spices that he associated with Cajun cooking. At the fourth floor, the car stopped short half a meter below the landing. One of his kidnappers grunted. The first sound he'd heard from them, it wasn't a French grunt.

Chairs and a table were dashed together in a corner of a loft used to store bales of silk. Bare mattresses were arranged in a haphazard bivouac on the floor. Eddie hadn't been taken by the police, unless kidnapping for ransom was what they did on their day off. Nor were his abductors Germans, who hadn't come to France to rough it. Nor the Milice, who would have taken him to their headquarters, where he could be tortured in middle-class comfort.

A familiar smell overpowered the odors from the lower floors. He wasn't going to be fed pâté. He identified the smell as cassoulet, a stew of meat and beans, coming from a coal stove presided over by a woman stirring a pot with a wood spoon. Anne Goudsmit turned around with a half-smile that wasn't for him, addressing the men in a language he didn't recognize. The way they answered, first with head-shaking, then nodding, he guessed that she wanted to know if he'd been trouble, and if everything had gone okay.

"Where have you been keeping yourself?" she asked him. "We went several times to your house. We didn't want to bring you here like this, but you gave us no choice."

"You had plenty of choices," Eddie said. "I'm not the only one in Paris who reads music."

She laughed a little. "So far, you haven't proved you can read it at all."

"Then you've got the wrong man."

"As we already have started with you, you will have to do. We can't pull people off the streets one after the other till we find one who understands the notes better than you do."

"What's stopping you?" he said.

The table was set for five. At one chair, instead of a plate and utensils, Eddie saw a brown accordion envelope tied up in string.

"If you won't try harder to help, that is your decision. The decision about you remains ours. You've already disappeared. You won't be missed."

He untied the string and slid the book out. Anyone watching him flip through the pages would know he was going through the motions.

Anne stepped away from the stove for a word with the men, giving him his first long look at them. Grubby didn't begin to describe them. They were dressed shabbily and didn't appear robust, or even clean. Their hideout was a dump. The cassoulet came from dented cans that he saw in a paper bag on the floor. If they believed they were the army that was going to turn back the Germans, they were delusional. Eddie understood why Janssen had been in a lousy mood all of the time. The drummer had foreseen his own doom.

He didn't know who they really were; maybe one of the obscure left-wing factions shouting loudest for war against Hitler until it came straight their way. He sympathized with them, but never took on a cause grander than saving his own skin. Their battles weren't his. His had been fought in Louisiana and points north, and he'd been defeated on every front. People willing to die for something larger than themselves perplexed him. Unless jazz was their cause, music the filter through which all things became explainable. Because he considered himself an artist, he had an aversion to ideologues. In the long run they were his sharpest critics. All political factions were, all bourgeois. All squares.

There was nothing in the damn book but damn tunes. The woman knew it, but was afraid to confess it to the others, and to him. To herself.

"You've stopped looking," she said.

"It isn't here."

"In Russia," she said, "they call your type useless eaters and let them starve." She took away the book, poured half of what was on her plate on another, and put it in front of him. "We will feed you just the same."

Their nerves were raw, but he wasn't afraid of them. They were out to kill Nazis, not jazzmen, though Janssen, who knew them best, probably had believed the same thing. He could argue that they were providing him with a new hideout while he waited for the next train to Switzerland, but would be arguing with himself.

"Who are you?" he asked.

A few bites, and they were almost done eating. Anne said, "How does it matter? I don't think anything matters to you."

"Where are you from?"

"Same answer," she said. "It's enough to know that we are enemies of the Germans and won't be stopped."

"From doing what?"

She licked both sides of the spoon. As she carried her plate to the sink, Eddie saw her glance toward the envelope. Her faction were monks deprived of the language of their bible, who adhered to arcane ritual while hoping to regain its meaning. Eddie Piron had been appointed their exegist, the prophet to lead them out of the wilderness. Without him they had nothing besides ceremony. They were nothing.

Blind hope was their god, and Goudsmit had been Christ, his plan for them their gospel. Eddie, the idol worshiper who bowed down only before the golden Selmer trumpet, looked at each one of them. The men looked back innocently, but not Anne, who knew that he recognized their helplessness, and that if she acknowledged it she would lose the others for the cause. He felt sorry for her but couldn't help. He had a train to catch.

The men rinsed their dishes, and then two of them went out. The one who remained to stop Eddie from escaping—Guy, Anne called him—went to a window, walked away, came back thirty seconds later to see if the skyline had improved.

The view was as squalid as what Eddie saw from his old place on the south side of Chicago within smelling distance of the stockyards. A prettier picture was Anne, who shone in mean surroundings. He had no good idea of what motivated her to take on an impossible struggle. She wasn't a Frenchwoman and could have avoided an active part in a war she'd chosen to fight. No wonder she despised him.

Guy kept close by to keep Eddie from fleeing, or trying to make love to his boss.

Anne walked across the factory floor, waited for Eddie to join her between the bales. "Do one thing for us," she whispered, "and we will let you go."

"What's that?"

"Give us the name of a French patriot who reads music better than you do, and also knows mathematics, who has been in the military, and isn't a coward."

"Beethoven couldn't help you," he said, "if he had Napoleon and Einstein backing him up."

"How do you know?"

"There's nothing in those arrangements but music. Music's all it is."

"That simply isn't so," she said. "Everything we need is in the envelope. I was told by people who don't boast, or make mistakes. The fault lies with you."

"What am I trying to find?" Eddie said. "Maybe if I knew—"

"It's technical information of no concern to you. You wouldn't understand it."

"How do you expect me to find what I don't know I'm looking for?"

"You would recognize it as something other than the music. That much would be clear."

"If I did find it," he said, "you'd never let me go."

She tried an innocent look, shaking her head, a dismissive laugh, her best smile, but gave up when they left him unpersuaded. He went for his trumpet case, popped open the snaps, and examined his instrument. As he buffed it against his sleeve, Guy made a grab for it. Eddie let him have it rather than risk damaging it in a tug of war.

"He doesn't like music?" Eddie said.

"You are American," Anne said. "It could be that he thinks you are going to blow it to summon the cavalry to your rescue."

"Yeah, and General Custer will finish off the Nazis like he did the Sioux."

She went back to the kitchen area, plugged in a radio that gave off bursts of music above harsh static. She tilted it in every direction, and Eddie heard, "This is Radio Londres, the voice of the Free French Forces," in the plummy tones of a British Broadcasting Corporation news presenter. He squeezed beside her, and she turned up the volume on the frail signal from across the English Channel.

"Before we begin," the announcer said, "please listen to some personal messages."

Anne lowered the sound to cut down on distortion. "Paul LaGrande, in Provins," the announcer said, "take the children to school. They aren't learning anything at home."

Eddie started to say something to Anne, who said, "Shush."

"Marie Clermont, the dog needs to be taken to the veterinarian immediately. If she does not receive the best treatment, then we cannot be held responsible."

Anne put her ear close to the radio. There was an extended eruption of static before the next message came in faintly. Eddie scarcely could make out the warning for Paul Beaudry to hurry to the baker in Clichy before the bread burned.

Eddie had spent sleepless mornings in bed listening to the coded messages from Radio Londres without making more sense of them than he did now. Anne looked up unhappily as the announcer signed off, and patriotic French music filled the airwaves. Guy dialed Radio-Paris, the Nazi station, and they listened to German swing, an Irving Berlin melody set to lyrics mocking President

Franklin D. Rosenfeld, which wasn't awful, Eddie had to admit, though it was hard to take for more than a couple of minutes.

"You expected a message from London," he said. "It was connected to the book?"

Anne shook her head.

"You pay close attention for someone who isn't expecting anything."

"I don't know what I may hear. That's why I listen."

He turned up the volume again on a syrupy intro to Louis Armstrong's big hit from a few years back, "I Double Dare You." The trumpeter was no Armstrong, but only one man on either side of the Atlantic was. Eddie hated the slow tempo and stodgy syncopation, the heavy-handed drumming that were hallmarks of National Socialist-approved jazz. He was trying to identify the band when the vocal came in, and he snorted as he recognized Karl Schwedler fronting for Charlie and His Orchestra, the top combo on the Nazi hit parade.

Anne shook her head at him. "This," she said, "this is what offends you?"

He couldn't deny it. It was all over his face until the negermusik gave way for a news reader detailing the relentless advance of the Wehrmacht on all fronts in his flawless Parisian accent.

"German propaganda," Anne said. "Shut it off."

Guy had his hand on the plug when Eddie caught it. He tuned back to Radio Londres, which offered the news with a less disastrous slant.

"If you want to know what is going on in the world, the Nazi station is better," Anne said. "Their lies are closer to the truth."

"You work for the British, and that's what you think of them?"

"They are fools," she said. "They could have prevented this war— could have won it before it began, but were too good to pick a fight with Hitler, too civilized. They are really worse than fools. They are Anglo-Saxons, first cousins to the Germans."

"Who are you?" Eddie heard the thrum of the cable as the elevator began to rise.

"It's too soon for them to be back," Anne said, and killed the radio.

Guy drew a gun. Anne nodded approvingly, but didn't show one of her own as the car continued its ascent. Eddie refused to be alarmed till Anne clutched at Guy's arm, and he realized they had only the single weapon. The elevator stopped one floor below. The floorboards creaked as more than one person, heavyweights, explored the spice loft. Eddie made out a single German word, "Rien," and the car resumed its climb.

The shaft resonated with voices that were boisterous and unafraid. Guy squeezed between the bales, keeping a clear view of the elevator. Anne positioned herself behind him. He scolded her in their language and she backed away, whispering to Eddie to follow.

Before he could move, he'd lost her in a maze of silk that gave off the faint tang of mulberries. The elevator arrived at their floor, announcing deadly threats in working-class accents soured by alcohol. Eddie spotted Anne crouched among the bales and moved toward her on his toes, came down flat-footed as a single shot inaugurated a barrage that went on for twenty seconds, so many bullets fired so fast that he lost count, and ended with someone bragging "That finishes the bastard."

A sober voice answered, "He isn't alone. Find the rest. Finish them, too."

Eddie went for his trumpet, had second thoughts, and pulled Anne to windows that hadn't been cleaned in decades except for a streak where the side of a fist had cut through layers of grime. "I'm sorry," she said, "I seem to have misplaced my rope ladder."

He started her moving to the front of the loft. She heard a scraping sound as the window was forced open, and the breeze rushed in.

"Quick, before they throw themselves out," one of the invaders shouted.

Three or four of them stampeded down an aisle on Eddie's left as he crouched beside Anne, hoping that others weren't coming head-on. When they'd gone by, he rushed her toward the elevator, where Guy lay in a mess of blood. A militiaman decked out in a wide blue beret, brown shirt, and brown tie under a German flyer's leather jacket patrolled around the corpse, rewarding himself from a flask. Exchanging it inside his waistband for a gun, he went in search of more action. Eddie came out from the bales and stepped over Guy's body. Anne circled it. As she entered the elevator, Eddie pulled the handle all the way to the left.

"They're in the elevator." The sober voice in command.

"Take the stairs."

The building shook as the Milice galloped to the street. Eddie stopped at the spice loft, a warren of intense flavors that stung his tongue. He opened a window and looked down as four militiamen burst into an alley and were brought up short by brick walls. They hurried back inside, and he hustled Anne to the stairs. "Faster," she cried, "they're coming." It was her mantra. She didn't give it up until she was in sunlight on the roof, and then not right away.

The roof, paved in pebbles, gathered the weather through skylights that had lost glass and were patched with cardboard or not at all. Pigeons fluttered in and out of the empty panes and roosted in the top story. Anne hurried ahead of Eddie, who was fascinated by the birds who'd built nests in abandoned machinery, and was looking the wrong way when she screamed.

He didn't see her at first. Then he did, the upper part of her body where she'd broken through a section of the roof surfaced in tar paper and nothing underneath. With one hand she clung to a skylight, treading air. "Hurry," she shouted at him. "But be careful."

He took a quick step, several cautious ones as the tarpaper sagged. Flattened against it, he inched toward her on his belly. Through tears in the paper he saw the fragile lattice holding everything up, the wood discolored and cracked from exposure to the elements. Anne kept still and adjusted her grip on the skylight. Not a strong grip. Eddie saw it slipping.

The hole widened around her, and she brought her free hand out clutching the envelope. It was the right place, perhaps, but not the best time to mention that she was jeopardizing their lives for garbage. She skidded it toward him, reaching for his hand. His fingers brushed hers, walked across the back of her hand. A deep breath broadened his chest, and he caught her wrist, locked onto it. Letting go of the skylight, she was drawn through the paper to a patch that supported her weight, where she pulled herself up alongside him.

"Thank God," she said.

Eddie said, "Don't I deserve some credit?"

"You, too."

The roof was edged by a wall a meter high plastered with tar and topped in brown slabs of terra cotta. Across an air shaft stood a building almost identical to theirs, but somewhat shrunken, one story less in height, and not as wide. They knelt beside each other, the sun and soft breeze against their cheeks reassurance that they were alive. Far from the worst place to be, thought Eddie, if not for the damn footsteps on the stairs. Anne looked at him with something important on her mind and said "Merde."

"Can you jump it?" Eddie said.

"What? Can I fly?"

He shook her hand from his shoulder, from his hip, and from his leg as he stepped up onto the terra cotta and leaped onto the next building before fear anchored him. Coming down with his knees tucked under his chin like Jesse Owens in newsreels from the Berlin Olympics, it occurred to him that this roof, too, might be clad in tarpaper. He landed on pebbles, and something solid underneath, raking his back as he skidded over them. Immediately he was on his feet, waving Anne to come over.

She put a tentative foot on the terra cotta, and Eddie saw it wobble as she brought up the other. "Don't look down."

She focused on the bottom of the airshaft, flapping her arms to maintain balance, or attempting a takeoff, then rocked back on her heels and flung herself into space. She arrived where he'd landed, but on her feet, the gold medal winner for style. Across the air shaft, the roof door opened. There was no sound of footsteps, the militiamen too knowledgeable about old buildings to dash onto tarpaper quicksand. Eddie had a sense of their heads turning every which way, like owls, as they hung at the door. But it was pure imagery. Crouched below the wall where he couldn't be seen, he couldn't see them.

The door shut, and he sat up with his back against the wall. "What if they figure out where we are and come up the stairs?" Anne asked him.

"Don't think about it."

"Aren't you?"

"Pray. You can do that." Because he'd stopped believing in God, that option wasn't available to him. Soon, he said "I think it's safe to go down now."

"What makes it safe?"

None of her questions lent themselves to good answers. He wanted to be encouraging, not to brush her off with glibness, but couldn't think of anything. He picked himself up and led her downstairs, as if that were answer enough.

"I left my trumpet," he said. "I'm going back."

"You're out of your mind. Get killed for a musical instrument?"

He could have said the same thing about her book, but he hadn't. He didn't now. "Wait in the alley," he said. "I won't be long."

"I'll come with you."

"Why?"

A question she couldn't answer. On adrenalin's dregs they sprinted up the stairs. At the silk loft, Eddie's strength ran out. He was unable to open the door more than a few centimeters, pushing against something blocking it from the other side. Anne threw her weight on top of his, and a space opened wide enough for them to squeeze in.

Two fresh bodies lay behind the arc of the door, tangled obscenely where Eddie had just swept them together. The faces were purpled and broken, destroyed in a beating, but from their clothes he recognized the men as his other kidnappers. The hair at the base of one man's skull was singed by a bullet fired in a downward angle at very close range. He didn't care to pull them apart to be certain they'd both been killed that way. Anne stared at the floor, not focused on the men, but near them. Her lips moved. He thought it might be the prayer that had eluded her on the roof.

"Rotten timing," he said, "coming back when the Milice were here."

"Find your trumpet, and let's get out."

They returned to the street without anything to say. Horror spoke eloquently for itself. It was the humdrum stuff, in Eddie's experience, that generated the most chatter. Okay with him if Anne didn't want to talk. It meant no more questions without answers.

The cab was in the alley with the key in the ignition. He had the driver's door open when Anne said, "We stole it this morning. The Sûreté will have been looking for it all day. We'd better walk."

"Where are we going?"

It was a question designed to have no answer.

"Yes. Where?"

"I have a train to catch," he said. "I was leaving for the station when your friends sidetracked me. So, if you'll excuse me, I'll be on my way, and you can be on yours."

"It's too late to make your train. Where will you spend the night?"

"You're concerned with my well-being now?"

"Yours and mine. We should spend it together." She was brought up short by a change in his expression. "Don't be ridiculous, that isn't at all what I mean." She didn't smile, no room for humor or self-consciousness in her makeup. "It will be safest if we don't split up yet."

"You've got it backward. If we separate, and one of us lands in the soup, she—or he—can't give up the other."

"As a couple, we'll arouse less suspicion than we will alone."

"What you're saying," he said, "is you're out of hideouts. Out of comrades as well."

"I'm no communist."

"It's a load off my mind. I wouldn't want to be mixed up with reds."

"We can't stay here all day bickering. Let's get moving."

She had nowhere to go, and no friends left alive, probably no money either. He doubted there was anything she wouldn't say or do to change his mind about leaving her. He didn't want her clinging to him. Still, they were on the same side in the war—or would be if she threw her support behind the Eddie Piron faction. Whoever she really was, he couldn't help feeling sympathy for her. "I can let you have some francs," he said.

"It's you I need."

"You know I can't help with the book."

"Just you," she said. "It's suicide alone on the streets late at night, or to check into a hotel by myself without luggage, and attract attention I don't want." She waited for him concede the logic of what she was saying, but he remained unmoved. "Don't think it will be different for you."

"Who are you?" he said.

"Everything you need to know about me, you know. More."

They came out onto the street as a car turned the corner, a glossy limousine that stuck out like a flamingo among the pigeons in the run-down neighborhood. It slowed, and men wearing German gray eyeballed the couple on the sidewalk. Showing her back to them, Anne put her face in the way of Eddie's and brushed lint that wasn't there from his shoulders, stopped to straighten his lapels till the car resumed speed.

He caught her wrist for a look at her watch. "You're right about the train," he said. "Do you know any hotels here?"

"For us, these dumps are death traps. You offered me money to go away. Use it instead for a nice room."

Eddie looked at her as he had when she'd first suggested spending the night together. She surprised him with a smile. It was wry, and evaporated quickly.

"We're entitled to some luxury after all we've been through," she said.

"Oh, is that how I should get rid of it?"

"Your money won't do you any good tomorrow," she said, "if tonight is your last on earth."

Hunting for a place to stay, Eddie became adept at spotting other couples like themselves, mismatched partners, joyless strangers not talking, uncomfortable with each other, well-dressed women on the arms of shabby young men, and girls alongside much older men who weren't relatives or lovers, if mutual awkwardness was a good indicator. On almost every block a commercial building had been converted into a cheap hotel or pension. Faces half-hidden behind linen curtains peered out at the street and drew back when he looked too intently at them. "Death trap" probably wasn't far off the mark. The guests—they reminded him of inmates—knew it better than he.

At a Metro stop they pushed through the turnstile and hurried down the stairs to the platform. A passenger in their crowded car stole glances at Eddie and squeezed near for a better look. Eddie glared at him. Undeterred, he closed in.

"Who's that mec?" Anne whispered.

"I don't know him."

"Then why is he looking at you like a long-lost brother?"

"He's a jazzhound."

"A dog?" she said in English. "Make sense."

"A fan of the music."

"All fans are yours?"

"I used to wish they were."

The man went through his pockets for a handbill, folded it to the clean side, and stepped over other passengers' feet, pointing a pencil at Eddie. "My God, he wants your autograph," Anne said, and pulled Eddie out of the car at the next station.

They crossed the platform to another train and rode across the city to the Champs de Mars stop near the Eiffel Tower. Anne slipped her arm around Eddie's hips, and they walked the tourist streets feeling as obvious as the doomed couples they'd left behind. Her hand was cold, not soft, and prodded him whenever he dropped the pace. As a caricature of affection it was as believable, he thought, as a revolver pressed into his flesh.

CHAPTER NINETEEN

At the four-star Auberge St. Viateur, the girls working a convention of Bavarian chocolatiers were demure and well-mannered and spoke second-hand German punctuated with barracks curses. The desk clerk smiled familiarly at Anne, and at the trumpet case that was Eddie's luggage. The rates were as obscene as the prostitutes' chatter, but Eddie felt secure in a hotel that kept out the riff-raff, catering to a better class of Nazis. He thought up a name for the register, and Anne preceded it with Mme where it was her place to sign. In an elevator smelling of bon-bons and cocoa, a man with plump, hairless cheeks and jeweled swastika cufflinks recited a story that ended in a one-word punch line that sounded to Eddie like "Palesteena." Other sweet-smelling fat men couldn't stop laughing. "Palesteena" was an Original Dixieland Jass Band hit built around an oriental riff, but Eddie doubted the Germans knew any of that. Anne looked hard at the comedian. Eddie saw her look at all the laughing chocolate men, sorry that she didn't have a real revolver to use.

Their room was immense, cream-colored with gold trim, stuffed with Louis XIV reproductions, a set for a boudoir farce. The bed was in keeping with the outsized scale. The carved, painted headboard forced Eddie into comparisons with the scoreboard behind the sun-bleached outfield at Heinemann Park by the New Orleans railyards, where the Pelicans played ball. Anne gave it a wide berth, circling toward an easy chair beside the window.

The Philips radio on the mantel was fixed on the German station. News of the Wehrmacht's latest triumph gave way to a broadcast from Berlin, a fulminating Katzenjammer Nazi. Eddie turned it off. Anne said "Put it back on," and he tilted it toward the door to keep their voices from being heard in the corridor.

"Since we have no choice," she said, "I can't object to staying here."

Eddie said, "I could get used to luxury like this."

"You mean if everything was different. If the Germans hadn't taken over."

That wasn't what he'd meant. He didn't mean anything he hadn't said. He didn't care for Germans any more than she did, hadn't a taste for luxury even when Carla had tried to make him a slave to it.

"The world is what it is," she said. "What anyone hopes for is irrelevant."

"Give yourself some credit for trying to make it different."

"I'm irrelevant."

"Me," he said, "I'm hungry."

She didn't like his flip attitude, but didn't object to ordering from room service.

"The clerk won't be happy that he can't rent this room a second time tonight," Eddie said. "You saw how he looked at us. He expects to pocket a second fee."

"These days everyone chisels. I can't blame him."

She'd had little to say since he'd stopped being her captive. With his pocket full of money and hers empty, she'd become his. They sat looking at each other across the white carpeting till there was a knock on the door, and Eddie brought in their food.

Anne wolfed her meal, yawned, and put her plate on the floor.

"Time for a nap," Eddie said, and moved over to make room for her.

She gave him the same look she'd had for the Germans in the elevator. "I'm comfortable where I am."

He didn't undress. His money was in his pants. The best way to guarantee that it still would be there along with her when he woke was to leave them on.

She was out cold instantly. Probably, she'd learned to sleep under conditions more troubling than those keeping him awake. If he could be like her. . . . Why consider it? Someone had to put her neck on the line fighting Nazis, and someone had to stay up till dawn in smoky clubs entertaining people who didn't much give a damn about what was happening in the world. That was how it was.

He was still awake when her chair creaked. "I can't sleep," she said. "I keep thinking about—"

"Guy? And the others?"

"How I failed."

"At what?"

"Everything—leave it at that. And don't ask who I am."

"Tell me about Goudsmit," he said. "And Janssen. Nothing can happen to them where they are now. Who were they?"

"Go to sleep."

He patted the mattress. "Thanks the same," she said, and rearranged herself on the chair. Eddie's eyes closed and he felt himself drifting off. "You really don't know about them?" she said. "Borge didn't try to make a convert of you?"

"Huh?" he said groggily. "Janssen? All the time. He despised me for not being political. As for what he wanted to convert me to, I never learned more than that he hated Germans a good deal more than the average Frenchman does."

"He talked too much. He had no discipline."

"Is that why he died?"

She yawned again. Eddie expected another brush-off, but then she sat up straight. "Yes," she said. "But not what you're thinking."

"What should I think?"

What was the use in asking? Hadn't she made it clear a thousand times that she wouldn't speak about herself and her organization? He was stretching out again when she said, "He was going to help me create a resistance against the occupation."

His back hurt, but he held as still as he had in his great-uncle's blind in the long-leaf pines when a white tail came into his sights and the slightest movement would send it bolting.

"But he got himself killed," she said. "He was a reckless man who died for nothing—nothing having to do with why he came to France."

"Goudsmit was like him?"

"You insult Anton's memory. Anton was brilliant without being stupid, traits found in combination in too many smart men. You heard him at the keyboard, how meticulous he was with each note. That's how his brain met every challenge."

"The challenge of being your husband while you lived with Janssen?"

"He was a free-thinker who looked down his nose at marriage. We were closer than man and wife, although I was not attracted to him physically."

"Yes, I see now," Eddie said. "Very brilliant."

"You didn't know him. His ideas had real value. Janssen was a prototypical red, a vehement proletarian, once you overlooked that his father was a dentist and his mother came from the minor nobility. He styled himself as the Danish Lenin, and weren't we fortunate to have enlisted him in our plot. His ideology was wet—"

"I'm unfamiliar with the various leftist factions," Eddie said.

"It came from the bottom of a bottle," she said. "He couldn't keep his mouth or zipper shut and needed to be iced down when an attractive woman, or the other kind, passed within arm's reach."

"You lived with him?" Eddie said. "Not Goudsmit?"

"We all sacrifice for the cause."

"He didn't strike me as someone who would kill himself."

"He didn't strike himself as that type either," she said. "Anton knew him before the war through jazz circles. He didn't have a good opinion of his politics, or his talent as a musician."

"He wasn't too bad—"

"Or of yours," she said. "It isn't as though we could place advertisements for underground fighters who were committed, brave, and sober. We took whoever was willing to carry out a dangerous job. Janssen wasn't the worst. Not by far."

"So you killed him."

Her foot hit the floor. Her heel, landing in the plate, shattered it. She collected the broken pieces and wrapped them in a napkin, and then used the napkin to blot a trickle of blood on her foot, all while Eddie wanted to kick himself. He'd gotten her talking, but it wasn't enough. Attempting to show that he wasn't a dope, he'd managed only to put her on guard.

"You were saying. . . ."

"The credit goes elsewhere," she said. "I don't know who she was."

"She?"

"Once, returning from a meeting with Anton, I saw a girl, not the prettiest, leave the apartment. The bed was damp when I got into it, and it reeked of hand-rolled cigarettes and cheap fragrance. The second time I saw her was when she stopped me on the sidewalk to mention that she would pour acid in my face if I didn't let her have Borge. A real proletarian. A student, he told me, though I'm skeptical. More likely they found each other at the club where he played with you."

"It would seem that you should have let her have him."

"It would seem she did everyone a favor." Anne stopped talking to press the napkin against her heel. "That was unfair. Janssen was a sad excuse for an underground fighter, but didn't deserve what he got. She was jealous over nothing. I wasn't his lover any more than I was Anton's. We lived together for appearance's sake, when nothing could have been more inconvenient. After she threatened me, Janssen had no choice but to tell her to get lost. A day later he was dead at her hands, or her brother's, or her pimp's. Another lover's, for all I know.

"Consider my situation," she went on. "A stranger in Paris to build a resistance movement, one of my key operatives is murdered in a stupid lovers' quarrel. With the Germans breathing down my neck, I'm stuck with a body that will stink if I don't get rid of it fast, and my organization will decay with it."

"Wouldn't it have been easier to dump it in a field or bury it in the basement, instead of taking it to one of the most picturesque bridges over the Seine and hanging it for everyone to see?"

"I, myself, though not at all brilliant, am not smart either," she said. "Anton was already dead. With Janssen gone, too, there was no one I had worked with longer than a few days, or who had my full confidence. I thought if we made a public display of Janssen's death, the Germans would think our operation had collapsed and lose interest in hunting for us."

"They weren't fooled."

She shrugged. "Janssen's death began a run of bad luck. Explosives he'd stored improperly went off in the basement, nearly killing me, and then . . . never mind. As you see—" She lifted the napkin and dabbed at the cut, which was bleeding again. "It hasn't changed."

"Where do you go from here?"

"I can't tell you," she said.

"Because you won't say more about yourself?"

"Because I don't know. What's the hurry?"

"We can't stay forever."

"*Now* you mention it."

Her smile, when he finally had it unblemished by cynicism, was not French, the ideal instrument of the irony that shaped it, well worth the wait for the second or two that it lasted.

"I should try to sleep," she said. "I don't often have a safe place to catch up."

Again he patted the bed. "It's not damp, and doesn't smell from cigarettes or perfume. There's plenty of room."

She reached for the envelope. The last thing he saw, shutting his eyes, was the book in her lap as she turned the pages mechanically. They opened again as she bumped against his leg. "Change your mind?"

"The chair," she said, "it's a crippler."

His arm crooked around her shoulders and turned her onto her back.

"No." She wrapped herself in the extra blanket. He brushed his lips against the base of her neck, and she caught his hand riding along her hip and pinned it against the mattress.

"It's understandable that we are anxious tonight," she said, "not knowing what tomorrow may bring. It would feel so good to make love and relieve those tensions."

He snuggled close. "Some of them, yes."

"For me it would create others," she said. "Relieving your tensions is not the purpose of my existence, and I can endure mine without help, thank you very much. I wouldn't make love for such a slight excuse."

"What for, then, only to have babies?"

"Not only."

"What am I missing?"

"Everything, I should say. It is called making love because that is what it should be. It isn't called relieving tensions."

"Do you find me repulsive like Goudsmit? Maybe stupid like Janssen? Or have you discovered something else to dislike?" Eddie said.

"I don't know you. Therefore I can't love you. There is no good reason to have sex with a casual acquaintance, not for me. Whether or not I may be physically attracted to you, don't bother to analyze it. It goes nowhere. The time will be put to better use in getting your rest."

"Did you deliver that speech off the top of your head, or was it prepared in advance for when you find yourself in bed with a man?"

"You should feel flattered to know that you are my muse."

He wasn't ready to let her have the last word when it was no. "A modern woman," he said, "you can't be serious."

"I don't give the impression of seriousness? Please let me know where I'm vague. I will try to be more clear."

In the middle of the night when he woke to massage a cramped leg, her blanket had come undone and she lay on her side with the top of her head just below his chin, so close that he felt each breath. A moan tickled the hairs on his chest, and then she hoisted herself onto her other side, rubbed against him like Josephine Baker doing a somnambulistic turn till her rear was nestled against his hips. Whatever tortures the Germans had in store for him couldn't be as agonizing. He reached out for her again. Less than awake, her objections might not be strenuous.

He berated himself for what he was thinking while he thought more about it. Trying for sleep was an ordeal in a bed that reeked of a nubile woman in her full efflorescence, so he took her place in the crippler chair. After twenty minutes, he got up to ease an ache in the small of his back and tripped over something in the dark. Using his toes, he sized up her precious book and kicked it across the floor.

Soccer wasn't his game. A better kick would have sent the book out the window. Easy enough to do that yet. Not so easy to face Anne in the morning when she asked where it was.

He turned on the light. Yanking the book out of the envelope, he sliced through a taped seam, the heavy paper curling back to reveal foreign script in a meticulous hand. He stripped the tape from the opposite crease, folded the paper on the remaining hinge, and spread the envelope open with its stained, filthy side against his lap. The other side was clean, a buff canvas for a schematic drawing, lines, arrows, and mysterious symbols as incomprehensible to Eddie as the notations in the unknown language.

He managed not to shout. What he understood of Goudsmit's writing was that it was a death contract for a woman acting alone— for anyone trying to put it into action. What flaw in his character prevented him from dropping the envelope out the window while encouraging Anne to continue probing the book of music for its hidden meaning? It was a conundrum requiring almost as much analysis as her feelings about him.

"Why is the light on? Come to sleep."

She was still on her side, her head propped up on one arm and a hand cupping her ear, a beautiful woman calling him to bed while he put his brain through gyrations about bombs and plots.

"You woke me," she said. "What are you doing?"

Uninterested in the answer, she bunched the pillow and buried her face. His knee depressing the mattress and his hand on her back caused her to ready an elbow for him. The lamp on the nightstand came on, and she turned toward him, shading her eyes with her hand. "Why won't you sleep?"

"I have it."

"You do?" She yawned, and behind her covered mouth asked, "Have what?"

Eddie opened the envelope over the sheets, and she squinted at the diagram through sandy eyes. "What am I looking at?"

"Your holy grail."

He put her hand on the paper, as though it were braille and she needed help in finding her place. She couldn't see clearly, still unaccustomed to the light. She rubbed her eyes, blinked them into focus, and sat up suddenly wide awake, her breast spilling out of her blouse a holier grail, the picture more entrancing than the one she examined now from every angle.

"Where did you—?"

"The inside of the envelope the book was in," he said, "that's what you're looking at. It's Goudsmit's plan?"

"Didn't I say he was brilliant? Who else would have thought of hiding it there?"

Too brilliant. Eddie kept it to himself. "Will you tell me now what it's for?"

She shot an unpleasant look as her hand went to her breast. She buttoned her blouse, and then she examined the paper for a full minute before turning it 180 degrees, so that she was viewing it upside down, or else had been before. Then she turned it back the other way.

She stifled a laugh. Eddie didn't share her sense of humor, how anything connected to a bomb plot could be funny. The frustrated laugh came with tears that weren't tears of joy, and she wiped them

away, and lowered her head over the drawing the way she'd scru-
tinized the musical arrangements when she couldn't figure why
Goudsmit's secrets eluded her. She muttered two or three words in
a strange language. Though Eddie didn't understand them, couldn't
tell where one ended and the next began, there was no mistaking
that they were curses.

"I can't do it," she said to him. "Not the slightest part."

"Do what?"

"Blow up this place."

"You don't have explosives? Wires? Batteries?"

"Building a bomb is easy. Getting it to where it can do the most
good—the most destruction," she said, "that's the trick."

"What's this a picture of?"

"Anton said he'd devised a foolproof scheme for bringing down
SS headquarters at the Jeu de Paume. It's a schematic diagram
of the basement, pointing out critical places where we could
collapse the entire structure."

"It's no good?"

"With Janssen, Guy, and two or three of the others to help, and
Anton to oversee things, there's an excellent chance we would suc-
ceed. After he was killed, we tried on our own, but the bomb went
off before we could get close to the musee. I was convinced that
when I had this drawing and Anton's notes, we—I'm the fool. They've
doubled the guard. I can't approach within a hundred meters."

She inspected the envelope again. Perhaps the error wasn't in the
plan, but was hers, a misunderstood word, or else a line interrupted
where coffee or wine had seeped through the paper, mistakes which
could be overcome. Soon she shut off the light, and the curses began
again. Eddie said, "They can hear you through the walls," and she
pressed her face into the pillow.

"There aren't easier targets, not as well-protected, where you can
slip in with a smaller bomb?" he said.

"I didn't come to Paris to make a small explosion."

He tried to look like he shared her disappointment. It was easy, talking to her back. "You believed you could defeat Germany? A handful of saboteurs?"

"If we could hurt the SS in their stronghold, the symbol of the occupation, it might inspire resistance."

"The Germans would send in more men," Eddie said, "and billet them behind thicker walls. Institute harsher laws against the people."

"It might wake them up. The French are complacent, content to go on as close to normal as they can. They don't really mind the Germans. Do I have to remind you that many support them?"

"You're not French yourself?"

"You're still determined to have my biography? Chew on this: I used to think I was."

"How can someone not know what she is?"

"I came by it honestly," she said. "An honest mistake."

"You know better now."

"I suspect I always did—that I'm Palestinian."

"From which land?"

"You've never heard of it?"

He shook his head.

"It doesn't exist yet as a country." She flopped onto her back and bent the pillow behind her. "Had I realized you wouldn't know what to make of my story, I'd have confessed everything."

"If it's not a country—"

"I don't live there only in my mind, believe me. It's a British colony in the holy land."

"Then you're British."

"As much as living under the Nazis has made you German, that's how British I am."

"No, not German. Not American either."

"The renowned jazz trumpeter from New Orleans isn't American? Oh, I see, a Frenchman. I hadn't heard that America sold Louisiana back to France."

"I took it for granted that I was what they said I was where I was born," Eddie said. "Another honest mistake."

"But you're going back," she said. "Back home."

"If that's what you want to call it. How did you come from Palestine to France?"

"It's a military secret. Part of this." She sat up, fingering the diagram. Then she tore it lengthwise, and again from side to side, shredded the scraps till they were too small to make smaller, got off the bed, and went quickly to the bathroom. Eddie heard the toilet flush, and she came back whisking her hands one against the other.

"You've declared a truce in your war on the SS?"

"Not for a minute," she said. "But as a civilian again, I can answer your question. I was flown here from England."

"You're poking fun at me," Eddie said. "English planes don't fly into occupied France."

"They fly over it. What they don't do is land. I jumped out."

"You?"

"Not many proper English gentlemen volunteer to do it."

"Why did you?"

"At my school in Palestine, the Girls' Agricultural School at Nahalal, where I was a teacher, I was noticed by the British SOE— the Special Operations Executive—as a fluent French speaker who might blend in here, who knows France and the people, and like all Palestinians is especially motivated to do something to help in the fight against Germany. With a few others, I was taken to England for training."

"In building bombs?"

"In writing letters in invisible ink. In sending and receiving wireless messages in Morse code, in hand-to-hand combat, in all

manner of useless things. The British are enamored of having operatives in Paris, but they haven't figured out what to do with us. The
operation was a *balagan*—a mess—from the start. We were dropped
over Brittany. German spotters had picked up our plane over the
Channel and were shooting at us before we reached the ground. I
was the only one of my group to reach Paris. That's where I found
Goudsmit, who had put together his own cell of anti-Germans. The
rest you know enough of."

"You'll go home now to Palestine?"

"Back to England would be a good first step."

"I'm trying for Switzerland myself," Eddie said. "You're welcome
to come along. It's easier to reach."

"But not to get into. The Swiss have become particular about who
they allow in their country. And my passport isn't the best. Anyway,
Switzerland is like a rat trap. After you've tasted the cheese, there's
no way out."

"Where else in Europe don't you find the Germans in control?"

"Spain."

"You expect Franco to welcome you with open arms?"

"He's not the humanitarian of the year, but he's no lackey of Hitler's. They say he's of Jewish descent. Unlike the Swiss, he doesn't
turn away refugees or send them back across the border. You're
welcome to accompany me."

"I'll think about it," he said. "Will you consider Switzerland?"

"No. But I will let you buy me a ticket for Vitoria-Gasteiz, in
Spain."

They agreed that he would take her to Gare Austerlitz, the hub
of the Paris-Bordeaux line, where she could catch a train for the
unoccupied zone. He'd never experienced such loneliness in the
company of a beautiful girl as he did on the long taxi ride across
the city. He didn't fault himself for doing nothing to oppose the
Nazis. Anne was a romantic, possessed of the freakish courage to

drop from a plane onto a continent under the boot heel of invaders who showed no mercy to their enemies. As a realist he knew better. Tossing a wrench into the most powerful military machine in the world wouldn't slow it. Only because he lacked a home to return to had he overstayed his welcome.

For no reason a record began playing in his head, an Al Jolson side from twenty years before with primitive blowing from a cornetist he was unable to identify to this day. It wasn't the melody haunting him but the lyrics, and he conjured a duet in which he made painful harmony with the exuberant Jolson.

"Swanee, how I love you, how I love you,
My dear old Swanee,
I'd give the world to be
Among the folks back home in D-I-X-I
Even know my mammy's waiting for me, praying for me
Down by the Swanee."

Swanee. Being stuck in the Alps for the duration of the war, or even for eternity, wasn't cruel punishment. In the Swiss rat trap the cheese was fondue, and the chocolate was the best.

CHAPTER TWENTY

The high-ceilinged waiting room at the Austerlitz station made for excellent acoustics for German snores. Soldiers in gray sprawled shoulder to shoulder on every bench, heads thrown back. Eddie's trumpet provoked derision as a symbol of impotence second only to a baguette tucked under the arm. Every glance at Anne was a leer. On the ticket line she turned to him and asked, "Have you thought about what I said? You're making a mistake, you understand."

"Is there an address where I can write to you," he asked, "so I know you made it out of Europe in one piece?"

"In one piece? Really, you expect too much." Then her mood turned glum again. "You won't hear from me."

He paid for a second-class carriage to Pau, the last stop before the Spanish frontier. There she would determine whether it was safe to go farther by train or to try the mountains on foot. Suddenly she embraced him, and when he touched his lips to hers she allowed them to linger. The German corporal watching them from the information kiosk lost interest around the time Eddie did. It was a dry kiss, delivered with wide-open eyes. Anne wasn't a natural actress, beyond her range in the role of a tragic Frenchwoman wrenched apart from her lover. When she pushed away, Eddie took his money from his pocket and forced most of it on her. It didn't buy a better kiss. A quick squeeze of his hand transmitted warmth absent from her embrace.

A train rolled into the shed, a fleet of freight cars shunted to a side track as though it had wandered lost from the countryside, and stopped at the passenger terminal seeking directions. Eight minutes later, a German locomotive glided up to the opposite platform hauling panzers and field pieces on flatcars stretching from the vanishing point on the horizon. Anne looked at her watch as Eddie told her, "With all that's going on in this war, you can throw your timetable out the window."

A blur of red, black, and silver defined as boxcars, coal hoppers, and chemical tanks pulled in to the station for a few minutes, then resumed motion in the direction from which they had come. A whistle sounded three short blasts, and Eddie looked up the track. "Only half an hour late," he said.

Air brakes shrieked. Wheels ground against the tracks where the military train had stopped. As Anne started to the platform, a German soldier got in her way.

"Nein, Mademoiselle, this train is not for you."

A dozen third-class carriages lagged behind a steam engine emblazoned SNCF, Société Nationale des Chemins de Fer, the French national carrier. Two conductors hopped down from the car behind the coal tender. Eddie saw them slip inside the dispatcher's shed at the end of the platform while a convoy of green and white municipal buses drew up behind the station. Gendarmes sealed the area. After ten minutes the doors opened and passengers swarmed out, not so much a cross-section of society, but a mishmash that had entered the buses as families, and been sloshed around inside, women with men who appeared to be strangers, youngsters in the care of adults looking nothing like them, and everyone with the same dazed expression, blinking and confused, as if they'd emerged from a pit. Mothers screamed louder than the babies they were unable to hush. The gendarmes prodded them with batons as they sorted themselves out in the street. Eddie heard "Vite, vite, vite," along with "Mach schnell," and the crowd was rearranged into lines and marched through the great hall of the station to the waiting train.

He took Anne aside to avoid being swept up in the mob. Luggage consisted of a single bag, or a parcel wrapped in brown paper tied with twine. Conspicuous were a handful of women in high fashion and men in tailored suits, who looked to be embarking on short notice on a vacation with the poorest of the poor. The children wailed at the gendarmes patrolling the ragged lines. An aged man with the lapels of his Norfolk jacket festooned with military decorations propped up an elderly woman who had fainted in his arms. He asked something of the closest gendarme and received the answer from his baton.

"Another roundup of foreigners," Eddie said to Anne.

"Foreign Jews, I should say."

"They don't all look like Jews."

"How should Jews look?"

"Some of these people are quite dark. Not Jews, but Gypsies, am I right?"

"You're wrong."

"I've never seen dark Jews before."

"I bet you have, but didn't know what they are. They're North Africans."

"African Jews?"

"From Morocco, Algeria, Tunisia. Since Vichy took over administration of French possessions, the Arabs have been subjected to Nazi propaganda, who have made their lives miserable. It used to be that no one ever noticed them in France. Now everyone does. Soon you won't see any."

"How do you know so much about them?"

She rolled her eyes.

"Yes, of course, but—"

"They've begun to make their way to Palestine with terrible stories."

"Where are they being taken now?"

"A concentration camp has been established at Pithiviers, near Orléans. They'll be held there for a time."

"And from Pithiviers?"

"No one knows."

"How can that be?"

"No one has ever come back to tell."

He reexamined the mass of people. The lightest weren't lighter than he was. The darker he would take for Arabs, if not Gypsies. Probably he'd seen them on the avenues and assumed that was what they were. If he had thought about them at all. Django's Gypsy girlfriend, Sophie Ziegler, was wrongly assumed to be a Jew. He searched the platform for a short, dark woman in the company of a darker man with a trim moustache, and a hand mangled and nearly lost in a fire when he was eighteen, which had forced him to relearn his instrument in his brilliant idiosyncratic manner, perhaps clutching a guitar case as Eddie Piron clung to his trumpet, impotent for all the world to see. He turned away from Anne, but tears in her eyes made it unnecessary.

"I failed at everything I came to do," she said. "All I managed to blow up was my house. I'm leaving without injuring a single German, let alone the SS. Without rallying the French. Nothing. I accomplished absolutely nothing. Assuming the road to hell is paved with good intentions, I'm well on the way to—Never mind. Plenty of dynamite is left. If I had a gram of courage I'd go back. Then at least I can say—"

"That you got yourself killed for more of nothing."

"Not for nothing."

They were shoved back as the mob was stalled at the entrance to the train. Several of the Jews tripped over each other, bringing down more at Eddie's feet. A gendarme knocked off-balance clubbed them again and again, screaming for them to get up. Eddie caught his wrist on the upswing and snatched the baton away, was whipping it at the gendarme's head when he felt Anne's hand on his shoulder, and let it fly.

"Careful, monsieur." Eddie pulled the gendarme upright. "You don't want to fall and hurt yourself."

A German military policeman retrieved the club and stood shoulder to shoulder with the gendarme, his hand against the butt of his big service revolver. A feeling that a place was reserved for him on the train to the camp remained with Eddie until the soldier and then the gendarme walked away.

"We should get out of here," Anne said.

"You'll miss your train."

She looked toward the platform, at the gendarme with his back to the Jews pounding his stick against his palm. Then she took Eddie's hand and pulled him to the street.

"I must be crazy to have believed I could go on excursion out of occupied France," she said. "And you, what were you thinking back there?"

"Obviously I wasn't."

"Obviously."

"No, that isn't true. I was thinking about my brother."

"He's in Paris?"

"Just a thought I had."

They walked away from the station along the Quai d'Austerlitz. Anne freed her hand from his, struggled to keep up as Eddie picked up the pace. They went for blocks studying their shoes on the pavement, avoiding faces.

"You're too quiet," Anne said. "Say something."

"What do you want to hear?"

"That this damn war is over."

He turned his head toward her. "Look out," she said, and he turned back as he was about to step off the curb in front of a truck. "You won't tell me about your brother?"

"Forget I mentioned him."

"I'm not a forgetter."

"Then don't. Think I care?"

"Why are you always so mysterious? Janssen said you gave away less about yourself in the bright lights than any of us in the underground."

"All there is is less," Eddie said. "Less and less every day."

"Oh, that explains everything."

She stopped at a red light. Without breaking stride he caught her hand again and pulled her onto the Pont d'Austerlitz. A gang of laborers, paint-spattered, reeking of turpentine and a liquid lunch, came toward them on the walkway, giving Anne the eye complete with lewd remarks, until a flock of nuns walking arm in arm sent them away.

"I was born in Picayune in the state of Mississippi," Eddie said in English when they were alone again.

"What? You're muttering."

"That's a few miles northeast of New Orleans, Louisiana, in 1908." He stood at the railing and looked down into the river, at red and blue barges like flooded boxcars parked alongside the quai. "On my mother's side I'm as French as anyone in Paris, but more so. We Pirons are *laine pur*, pure wool, who never trucked with foreign invaders as folks here seem to take to naturally. We left for the United States, which was French North America two hundred years ago, did all right for ourselves in sugar before backing the wrong cause in the American Civil War."

"Your father's side? They were pure French also?"

"Pure niggers. House slaves mostly, which made them a manner of aristocrats, the property of my mother's people. They were the Pirons."

He looked hard at the girl to deter her from studying where the refined planter left off and the descendant of wild jungle tribesmen began. The hard look had no effect on hers.

"It happened a lot in those times?" she said.

"Ever get an eyeful of the Africans you have in Paris?"

The girl shook her head.

"There aren't as many as there were. Run into some, you'd notice right off how black they are. There's none like that back home. The boys in some of my old bands, Americans I played with here, for instance, you wouldn't find a one of them close to that color. One hundred percent of American Negroes've got white granddaddies, or great-granddaddies, what have you, that owned grandma and had his way with her."

"We were slaves too," she said. "Slaves in Africa. Perhaps your ancestors owned mine. We didn't have relations with them, but we never forgot what it's like being under another people's thumb."

"Your people didn't hang around Africa. Cleared out the first chance you had."

"The first chance God gave us, yes."

"We had no place to go. We continued to live among those people who bred us and worked us like animals. As we look fairly much like them, once you get past the color, they gave us their names. That's how it is in the best families in New Orleans, white but also black, the whites resenting us for not disappearing like history never happened."

"I see."

"Not in your worst nightmares," he said. "Your people lit out for their own country where they could live with nobody over them. As Africa was no longer our country, we stayed with those people that had owned us. They still owned us, only now they called it something else. In New Orleans, things were better than in most places in the South because we are all blood-related. But there's just so much you can get away with before they pull your horns in."

"Of course, we—everybody has heard what it's like there for you."

"Not for me," he said. "I made my way as I saw fit, not trying to pass, mind you—"

"Pass? I'm unfamiliar with this expression."

"To fool people into thinking I was white. Till I was thirteen, fourteen years old, it was like I was white. All my friends were. I never gave being colored a thought."

"What happened then?"

"I started noticing girls is what happened. Young colored boy is expected to act like a capon around white females. That's the rule, you see. I had no argument with it. My argument was that I didn't believe it applied to me."

"It made you angry?"

"Angry at white folks? It would've, if they looked down their nose at me, and me as fair as them. That day never came. They were blind to what I was, those that didn't know me. It'd've been different if I was one of those uptown niggers. How white folks treat them is a crime, but it isn't my problem. Never was."

He stopped to look at her again. Though it was a gentle look, he held it until she lowered her eyes. He needed her to hear his confession, this girl who'd never visited the South, or been to the United States for that matter, who was raised among her own kind, and went to help them build a country of their own, who'd never known anyone before him who wasn't white, and on whom it had fallen to hear his story, and to make sense of it for him.

"What is an uptown nigger?" she asked.

He dismissed it with a wave of his hand. "I had a brother. You wouldn't think we were related, that's how dark he was. Funny thing. White folks who knew what I was didn't have a bad opinion of me for being colored, but sometimes my brother did because I look white. These things come up in Creole families. Come up all the time."

"You don't have to tell—"

"Listen," he said over her. "We didn't look at all alike. Not alike in any way. The most important thing for me was my music. Sit me down with my horn someplace where I can practice, even as a child I didn't want for anything. My brother was the opposite. He couldn't help but look for trouble. Nothing criminal, mind you, just general hell-raising, making a ruckus."

"Where you come from, a black boy can't do those things?"

"He'll do it till he can't any more, provided he's prepared to pay a heavy price," Eddie said, "something I could get around on account of how I look. Tom, my brother, he was out to provoke white folks. It was his hobby—no, his business, you could say, his jazz."

"Regarding white women?" Anne said.

"They are the crème de la crème of trouble," Eddie said. "Trouble that will get you killed. Tom knew better than to look for that kind of trouble, except when he was drinking. Or when there was no other trouble to be had.

"Around the time he turned sixteen, Tom began seeing a pretty little Creole girl, name of Carmen, a kitchen maid for a rich white family in the Garden District. To look at her, you wouldn't think she wasn't pure white. Light as me, but with blue eyes, and dirty blond hair. But under the one-drop theory that they have there, she was colored."

"One drop of what? What is that?"

"Blood," Eddie said. "Somebody with a single drop of Negro blood is colored as far as the State of Louisiana is concerned. There isn't any appeal from that law."

"Your brother thought Carmen was white?"

Eddie shook his head. "Tom wasn't suicidal. It was plenty that she looked white. Being with her was eating his cake, you might say, and having it too. It drove white folks crazy to see him on Canal Street with the most beautiful blonde in New Orleans, and there wasn't anything they could do about it. It even drove his brother crazy. That might've been the best part."

"I think I see," the girl said, "where this story will end."

"Everybody could," Eddie said, "aside from my brother. All that was lacking was how it would get there. Carmen liked to tell people she was an Italian girl from a family on Bienville Street that had fallen on hard times. It was a bad joke that became dangerous when people fell for it. White boys seeing her on the street with Tom, they fell for it."

"They were outraged?"

"Murderous would be a better word. Not just the rednecks. Consider Tom sporting Carmen on his arm past a new cop name of Reed Jackman, who'd come to New Orleans from the Mobile, Alabama, police. Each time he spied my brother with his sweet blond girlfriend, Jackman's blood would percolate, you know, he couldn't abide them being together. New Years Eve I went down to the French Quarter with Tom and Carmen to hear the marching bands and watch the fireworks on the river. I had just ducked inside a store on Royal Street to pick up a pack of Juicy Fruit when Jackman called my brother over and asked him what he was doing with this young white girl.

"'Season's greetin's, and a happy 1929 to you, Officer Reed,' Tom said to him. It left Jackman's jaw hanging slack. In his thirty-five years on earth, I don't believe he had ever heard a colored boy speak to him like that, like they were born of the same kind. Tom wasn't being his uppity self. It was New Years, he was out with his girl, having fun, and all he meant was for Jackman to be happy, too, wasn't it great being alive. I came out of the store with my gum in time to see Jackman trying to make up his mind what to do. That's when Carmen put one of those streamer horns in her lips and tooted it. It made the buzzing sound that they do as it unfurled, and the end of it, it hit Jackman on the tip of his nose. Snapped him out of his trance, you could say."

Eddie stopped for the girl's questions. She had said that she knew where the story was headed, and now she wanted details. He would let her have all she could stand with his take on them.

"He arrested your brother?"

"Cops don't arrest a Negro without humiliating him first, making him feel he isn't worth what you scrape off your heel on the curbstone. He asked again where he was going with this blond young lady."

"None of you told him she wasn't white?"

"Tom had exhausted his good cheer," Eddie said. "He said, 'Ain't no law against it.'"

"What about Carmen?"

"He wouldn't let her say anything."

"Why didn't you?"

"There is no law against it."

"You're as stubborn as he—"

"From time to time in the South, you will come across a white girl out to scandalize polite society by having the thrill of getting too close to a genuine Negro. Encouraging disaster is what it is. Not for the girl, of course, but for the fellow who is accomplice to such foolishness."

"You aren't allowed even to do that?"

"To my knowledge, no one has actually been charged and convicted of walking on the public street in New Orleans in the company of a white woman. You have to sleep with her, which is a violation of the miscegenation law, which they also have there. It means—"

"I know what it means. There are laws like it now in Germany."

"How is anybody going to know, unless they are peeping through a window, or one of the parties blabs, or it results in a baby? Cops like Reed Jackman are the guardians of morality and racial purity, bound and determined to stamp out miscegenation and its evils before, after, and while it is taking place. They go about it by separating colored men from white women at every step of the way. 'Stop where you're at,' he said to Tom. 'I'm taking you in.'"

"You're the older brother, you should have told him the truth about Carmen."

"Tom asked him, he said, 'What for? I haven't done anything.'

"'Gonna let a technicality get in our way?' Jackman said. 'You'll help me come up with something.'

"'What you want to spoil New Years Eve for, Officer Jackman?' Tom said. 'Why you want 1929 to get off on the wrong foot?'" Eddie broke off, looking at river traffic.

"Then what happened?" Anne asked.

"I could see Jackman's lips working," Eddie said, "but the best he could do was 'Wrong foot for you is the right one for me.' Tom wasn't listening. He took Carmen by the arm and started down the street, which is when Jackman removed his billy club from his belt loop and whipped it across Tom's ear."

Eddie saw Anne nod. Assuming she wasn't telling him that Jackman had acted properly, this was a part of the story she'd foreseen.

"He was ready to swing it again," Eddie said, "when Carmen yelled. It distracted him, and my brother lunged for his service revolver. I don't think Tom had strength left to pull it out of the holster. Jackman sidestepped him and split open his head like a watermelon, blood pouring into the street. He had raised the club above his shoulder again when—"

"When you rushed him," the girl said.

"How did you know?"

"Your brother's not the only Piron who isn't hard to understand."

"Want to take it from here?" Eddie asked, not sarcastic, curious about what she thought of him and what she figured had happened next.

She pursed her lips.

"I came up on him from behind and snatched the billy out of his hand. It was that easy, but, like having a tiger by the tail, too dangerous to let go or back off from what I had taken on. He threw a punch below the belt that made me see stars. I brought the stick up into his face and knocked his upper plate half-way to Bourbon Street.

"He didn't go down. He had a hand inside my shirt, clawing at my heart, it felt like, going for his gun with the other. I pounded him I don't know how many more times till he was at my feet, and Carmen grabbing my arm, saying, 'You better get out of here, Eddie, cause you surely have murdered this white cop.'"

Anne bit her lip.

"I hadn't, thank God. Busted open his skull, and cracked his elbow so it won't ever bend, but he was still breathing, although I didn't find out till I picked up a *Times-Picayune* at the out-of-town newsstand in Central Station in Chicago, where I had arrived on the first train headed north, the Panama Limited, traveling on the Illinois Central line. I haven't been back to New Orleans since."

"And your brother?"

"You know."

"That police officer didn't kill him."

"Not through any fault of his own," Eddie said. "I should say both of theirs."

"Who did?"

"It was a trusty at the Angola prison where they sentenced Tom to fifteen years at hard labor for assaulting an officer in the performance of his duties with the intent to kill him. He lasted three weeks less two days."

"How did he . . . did it happen?"

"Jackman's friends on the police took up a collection and gave this other prisoner's uncle two hundred dollars cash, and a Smith and Wesson revolver, new suit of clothes, and a Borsalino hat taken from the body of a suicide off the Walnut Street ferry as payment for him stabbing Tom."

"I knew it would end like that," Anne said. "Didn't I tell you I could see what was coming?"

"Yeah, you did," Eddie said. "Remember what I told you?"

"That everyone could? Everyone but your brother?"

"Even him."

CHAPTER TWENTY-ONE

Boyishly handsome Albert Speer, builder of the Reich chancel-lery and the Führer's private residence in Berlin, thirty-six years old, with an IQ of 128 and the breeze in his fine blond hair, told his driver to stop beside the fountain in the Place des Vosges. Sighting through the viewfinder of the bellows camera strapped around his neck, he fired off several pictures of the cobbled plaza and the old buildings surrounding it.

"Seventy-five years ago, all of Paris looked like this," he said as he advanced the film to the next shot, "a medieval anachronism. Napoleon III instructed Baron Haussmann, his favorite architect, to make the capital what you have today, an airy metropolis of broad boulevards. The City of Light. Monsieur de Villiers is well acquainted with this morsel of history, but you," he said to the two of the three men in the open back seat wearing leather topcoats with the collar turned up against the wind, "you would not be.

"The Marais," he went on, "is built over a swamp. Due to a problem with drainage that stumped engineers of the last century, this part of the city wasn't incorporated into Haussmann's design. Frenchmen with nostalgic feelings for the area do not recognize that it is a remnant of the primitivism of the middle ages. The narrow streets don't charm me. I see them as the old cowpaths that they were, winding in circles among structures of no distinction. Real Parisians have long shunned the area, leaving it to foreigners and Jews. No one will miss it."

"Won't the Jews?" de Villiers said.

"Who will miss the Jews?" Speer answered. "If we were to empty the Marais of its population without rebuilding it, we would be doing France an invaluable service." He swung around in his seat. "You appear somewhat reserved, Monsieur. You have second thoughts?"

"Certainly not. But I don't want to vex anyone. I have no love for Jews, but to turn out tens of thousands of them into the streets—"

"German industry needs labor," Speer said. "With so many of her sons on the battlefield, replacements are in short supply. Foreign Jews who have invaded French soil will find employment in our mines and factories. As an officer of the SS myself, let me assure you that we have plans for every Jew in France. It is why Major Weiler sought my involvement in your project. I can move the bureaucracy to expedite the removal of all foreign and French Jews as soon as you have obtained the building sites from their owners."

"What do you have in mind for the Marais, Herr Speer?" asked Weiler.

"I envision a modern Cité du Führer, stretching back from the Seine a good half-kilometer. Medievalism will be replaced with sound fascist architecture. Like the people they inspire, fascist structures disdain soft edges and ornamentation. Buildings on such a massive scale are out of place on cobblestone lanes. The streets will be widened as in the rest of Paris."

"Wide arteries permit the easy movement of armies and artillery pieces so the lower classes may be controlled and the masses made to feel impotent in the face of authority," de Villiers said. "Isn't that so?"

"You are a student of architecture yourself?"

"Of history."

"I am a student of the future," Speer said. "The Cité du Führer will be built to endure for millennia. When do you think you will have obtained sufficient property rights for demolition to get under way?"

"The process is not moving ahead in a timely manner. Many landlords are reluctant to sell."

"You see, Herr Speer," Weiler interrupted, "the influx of foreign Jews, while a tragedy for Paris as a whole, has created something of a boom in the Marais. The landlords cram additional residents into every apartment, and still there are more Jews clamoring for space. The landlords refuse to sell because they are making greater profit."

"What do you propose to do?"

"The landlords will be ordered to evict the Jews. The increased vacancy rate will be an incentive to divest themselves of their properties. With more Jews joining the thousands already sleeping on the sidewalks, the stench and the noise, the assault on public hygiene will heighten pressure for their immediate removal. Not only the Jews, but also other social undesirables, impecunious artists, Gypsy fortune tellers, street performers."

"You might want to retain a few of those," said Speer. "A city without mimes, who would want to live here?"

"Perhaps a smattering."

"You are to be congratulated for forging relationships unique in Europe under the new order. It sets a splendid example when French businessmen and the SS join in a partnership. Germans will be in France for a long time, perhaps until the new buildings turn to dust. There should be cooperation in every field."

"The redevelopment of the Marais is not our first venture," de Villiers said.

"What is?"

"As an experiment, I put up the financing for the purchase of a nightspot on Place Pigalle. A jazz club called La Caverne Negre."

"I am a partisan of the music myself," said Speer. "It is not impossible to be a good Nazi and to appreciate jazz, although it is easier here than in Berlin. Your club has the potential to do well?"

"I can't say that I have high regard for the music, or the musicians, if that's what you wish to call those who make it," said de Villiers. "For me it is the noise of the jungle, but I am not averse to profiting from it. The club will be enlarged, modernized, and with proper management will be the first success in our partnership."

Speer instructed his driver to continue around the plaza.

"Unlike the situation in the Marais," de Villiers went on, "work at Place Pigalle is ahead of schedule. The club will reopen Friday night, a gala event with the leading lights of the occupation and SS as invited guests. I would be honored to have you at my table."

Speer's hand was on the arm of his driver, who stomped on the brake, throwing the men in back against the front seat. Speer stood up, pointing his camera at a faded mansion. "What is that house?" he asked.

"The Hotel de Rohan-Guemenee," de Villiers said. "The writer, Victor Hugo, lived there."

"I think we should save this one, gentlemen," Speer said. "What do you say? The old pile will make an excellent public pissoir, no?"

Avoiding main thoroughfares, Eddie took Anne away from the Seine through the eastern part of the city. He couldn't say that he'd been to the eleventh arrondissement half a dozen times. North of Boulevard Voltaire not even that often. Here the buildings did not seem Parisian, the faces not particularly French. Pressed, he would have difficulty saying what a French face should look like, aside from his and those he missed in Montmartre. At Boulevard Menilmontant he and Anne had the same idea at the same time, and they turned together toward the entrance of Cimitiere Pere LaChaise.

He felt at peace immediately. The peace of the grave. Cemeteries rarely had that effect on him, not those in New Orleans shaded in live oaks tangled in Spanish moss, and haunted by the spirits of the witches and voodoo queens interred in the ovens where they cheated the subsurface rivers washing buried cadavers to the Gulf. There was nothing sinister about the hallowed ground of Pere LaChaise. At the Mur des Federes he stopped to examine the memorial to the insurrectionists from the Paris commune massacred in 1871. Anne walked by without a second look but lingered at the graves of Frederic Chopin, Georges Bizet, and of Sarah Bernhardt, and the caricaturist Daumier. A monument covered in cupid's bows stamped in lipsticks of various shades marked the grave of Oscar Wilde. Anne leaned so close that Eddie thought she was going to add her kiss, but she pulled back after placing a pebble on top.

"We should be safe here," she said. "The police and militias don't come where there already are corpses. They prefer to make their own. Besides, a cemetery is a place we should get used to."

"I'm not ready for it," Eddie said. "The British wouldn't have dropped you in France without a plan to get out, and a backup. How can it be that you're stuck?"

"They were as unrealistic about evacuating us as they were in what they expected us to accomplish. We Palestinians knew we were entrusting our lives to amateurs with no concern for us as individuals. It didn't matter. We had to return to Europe to do whatever we could. Among ourselves we discussed how we might escape. If we could reach the Pyrenees, we would be in sight of Spain. From Spain we could walk into Portugal, and from there we could get on a ship. My mistake was in thinking I could roll across the border on a French train."

On a leafy path at a monument under a plane tree, Eddie stopped again.

"Whose grave is this?" Anne said.

"Judah Benjamin's."

"Should I know the name?"

"He was a big shot from my city. New Orleans. A U.S. senator."

"Why is he buried here?"

"During the American civil war he quit Washington to be a minister in the rebel government. After the defeat he ran away to England. I wouldn't have thought I could have sympathy for a man like him, a slaveholder, but I'm starting to understand how he felt stuck here."

"He wanted to go home?"

"He had no home."

They sat on a bench beside the grave of Ferdinand de Lesseps, excavator of the Suez Canal. Eddie said, "Something I was going to tell you, but I forget." Then he snapped his fingers. "Roquentin, my old boss at La Caverne, is going back to Toulouse in the south. He'll give us a ride."

"He has a car with room for two more?"

"I don't know how he intends to travel, but we'll be welcome to come along. Spain was his idea, too."

When the gates closed, they were among the last to exit the cemetery, attaching themselves to mourners from the burial of someone who was not among the pantheon, if the small number of vehicles in the cortege was an indication of earthly status. An elderly man for whom French was not a first or second language asked if he could drop them off.

"If you can bring us close to Montmartre, we will be grateful," Eddie told him.

The man led them to an American LaSalle, stealing peeks at Eddie's trumpet but too diplomatic to ask why he needed it at a cemetery. Several blocks from Place Pigalle, Eddie thanked him, and they got out of the car. Though he'd been away for just a few days, he felt the same as if he'd returned from a long voyage. All that was lacking from an ideal homecoming was a new gig at La Caverne.

The man-ape swinging his club above the door was darker, devolved into a Neanderthal Sambo with heavy ridges over his eyes, a protuberant jaw, white rubber lips curled in a simpering grin. Slung over one shoulder was a woman, King Kong's sexpot Ann Darrow as Marianne, the chaste symbol of France. Brown paper was taped over the windows. The door was locked. When Eddie tried it, a voice called out, "Go away, can't you see we're closed?"

"It's me," he said. "Eddie."

It brought silence. Fingers appeared against the window glass, widening a seam in the paper. Anne said, "You don't know who's inside. It could be the—"

The door opened. Roquentin looked at them as though he was looking at a ghost, and the ghost had brought along an angel. "What are you doing here?"

"This is how you greet your old meal ticket?" Eddie said.

"It is when I want him alive." He pulled them inside. "You promised you were leaving Paris."

"I promise a lot of things I can't do."

"And never pass up those you can do to make trouble." He was looking at Anne. "I know you from someplace," he said to her, and left it at that. "What brings you back?" he asked Eddie. "Miss me, or the SS?"

"Getting to where I'm going is more complicated than I thought."

"And you respond by finding a beautiful young woman so no one will look twice in your direction, and returning to a business under the ownership of the SS."

"We need a ride."

"Anyplace in particular?"

"Wherever you are traveling suits us," Eddie said, "as long as it is out of the occupied zone."

"Ah, I see, you are trying to get me killed with you."

"Is that a no? I don't understand."

"You don't understand anything. I, on the other hand, understand everything but why I go along with you."

"Thank you," Anne said when Eddie didn't.

Eddie looked around the club. Changes made to the interior were no less drastic than those to the sign out in front. Newer, larger tables had replaced the old scarred ones, and there were more of them, closer together, covered in linen cloths. Additional banks of lights suspended above the riser seemed adequate to illuminate the Comedie-Française. There were new menus on the new tables inscribed with new prices. Posters promoting appearances by international stars, and shows headlining Eddie et Ses Anges were missing from the walls, which were now a gallery of not-very-good watercolors.

"I told them they are turning away customers," Roquentin said. "I don't know why I opened my mouth. There's nothing I would enjoy more than for them to lose their investment. I patiently explained that the charm of La Caverne is in its hominess. It isn't an art gallery, or restaurant, or concert hall, but a jazz club, where half of the patrons are pie-eyed and can't see as far as the walls. The Germans didn't want to hear. They believe that where there are conditions of order there is automatic improvement. I give the club a few weeks before it goes under."

"You can buy it back."

"No, I am gone for good. I will be happier in the unoccupied zone. Maybe I'll open a bar in Toulouse."

"How will you get there?" Eddie said.

"Did you know that Philippe is also from Toulouse? He has a truck, and I am going to load my things on top. There should be space for two more, if everyone takes shifts riding in back. If not, we can drop the piano at the side of the road."

"When do you leave?"

"After the weekend," Roquentin said. "The SS are preparing a grand opening and demand that I organize it."

"How is it going?"

"We won't draw flies. There will only be Germans and their guests. If I could get away with it, I'd poison them all."

"It's a reasonable idea."

"Unfortunately, I know as much about poison as they do about presenting good jazz. Leave mass murder to the Germans, and the music to me, then you can't go wrong. When no customers show up, they may want to murder me, too, but it's out of my hands."

"Is that a hint that you'd like me to play?" Eddie said.

"Certainly not. You can't show your face. You would be arrested in a flash."

"Because, you know, if you need me to boost the gate, I'll do it, considering all the risks you've taken for me."

Anne put her foot over his toes.

"I didn't take them for you to end up in the same place as if I hadn't," Roquentin said.

"Announce that I will perform. You'll fill every seat."

"Those are the last things I want to do."

Anne said, "You heard. You're not wanted. Why do you insist?"

"Inform the SS that I guarantee the successful start of their endeavor in exchange for the charges against me being dropped," Eddie said to Roquentin. "Ouch," he said then as Anne stepped on his foot with all her weight.

"Are you nuts?" said Roquentin. "They will use you and then kill you. You know them."

"Do it for me."

"No."

"Then I will set up shop on the sidewalk with my horn until I've drawn a crowd, and bring them in like the Pied Piper of Hamelin. It's up to you."

"When it comes to you," Roquentin said, "nothing ever is."

Anne said, "You're a fool. I'm leaving without you."

"Excuse me," Eddie said to Roquentin, and manhandled Anne into a corner. "Before you go, I ask one favor."

"Absolutely not."

"You mentioned that some dynamite remains hidden. I would like you to build a bomb for me."

"For you?"

"For me at first. And after for the SS. I'm no good with poison either."

She looked at him skeptically. "To what should I attribute this sudden conversion?"

"So that you will have a better opinion of me," Eddie said, "the next night we spend together."

She shook her head. "One thing has nothing to do with the other."

"So I need to find a better reason?" he said. "I'll leave it to you."

❧

Weiler said, "Roquentin says things aren't going well, there is little excitement about the new club."

Without looking up from his paper, Maier said, "Does it surprise you?"

"This does. He also says that arrangements can be made for Piron to come out of hiding to play for us."

As Maier turned the page deliberately, Weiler was unable to conceal a smile. Maier's responding to every question with another question, the delay in answering, his determination always to be deferred to, and his contempt for every idea other than his own had become old hat. It was intimidating until you got on to it and recognized it as the stagecraft that it was. He watched with amusement as the colonel folded the paper again and placed it precisely on the corner of his desk, squaring the edges before looking at him.

"Why would a wanted man put himself on public display?"

"He is at the end of his rope," Weiler said. "He tried to flee, to go underground without success—maybe even to kill himself only to find out he didn't have the nerve. If he doesn't come to an arrangement with us, he is finished. In attempting to curry our favor, he is seeking preferential terms."

"This is what you believe?"

Why couldn't Maier say he had a different idea, and tell him what it was? Why another damn question? He would give the colonel a dose of his own medicine and see how it went down.

"What other interpretation is there?"

"I'm not a soothsayer," Maier said. "Find out where he is and seize him. Leave it at that."

"Won't it be sweeter to allow him to think he has bargained for his freedom, and then to snatch it away? After using him to make a success of the club, why can't we hold up de Villiers for a larger share of the project in the Marais?"

"We can accomplish the same thing also by putting a gun to de Villiers's head."

Weiler scratched his ear. Twice the colonel had answered with declarative statements. Perhaps he had broken him of an obnoxious trait, one of them.

"Having Piron under lock and key will be sweet enough," Maier said, "without playing games."

"It would be diff—Would it not be different if it was your daughter he drove to kill herself?"

"Every case has its human aspects," Maier said. "If I were to act upon sentiment, my work would suffer as a consequence. I put my confidence in reason. However, I am human. As I shut my eyes in bed, my feelings often overwhelm my thoughts."

"Yes?" Weiler said. "What do you do?"

"Go to sleep."

"For me it isn't that easy. Piron is a beast, deserving of the harshest treatment."

Maier was staring at him without blinking. Had he actually contradicted the colonel? Why had he never shown his mettle before?

"I have already instructed Roquentin to inform Piron that we will accede to his request," he said. "The reopening of the club will be a huge triumph. I have invited everyone who is anyone in the occupation administration. De Villiers will witness the arrest of the man responsible for his daughter's ruin. If I know anything about human nature, he will reward us generously."

"Do you?" Maier asked.

"Sir?"

"Should it turn out that you only *think* you understand human nature, what then?"

"But I do," Weiler said. "It's a gift."

Maier still hadn't blinked. Weiler felt an overpowering urge to shut his own eyes. Even knowing that the colonel's constant stare was a trick, it was unsettling how he kept on with it for so long.

"Strange, then," Maier said, "that you don't have a clue about mine."

◆

"There, that house," Anne said to Eddie before the barking of a big dog sent them into the shadows.

In street lamplight strained through the bare crown of an elm, Eddie surveyed a box-like dwelling of native fieldstone, centuries old, with a sloping roof and iron shutters sealing the windows, one of thousands throughout the city, this one set back from the sidewalk by a scabby lot. Two bicycles preceded by the flapping sound made by a soft tire moved from right to left across his field of vision. "The dynamite," he said, pulling Anne deep into the blackness, "it's inside?"

"Do you think I could sleep soundly beside eight kilograms of high-grade explosives?" she said. "The old man, Monsieur Champenois, used to visit a prostitute in Clichy on Monday and Thursday afternoons. When he was gone, I made two trips to bring it from where we stashed it after stealing it, and buried it in the alley under my window."

"You wouldn't sleep next to it, but rested comfortably on top?"

"Understanding that nothing short of an earthquake would set it off, I slept quite well at times. It was fear of the militias that spoiled my rest."

"You didn't carry it in a crate in your arms with a shovel over your shoulder."

"The sticks fit in my bag like fat baguettes. The shovel I borrowed from Monsieur Champenois's shed. We can't dig in the yard without waking him, and I can't announce I'm here for the dynamite that I forgot when I ran away. How do you propose getting it out of the ground?"

"Something will come to me."

"What am I to do while you are waiting for inspiration to strike?"

"Go back to Roquentin's."

"I'll wait here," she said. "Should something go wrong, I can be of use in collecting your pieces."

"What would I do without you?"

He went across the street, pounded on the door with no idea what he would say when it was opened. The pounding triggered renewed barking inside, the frenzied scraping of claws against a bare floor, and slippered feet slapping it, followed by "Silence, Fido," and then, for human ears, "Who are you? What do you want?"

Good questions.

"The police."

"Un moment," came from inside the house, and there was more barking before Eddie looked down at the massive black-brown head of a Rottweiler as sturdy as a hippo. Slobber dripped from the snarling jaws as it fought the old man for slack. Fido? Cerberus was a better fit.

Champenois was seventy-five at least, pinch-faced without his false teeth, not an imposing physical specimen in his struggle to control the dog. Eddie speculated about his whore, her looks, and the strong stomach required in a profession that prohibited rejecting even such a client. A frayed robe hanging from the old man's shoulders dragged against the floor, and on his head was what looked to be a knit dunce cap. It puzzled Eddie till he realized that he was the dunce, and it was a night hat. "You're here about the Jewish bitch," Champenois said.

"The woman you kept hidden."

"I hid no one, and nothing. During the time I let her stay with me, I didn't know what she was."

"I am sure that you didn't," Eddie said. "Others may not see it from your perspective. Cooperate with me, or you will be taken to the station to convince them."

Eddie felt Fido's hot breath through his pants. Champenois snapped the leash. Fido didn't notice.

"I told my story at the time she disappeared," the old man said. "You'll find nothing of hers here. After she left I—All right, come inside. Look to your heart's content."

Champenois dropped the leash. The dog jammed its muzzle into Eddie's crotch, and the big jaws opened. Fido sniffed, shook himself, then skulked away. Eddie was taken to a room as bright and airy as a punishment cell, where he made a pretense of disappointment losing out to anger at not finding anything.

"She didn't leave—?"

"Not a button, Monsieur," Champenois said. "The room was as empty when she vanished as the day I let her have it."

"That isn't what she claims."

"What are you saying?"

"She was captured less than three hours ago. She swears that you provided assistance in secreting some items on your property."

"That's absurd," Champenois said. "Why would I?"

"She is young and beautiful," Eddie said. The residue of vanity sparkled in the old man's smile. "Also desperate and lonely. I would venture that she was not the only one who was. I'm going to tear the place apart until I find it."

"It?" the old man said. "What is it?"

"You know very well."

"Come back in the morning when there is bright light and you are sober. It will become clear there is nothing here."

"Get dressed," Eddie said. "Leave some food for the dog."

"Go ahead, have your way. See if I give a damn."

"Give me your shovel."

"I haven't got one."

"In your shed."

Champenois fell back against the bed. Eddie considered that in his thirties he had found his real talent, and it was not as a musician, but as a character actor in the role of the hard-bitten flic. Leaving the old man with Fido curled up at his feet, he went outside.

A tin shed stood tall over a sea of junk in the tiny back yard. Here the street light didn't reach, and the moon stayed away. From a collection of garden implements sufficient to cultivate a small farm, Eddie selected a shovel with a broad blade. Fido came, and Eddie choked up on the handle. Champenois trailed them to the rear of the house, where he pointed out Anne's window. Eddie sent him inside to turn on the light and open the shutter.

Eddie wedged the shovel into the earth, pressed his foot against it, and pried out a pebbly load. The ground was moist, cemented with frost. The digging wasn't easy as he scraped out a space about a meter square, and then deepened it. Champenois went back to the house for a cardigan to throw over the robe, and cigarettes that he chain-smoked leaning against the wall. He was sleepy-eyed, eager for bed, a feeling that was contagious until the shovel bit against something hard, and he bent over the hole.

"It's a box." Champenois crossed himself. "So help me, I don't know what it's doing there."

He made a grab for the shovel. Eddie held it out of his reach, then flung it away. Fido ran after it, and brought it back while Eddie carved the soil with his fingers, carefully lifted the box, and set it down in loose earth.

As he raised the lid, Champenois leaned over his shoulder and struck a match. Eddie shoved him back, and the dog lunged. "Fido, no," the old man said without conviction. The box was filled with crumpled newspaper. Probing with his fingertips, Eddie traced the outline of a tubular object, then raised one end of a stick of dynamite. Chamepenois came near again, and Eddie closed the lid.

"What did you find?"

"As if you don't know," Eddie said.

"But I don't. I don't know anything. It is all a mystery. I curse the day I let the Jewess under my roof."

"Let's go," Eddie said. "My car is in front."

"Please, I don't want trouble," Champenois said. "It isn't my fault that it finds me."

"I should say it has. I advise putting on pants. You may not return home in this lifetime."

"You are being unjust."

Eddie shrugged. "I will wait for you in the car."

The old man's face was shiny with tears as he went inside again. Eddie hurried across the street. "Hey," he whispered, "where are you?"

The wind whistling through the trees answered. Had a real policeman happened by, or had the neighbors reported a prowler, unduly attractive, lurking on the block? "Shush," he heard, and Anne was suddenly at his side.

"You have it?" she said.

He showed her the box.

"What about Champenois?"

"He is dressing for the executioner. I feel bad playing tricks on a frail old man."

"He's a compulsive lecher. I couldn't undress for bed without his eye at the keyhole. His dog is worse."

"Yes," Eddie said, "his dog."

She handled the dynamite without tenderness, unbuttoned her blouse, and slid the sticks against her body. Eddie said, "Are you determined to die horribly?"

"If you have means of transporting them without keeping them close enough to blow us up, let me know. Put down the box, and let's . . ." She froze as another bicycle came down the street. "Let's get going . . . Something in the air—" A spasm racked her body, snapping her head back, and then she sneezed. "I'm allergic to."

CHAPTER TWENTY-TWO

A light shining through the papered windows gave La Caverne the soft glow of a Japanese lantern. Listening at the
door, Eddie was nearly certain no one was inside. In case he was
mistaken, he sent Anne around the corner before using the key
Roquentin had given him to let himself in.

The light came from an unshaded lamp on a blocky object
cloaked in a painter's dropcloth. A radio crackled with static, all
that was left on air after the broadcasters went silent for the night.
A half-eaten sandwich in a circle of empty beer bottles fed a swarm
of flies. Eddie stuck his head out and whistled for Anne, who came
back steadying the precious cargo against her breast. "It looks like

everyone was taken away without warning." She shut off the radio. "As if there was a roundup."

"More likely the painters went home early after their bosses left," Eddie said. "In a few hours they will be back. The old place looks almost new again."

She sniffed the pleasant linseed-oil scent of fresh paint. Eddie raised a corner of the drop cloth and drummed his fingers on the glossy surface of a new eight-burner stove. A tangle of electric wires sprouted through empty wall sockets, but not much else remained to be finished.

"They're working fast," he said. "We don't have a lot of time."

"What we have to do doesn't take much time," Anne said. "If you are willing to come onstage with the dynamite and a match to light it, and to toss the sticks into the laps of the enemy, it shouldn't take any at all."

"I'll keep it in the back of my mind."

"A delayed-action bomb will give us the chance to be away from the building when it goes off."

"That's more what I was thinking of."

"But not as uncomplicated. Two sticks of dynamite, strategically placed, could bring down the entire building, killing everyone."

Eddie said, "Isn't that what we want?"

"Everyone means everyone. Not only Germans, but waiters, the band, your friends. Anyone who stops by for a drink at the wrong time. Can you accept that on your conscience?"

"I'll consult my conscience later. What do you say?"

"You know."

"Kill every German?"

"Every damn one. Along with every collaborator."

"The rest—they're on their own?"

"Every one is your good friend," she said. "Is that it?"

"A few aren't."

"None are mine."

Eddie held his hand against the bulge in her blouse.

"What are you doing?"

"Trying to prevent you from going off. How good are you at building bombs?"

She slipped the dynamite sticks out of her blouse and lay them on the dropcloth. "My instructors in England were the most skilled saboteurs to have escaped from eastern Europe. Bring me an alarm clock, batteries, and copper wire, and I can topple the Eiffel Tower. Demolishing the club, it's child's play."

"I don't know any children who play like that."

"That's you."

"This isn't easy," Eddie said.

Anne didn't answer.

"For you?"

"Not as hard," she said. "Leave it at that." And when he still hesitated, wanting more: "I'll do what I can so you sleep well."

"How will you build your bomb?"

"Let me worry. The difficulty will be yours, in keeping alive those who don't deserve to die. I'm open to anything that kills the rest."

"I hadn't considered it till now."

"Consider this. You will be on stage. For many the last words they hear will be yours. What will you say to separate the others from them?"

"When I am playing God?"

"You don't strike me as much like God. You're more like Abraham, who begged God to spare Sodom if he could find fifty decent men there. When he couldn't, he dropped the number to forty-five, and then forty, and then to thirty, and to twenty, and to ten. Abraham failed to find even that many, and Sodom was destroyed. You will fail, too."

"How do I invite some people to continue their lives, and others to be blown to bits? This business of playing God, it stinks."

"Even for Him."

"There is a woman wishing to speak to you," said Weiler's adjutant, Pfluge, "about a matter of utmost urgency."

Weiler looked up from the menu of a seafood restaurant in Montparnasse recently transferred to German hands. He almost didn't recognize Pfluge, whose nose had been altered by the explosion several weeks before, though it was hard to decide where exactly it was changed. "Every Parisian has a half dozen at least," he said. "Why are you bothering me?"

"She isn't Parisian. Not even French, but American."

"The question remains. Why?"

"She's the woman raped by the trumpet player from Place Pigalle, and wants you to know she is en route to the Sûreté to file a formal complaint."

Weiler went to the window. As he opened it, a breeze sailed the menu to the floor.

"You won't see her? I'll send her away."

"As he is the star at the opening of our club on Friday while we seek his arrest, it's understandable that there is some confusion. I will straighten her out."

Reaching under his desk for the menu, he watched python-skin peep-toe pumps come near. The heels were run down. He suspected that the soles were patched with newspaper. After hearing from the woman about Piron, he hadn't looked into her story, satisfied simply to have it. Now he worried that too much might be made of it and would ruin the big night at La Caverne Negre.

"Good afternoon, Madame," he said in English when they were face to face. "What can I do for you?"

"Know what you can do?" Mavis stood with one hip cocked, and her hand pressed against it. The other dangled a beaded purse. "Ah, forget it. It's been . . . how long's it been, and I haven't heard a damn thing about Piron. Getting warm yet?"

"He's gone to ground. We are searching everywhere and will have him soon."

"Don't give yourself eyestrain. He's blowing his horn at his club on Friday. You Jerries own this town. What's the rub?"

"It isn't that uncomplicated," Weiler said. "Have patience."

"I'm fresh out. I've had it to here with Paris. I want to go home, but the gent who brought me left me high and dry. I told Piron I'd forget what he did to me for the right price—"

Weiler watched her grope for other words. If she could be bribed to forget something that probably never happened, then why should he concern himself with it?

"Not that I could forget. I'm scarred for life," she said. "Till you find him, I'm stuck in France without a pot to pee in. What I'm saying—"

"It is hard to support yourself as a tourist."

"What I'm thinking is I'm hoisting the white flag and surrendering to you."

"You overlook that we are not at war with each other. I may be able to arrange a work permit. What can you do?"

"Singing and hoofing," Mavis said. "A little acting. You need a Yank to play the heavy in one of your pictures, I'm your gal."

How utterly American she was in the forthright way of all Americans, unlike the native coquettes incapable of speaking frankly to a German. Colonel Maier would regard her as a primitive. He, himself, was not unsympathetic to a woman trapped overseas without means, and believed he could help. A Frenchman might find her captivating, as well as compliant in her sorry state.

"Paris is not lacking in entertainers," he said. "Nothing else?"

"That's about it."

"A beautiful woman? Not one thing more? Think."

Mavis said, "Am I reading you right?"

"Till Piron rights the wrong he did to you, you will have to do something to put food in your mouth. I may have just the opportunity you require."

"There's no reason to get fresh," Mavis said.

❖

In his old hiding place above La Caverne, Eddie laughed out loud as he turned the pages of a policier while Anne stared glumly at the walls.

"Don't be selfish, I can also use a laugh," she said.

"This Chandler is extremely humorous. His plot is complex. In places I can't follow it. But the language . . . you would have to understand English."

"We're speaking English now."

"American English, to get the joke."

"Since he is that brilliant, he might want to help with our plot," she said. "I am still stuck. A bomb that brings down the building will kill everyone inside. A ticking bomb delivered to the SS will call notice to itself, killing us. It's an either-or situation in which both alternatives are no good."

"Can you fashion a device I can smuggle in my trumpet case?"

"And blow up the band? Ask me again after I have heard you play."

Roquentin came in with food, but they didn't stop to see what was on the tray. Roquentin took the book from Eddie's hand, and Eddie said, "This is an excellent story, full of beatings and murder to take our mind off our troubles. I don't suppose you brought another."

"Be grateful for what you have. A Wehrmacht officer left it."

"Where did he get an American crime novel?"

"He had emigrated to the States as a child. When the master race took over Europe, he didn't want to be left out of the fun and returned to Munich. All he missed in America besides detective novels was the—"

"Don't tell me," Eddie said. "The jazz."

"The cheesecake at a restaurant on Times Square."

"I wouldn't mind some now."

"I apologize that there is none on today's menu," Roquentin said. "Will you settle for a slice of birthday cake?"

"What do you mean?"

"There's going to be a surprise birthday celebration during the intermission Friday night. You are expected to play 'Happy Birthday To You.' Will you?"

"It's so easy, I could teach you."

"I would rather that you played. The birthday boy is Colonel Maier, the investigator from Berlin. Any wrong notes will be yours."

"You'd like me also to dress like a clown and pull coins from the ears of his friends?" Eddie said.

"Play the song when we wheel out the cake. That will be enough."

"What kind of cake?"

Roquentin shrugged. "I'm thinking of telling the patisserie to use sawdust for flour."

"With arsenic for the frosting?"

"Never mind," Roquentin said. "You'll play? I understand it's demeaning yourself."

"You'll need a big cake for everyone to get a piece," Eddie said. "At least half a meter on all sides, I should think."

"Why this interest in cake?"

"You brought it up," Eddie said.

Anne tried to get in a word, but Eddie put his hand on hers and said over her, "Can you order one of that size?"

"Your first idea was better," Roquentin said. "I should poison it."

"Our big one will be harder for them to digest."

When they were alone again, staring down the food that neither had appetite for, Anne said, "It's an insane idea."

"You knew right away what I was getting at?"

"My mind isn't as quick as yours. It took half a second—"

"Not more insane than entertaining the SS, or Germans overrunning Paris, or this war."

"We can't hide a bomb inside a cake," Anne said. "Cakes aren't meant to tick."

"Put the clock in a container, and they won't hear it. Or as a decoration on top as the symbol of, uh, passing time." He didn't wait to hear what she thought. "We'll play so loud that the ticking is drowned out."

"Placing the bomb inside the cake and serving it up to the SS isn't a bad idea as far as it goes. However, detonating pastry isn't something my SOE training prepared me for."

"I can always light the fuse."

"It won't be cute, like getting a pie in the face in a silent movie," Anne said. "I'm going to forget about cakes and go back to what we had before."

"We had nothing before," Eddie said.

He wasn't like her, couldn't sit still racking his brain over a puzzle with no good solution. He read till she pointed to her watch. "Time for bed," she said.

He beat dust out of the mattress and let her have it along with time to invite him to share it. Waiting, he fell asleep on the floor. He was on chapter seven of *Farewell, My Lovely*, reading it for the third time, when Roquentin said, "Good Friday morning."

"I'd lost track," Eddie said.

"The cake is here."

"Let's see it."

"The electricians haven't finished," Roquentin said. "One of them may walk in at any time. Is it worth your neck to look at a cake?"

"Of course not. Just the same. . . ."

There were tears in the paper over the windows. Eddie saw the street for the first time in days, people trying for a peek inside the remodeled Caverne as they passed by. The cake was in the kitchen on a table out of reach of the mice, a double-tiered confection slathered in yellow frosting, and across the top German words scripted in red glaze.

"Herzlichen Glückwunsch und Viel Glück," Eddie read out loud. "Does anybody know what it means?"

"Happy birthday and much happiness," Anne said.

"Well, we'll see."

"What is this sudden obsession with birthday cake?" Roquentin said. "You still haven't explained."

"We want to ensure that Colonel Maier's party is memorable for everyone."

"I don't like the sound of it," Roquentin said.

Eddie hadn't stopped examining the cake. "Something's missing."

"A dancer from the Folies to jump out."

Anne frowned. Eddie didn't smile long.

"The number of birthdays is usually written on top," Roquentin said. "Maier is turning forty. It may not be something he wishes to be reminded of."

"Something else."

"Candles. We don't need them either. Can you see a colonel in the SS blowing out forty candles on a cake like a little boy?"

"Plus one for good luck," Eddie said. "What's a proper birthday celebration without them? Get some, will you?"

"I don't know what you're up to," Roquentin said, "but aren't you carrying it too far?"

"Not at all. I want to be certain everything goes off in a big way."

Someone had borrowed a couple of Wehrmacht 150cm anti-aircraft beacons and trained them over Place Pigalle. Watching the beams play among the clouds, Eddie wondered how many Parisians believed an air raid was imminent and were battening down against a flight of bombers. The light spilled over limousines parked on the cobbled square, and on couples overdressed for an evening of jazz pressing together on a red carpet outside the club. A man decked out for a round of golf drove by in a Mercedes-Benz 500K roadster in an insolent shade of red. Eddie took an immediate liking to him till he noticed German plates below the bumpers. Then an SS staff car pulled up, and he ducked away from the window without seeing who it brought.

The first show was scheduled for 9:30. That was half an hour ago, but Speer had yet to arrive. The long wait caused a case of nerves which Eddie suspected wouldn't improve his playing, although the tremolo it put in his singing voice occasionally won favorable reviews.

The other Angels were wrapped up in gin rummy in their small dressing area. He listened to them argue over each hand, Weskers the loudest, and always with the last word. Their nerves weren't on edge, their concerns no greater than hitting the right notes.

A hand slapped his shoulder and parked there. "Weiler must have invited every high Nazi in France," Roquentin said. "If any more show up, someone has to tell them all the seats are taken. Who do you think that someone will be?"

"You have nothing to be afraid of. All your troubles soon will be over."

"Think it's funny? You tell them."

"I want them inside," Eddie said. "Nothing I like better than playing before big crowds of SS. Tell them there's plenty of standing room."

"You're crazy."

It was a possibility, but from what Eddie knew of crazy people they never considered that they might be crazy, or had second thoughts. He, on the other hand, was filled with self-doubt and regret, some for events still in the future, feelings that were heightened when he spotted Carla's father. De Villiers looked like he'd been paid to model his evening clothes, the mourner's button on the lapel a reminder that his daughter had died of complications resulting from an overdose of Eddie Piron.

There were three empty chairs at the ringside table where Major Weiler and Colonel Maier rose to shake de Villiers's hand. Behind de Villiers, a woman squeezed through the crowded aisles, pausing to look into the faces at every table. Weiler snapped his fingers to get her attention, but she was staring at the bandstand then and couldn't be disturbed.

In darkness behind the bandstand, Eddie watched Weiler make introductions as Mavis arrived at his table. What new trouble did she bring? Had she crashed the gala in order to denounce him in front of all of Paris? Colonel Maier couldn't scrape up a smile, but de Villiers did, and kissed her hand. Mavis held on to a giggle as she was seated next to him and he whispered in her ear, which seemed to please de Villiers and Major Weiler equally, though Eddie couldn't say why.

Roquentin said, "I've got to check that everything is as it should be."

"You've done it a hundred times."

"Not enough."

"The cake, it's ready?"

"I've heard about the cake two hundred times. It's the least of my worries."

The cake was Eddie's worry, his and Anne's. He hadn't seen her since the club began to fill. She'd told him to stop worrying because worry was also the enemy, but didn't have advice on how to avoid it, and so he worried about everything, worry part of the plot now.

In an instant Roquentin was back, pulling at his sleeve. "Speer was recalled to Berlin. Get onstage. Can't you see we're running late?"

Looking into the crowd, Eddie's nerve deserted him, his lip gone soft and flabby. So this was what it was like to be in bed with a woman and find yourself capable only of excuses. He was desperate for a believable lie, as were many men in that situation. Better to learn these things confronting Nazis than an impatient lover. The idea made him laugh, and he felt his confidence coming back. As the Angels headed under the lights, he took aside Philippe, the piano player: "Forget the playlist. Open with 'Alligator Crawl,' your specialty number. Can you give them four minutes before I come on?"

"Close your eyes, and you'll hear Waller."

"Yes, I know. Let's hope the stage lights fail. Everyone will think you really are him."

"I would rather they didn't," Philippe said. "He's Negro, they'd tear me apart." Suddenly he looked confused. "Where will you be?"

"Leading the applause."

The opening bars brought foot-stamping and cheers that should have been Eddie's. He was furious with himself for surrendering the limelight. The other Angels didn't seem right, caught up in the nervous contagion.

Philippe sounded like Philippe trying to sound like Fats Waller, a credible impersonation for a couple of measures before his left hand took a wrong turn in the intricacies of the walking bass. Eddie blamed it on the limelight's glare, a place where few entertainers really were at home. A waitress came by, balancing a tray of aperitifs on her fingertips. Eddie snatched a glass and emptied it in a gulp. "Hey," the girl said too late. "What do you think you're doing?"

He came out in front of the band to big applause, exultant in the adulation of the crowd. He never had enough. Never would. Even coming from Nazi bastards who didn't think he was human, it was what he lived for.

He brought the trumpet to his lips, fit it against his embouchure. Though his mouth was dry, his sound was clean and powerful, reaching into the dark corners where applause lingered. He released the spit valve, and saliva poured out of the horn. Where it all came from he didn't know.

Leading off with "Apex Blues," he blew loud as the crowd settled. After stating the melody, he didn't have much to do besides tap his foot and look amiable while the clarinet played trills around him. Next on the playlist was "Chinatown My Chinatown." He shook his head, and the band held back till they heard the introduction to "I'll Be Glad When You're Dead, You Rascal You." Philippe came in with the drums playing softly alongside Eddie, who put down his trumpet after the opening chorus and began to sing.

The Angels were all over the tune, nerves an epidemic now. Philippe hit a clunker, throwing Eddie off-stride. Briefly, he forgot the words.

He stepped to the edge of the bandstand. The bigwigs were almost at arm's length, de Villiers and Mavis too engrossed in each other to listen and look. Weiler drummed a saltshaker against the tabletop to his own music. Colonel Maier stared dead ahead, stone-faced. No fan of jazz, he didn't miss a beat.

Eddie mopped his face with a white handkerchief. The crowd howled as he mimicked Satchmo Armstrong's signature mannerism, but the sweat pouring out of him was real.

The club was filled beyond capacity, the doors sealed to keep the overflow from storming inside. Waiters and waitresses were backed up at the service bar. Roquentin hadn't put on sufficient staff to handle the mob. Eddie noticed a waitress gesturing at a waiter, who abruptly stripped off his apron and disappeared through the kitchen. The waitress was Anne, who followed after him and came out with a tray over her shoulder. What compelled her to show her face to a room filled with Nazis looking to send her to hell? Where had she learned the obsequious smile that allowed her close to the unruly occupiers of the city like a matador testing sharp horns? A sidelong glance in his direction, and she ran back to the kitchen to take on the work of the waitresses she shooed from the club.

Next on the playlist was "Between the Devil and the Deep Blue Sea," which had been a huge hit for Armstrong. Even de Villiers stopped gabbing to focus on the stage. After the opening verse, Eddie skipped over the lyric. Everything he wanted to say was in the title.

The crowd hung on each note as it used to do in the good times before the Germans came. La Caverne Negre was Eddie's second home, or third, or fourth, and he would miss it. Miss what it had meant to him, what it had been. Tonight belonged to the new regime, and after tonight there would be nothing. His lament was for something that already had ceased to exist.

He closed with "Stardust," squeezing every drop of pathos from the gorgeous melody. Before the Angels could march off, Roquentin jumped under the lights waving for the crowd to stay put. "I wish to thank all of you for your loyal patronage of so many years," he said. "As you know, this will be my last night at La Caverne Negre before I give the club over to new friends."

Philippe struck a few chords as Roquentin bathed in the affection of the crowd. "Rest assured that I am leaving you in the best hands." The spotlight flashed, but he didn't surrender the stage. "We have a surprise," he said. "Don't anyone leave."

Eddie unloaded a flood of spit as the lights dimmed.

He popped a mute into the bowl of his horn, and "Happy Birthday To You" came out sweetly for one refrain, and again with a jazzy lilt. De Villiers and Weiler grinned at Colonel Maier, whose hard look didn't vary. A spotlight swept the walls and ceiling, the tables, the floor, and the stage before it settled on the kitchen door as the cake came out on a cart guided by Anne. Eddie stepped to the side of the riser, aimed the stagelights at the Germans' table, and watched them shield their eyes, squinting and blinking as the cake was delivered.

"Today," Roquentin said, "is the birthday of our dear friend, Colonel Maier, who has traveled all the way from Berlin to share it with us. Please, all of you are invited to celebrate with the colonel."

Eddie removed the mute, and the insipid jingle turned brassy. Through all of it, Maier didn't smile. Someone would pay for this foolishness, and the someone might well be the musician blowing in his face. Eddie marveled at his stern display. How the man didn't blush, or squirm, or acknowledge the cake arriving before him. Maier just sat, looking stiffly ahead, staring right through the cake while Roquentin signaled for quiet.

Eddie whispered to him, "Get out, and take the Angels with you."

"It's only the end of the first set. We haven't lit the candles for Maier."

"You can light others," Eddie said. "In church."

"It isn't easy leaving for the last time."

"It's easier to die here?"

Roquentin looked at the table where Maier and Weiler sat before the cake as if they had never been to a birthday party as children, and didn't know what came next. Eddie crooked a finger at the band, which followed Roquentin to the side exit along with the rest of the waiters and waitresses, Anne bringing up the rear. Weiler put a thin-bladed knife in Maier's hand. De Villiers took it away and pointed it at the unlit candles in the frosting.

Mavis found a matchbook in her purse, and de Villiers passed it to the colonel, who'd had his fill of childishness, and seemed ready to go home. Suddenly the house lights came on. Weiler bolted from the table and ran down Roquentin and his crew, collared the last of them like a card sharp dealing the ace from the bottom of the deck, and returned with Anne.

De Villiers said, "What is going on? If you will explain."

"This woman is sought on serious charges," Weiler said.

"Can't it wait?" de Villiers said. "Tonight is for pleasantness."

Weiler deferred to Colonel Maier, who nodded, and then turned to Anne. "Be so kind," he said, "as to light the candles for me."

She retreated, bumping into Weiler, who forced her back.

"You would deny me this honor on my birthday?"

Nothing of her jauntiness was left. Maier pressed the matches into her hand. "Light them."

She tore a match from the book and ground it against the flint. It didn't catch. Another crumpled when she struck it too hard. A third produced a flame that wandered along the edges of the cake. Maier caught her wrist and lowered it over a candle.

The wick took the flame, as did two more before the match burned down to her fingers, and she blew it out. She ripped another from the book, and Maier took her wrist again, and like bride and groom they lit a row of five candles. Eddie heard impatient chatter in the crowd, which was tired of ceremony, hungry for cake. The match flickered out. Anne struck another.

One candle refused to light. Three matches were used up before the flame sputtered and caught. Sizzling, it threw off sparks, melted much of the paraffin, and burned out.

No matches were left in the book. Anne plucked a lighted candle and brought it to the smoking wick.

Maier swept her arm aside. He yanked out the glowing candle, squashed it under his heel, and drove his hand into the cake. Eddie observed that he was no Jack Horner as he emerged with nothing. Maier looked up at Anne, considered that she might be a prize he wouldn't be cheated of, and shoved her away without a word before his humiliation was made complete. De Villiers, looking as though he was having second thoughts about his dealings with the Germans, moistened a napkin in a water tumbler, and Maier scrubbed his wrist and the back of his hand, examined each finger individually, and cleaned between them. Someone in the crowd laughed, and Eddie heard someone else tell him to shut up. Eddie blew a chorus of "Happy Birthday" with a bluesy inflection, the vocal provided by the crowd, which caught its collective breath after "Dear . . ." and then shouted, ". . . Colonel Maier, Happy birthday to you," and cheered as all but four of the candles were extinguished in a single blow.

Maier took back the knife and from the undamaged part of the cake hacked out a generous wedge and served it to Mavis. She displayed it like a trophy to the crowd, took a small bite, then put it down and sliced smaller pieces for everyone, while the colonel popped the cork on a bottle of Piper-Heidsieck and filled each glass on the table.

Weiler was pronouncing a toast when Anne slipped away.

Too late he made a grab for her, out of his seat when de Villiers stopped him. "I will not allow you to spoil our good time. Where can she run? You will find her to do with her what you must. But not now."

Weiler wouldn't repeat his mistake with Eddie.

"Come, have cake with us," he said to him. "You provided good entertainment."

The house lights came on, the customers afraid of the dark, perhaps, or if they were realistic, thought Eddie, of each other. The story of Abraham begging God to save Sodom for the sake of fifty good men was on his mind again. At La Caverne Negre, fifty was an impractical number. The bidding would begin at one. A single death that might weigh on his conscience, and he would argue with God rather than play Him.

Nothing about the Germans scored points in their favor. The fawning cravenness of their French lackeys counted for as much. La Caverne was theirs now, as were Paris, France, Europe. Still they wanted more. *Laissez les bons temps rouler* was their motto, but with a meaning that would be rejected in New Orleans. The occupation was the best of times for them, the good old days here and now. It was written all over the glossy faces that Eddie recognized from other places he'd been wrong to call home.

De Villiers couldn't contain his disgust for Eddie. Weiler poured Champagne for Eddie and then topped off his own glass.

"Give me a second to put my horn away," Eddie said, "and I'll be back for my cake." He tapped his pockets. "Can I borrow a cigarette? I'm fresh out."

Mavis picked a Gitane out of a tortoiseshell case, put it between his lips, and gave him a light from hers. "Don't go too far," she said.

From the bandstand he maintained his lookout for one good person. No one in uniform qualified. Neither did their friends, and anybody pretending to be one. He considered Mavis. Not the most admirable of women, she didn't, nevertheless, deserve to die tonight. Not for trying to destroy Eddie Piron. Therefore no one would.

He knelt over the trumpet case, popped the snaps, and raised the lid. Mavis wasn't there when he looked again. He spotted her in the back of the club making a beeline to the ladies' toilet. That part of La Caverne was the remnant of an ancient fieldstone inn that Roquentin had incorporated into the nightspot by knocking down a wall when he opened in the twenties. The toilets were the safest place to be in the event of an air raid or lesser calamity. A final survey of the crowd turned up no one else he would argue about with God for or against.

He was seized with a fit of coughing. He hadn't smoked since he became serious about the trumpet at eleven, and the cigarette scorched his lungs. He moved it to a corner of his mouth with a glance at Weiler, who was watching him over the lip of his glass.

Inside the trumpet case, four feet of fuse coiled around spindles in the lid were attached to two sticks of dynamite in the compartment where his horn belonged. He knocked a worm of ash from the cigarette, and touched the lit end to the fuse until it began to sparkle like a nigger chaser. After lighting it, he had fifteen or twenty seconds to get outside before it went off, Anne had said, unless the fuse was slow, or extinguished itself, or burned so fast that not even Jesse Owens was quick enough to outrun it.

Eddie would have to outwalk it.

"Stop him!"

Eddie looked up as Weiler slammed his glass on the table. It disintegrated in his fist, spattering blood on de Villiers. Shrugging out of de Villiers's grasp, he charged the bandstand.

There was silence of the kind, Eddie figured, that John Wilkes Booth had commanded on the stage at Ford's Theater. "Sic semper tyrannis," Booth had shouted after his awful deed. Though nothing in what he did at La Caverne Negre tonight was motivated by

Booth's bitter impulse, was in fact its precise opposite, Eddie wanted to shout the same words.

Instead, he shut the lid and ran.

La Caverne refilled with sound as the silence fell apart of its own weight. "Stop that man, get Piron," rose above the racket. The bandstand shook as two men leaped onto it. Eddie felt their footsteps before he heard them.

Maier pounced on the trumpet case as Weiler came after Eddie, who ran with his head down, concentrating on his footing. The way to the door was blocked by men braced for collision, a defensive backfield in Wehrmacht gray. A stout lieutenant lunging drunkenly at his hips was easily sidestepped, and Eddie lowered his shoulder into two corporals, crouched and nimble, and knocked them off their feet. Outstretched hands pulled him off-stride. They clawed buttons from his shirt and skin from his neck while his internal clock struck the final seconds. Punches transmitting equal pain to his fist and German chins gained two hard-fought meters, and then he stiffened his arm and used it like a jouster's lance to break through the human wall.

His steps lengthened; the exit remained distant. When at last he reached it, the door refused to open no matter how hard he pushed against it. Powerful hands spinning him around brought him face to face with Major Weiler. A short, straight punch drove him back against the door, and was followed by a looping blow that caught him between the eyes and relieved him momentarily of his intelligence. Weiler grabbed his lapels and jerked. A head butt was turned back by a fist landing over the major's heart. Weiler grunted but kept his grip. Eddie brought up his knee into Weiler's crotch. Weiler didn't seem to notice. Eddie did it again, getting Weiler's attention along with a spray of curses, and bloody snot, and Weiler's skull glancing against his cheek.

Over Weiler's shoulder, Eddie saw Colonel Maier tear open the trumpet case and reach in. How could it be that seconds ago too few seconds were left, and now there were too many? The puzzle distracted him, and Weiler's hands wrapped around his throat. Unable to dislodge them, he winged punches non-stop, connected with most. But he was dizzy, and hurting, and they had no snap, and caused little damage.

"You're done, Piron." Weiler spit the words in his face. "By all that's holy, your luck's run out."

It wasn't news. He clapped his hands against Weiler's ears and saw the major's face contort.

He threw more weak fists. Heavier hands hit back. Other Germans rushed to aid Weiler. A wall of SS closed around him, crammed the narrow space where he grappled with the major. A sensation that the building had begun to dance couldn't be blamed on the pummeling he was taking. The wall of storm troopers came apart with a roar ahead of shock waves from the detonating TNT that reached him, blunted by German bodies.

The explosion blew the door off the hinges. Eddie rode it locked in Weiler's embrace until the jolt of a hard landing. Weiler skated, cartwheeled to the gutter, stopped by a hydrant at the curb.

Eddie was of the opinion that Weiler was right, and he must be dead, taking his bearings in the afterlife with a birdseye view of the world he'd left. It was easier to believe than that he'd survived intact. More than he could say for Weiler, who had absorbed the brunt of the explosion.

His head ached. Pressing it cautiously between his hands, he was grateful that the shape seemed to be the same, only some patches of hair and skin missing from where they belonged. About the inside it was too soon to know. He winced as a bolt of pain passed through it .

Getting to his feet, he discovered he'd lost his shoes. In his brain there was room for just one thought at a time now, and that was how to replace them. Weiler had retained his, though not both legs. Eddie went first to one by itself on the street, and snatched a well-crafted oxford with a superlative shine. The other he took from Weiler's corpse. Not a perfect fit, but, then, what ever was?

A second inventory of himself was in order. The sleeves were missing from his shirt. Everything else seemed to be accounted for, yet something was not. Through smoke and dust he saw a handful of survivors, though he thought of them as something else, his failures perhaps, also taking stock. Their cries and groans were lost in the ringing in his ears. The ringing was all he could hear.

La Caverne Negre. Had the name ever been more apt? A black cave was what it was now. The roof, the section above the bandstand, had been blown sky-high, and the starless night pressed down, blotting the light from the street. In the mass of debris was his trumpet. He climbed over rubble slick with flesh. Yellow metal reflected in a passing headlight caught his attention, a lamp or light stanchion. In a hand above the pile where the riser had been was brass recast by immense heat, a musical instrument imagined by Salvador Dalí, the hand extending from the sleeve of a ranking SS officer. It was all Eddie cared to see of Colonel Maier. The trumpet was reclaimable as a souvenir, but Eddie had stopped wanting it. Maier could keep it. A fair trade for good German shoes.

Fire engines arrived ahead of cars from the Sûreté and a Wehrmacht troop carrier. Seeing the pumpers with flashing lights and firefighters rushing to link sections of hose, and not hearing idling engines and shouts, brought déjà vu from when he was a kid gawking at the silent images at the nickelodeon. For the third time he took an accounting of what he'd lost. His sleeves and his shoes. His horn and his hearing. Paris. Maybe his music. Gone for nothing if the French didn't take up the fight against the Germans. Who gave a damn? He had nothing here. Never did. No, that wasn't right. It was late for sour grapes.

A man from a car with German plates tried to get him to sit down. Eddie pushed him away. Anne was supposed to meet him around the corner if everything went okay, and it had. Hadn't it?

A truck pulled up, and Roquentin came around the front barking at him and gesturing for him to hurry. All Eddie heard was the ringing in his head. Gentle pressure where his arm was burned was agonizing. He yelled, but didn't hear that either. Roquentin gave him over to Anne, who pulled him onto the front seat, and they raced away from Place Pigalle on little-used streets.

"He's hurt."

He could feel her words on his cheek. In daylight maybe he'd be able to read lips. Now he might as well be blind as well as deaf. He held onto the door handle as Roquentin turned suddenly away from a roadblock, unable to let go as intimations of pain broke through the numbness where he hadn't known he was injured.

"I think he's in shock. He doesn't answer when I ask where his injuries are."

"Frankly, I never expected we would see him alive," Roquentin said.

"He was very good, very strong. I didn't know he would be so brave." She patted Eddie's hand, squeezed it, brushed her lips against the knuckles, and clapped his open palm to her face. "I'll make his pain go away, you'll see. I will fix him as good as new."

"You'll bring him to your country?"

"He needs false papers to get past the British. A new identity once he is living there. I can help with those—with everything." She held him tighter. "He will always have me."

"He's a proud man," Roquentin said. "It won't be easy, pretending to be other than himself."

"He has no place else," Anne said. "How hard can it be?"